What was she *doing*?

Encouraging liberties from a Berowne! Was she mad? What could be more compromising?

Dragging back a little, Louisa said sharply, 'Beware! I said *friends*, nothing more.'

Septimus dropped her hands abruptly. 'How wise of you to warn me! I was about to throw you to the turf and do my worst.'

A faint flush stained Louisa's cheeks. 'Indeed? I thought you meant only to kiss me. It just shows how wrong one can be!'

Dear Reader

We launch a Paula Marshall trilogy this month, following the Schuyler family, who are American, but base their lives in England. We begin with Gerard, a real buccaneer, and his efforts to discover the truth about Victoria. We have a wonderful romp from Elizabeth Bailey, and our two American authors are Donna Anders, with the first of her mother/daughter duo set on Hawaii, and Marjorie Burrows, with a story of Montana in 1876. A wonderful month's reading to welcome the spring!

The Editor

Elizabeth Bailey grew up in Malawi, returning to England to plunge into the theatre. After many happy years 'tatting around the reps', she finally turned from 'dabbling' to serious writing. She finds it more satisfying for she is in control of everything: scripts, design, direction and the portrayal of every character! Elizabeth lives on the border of Kent and Sussex and, in time spared from writing, teaches GCSE and A level drama at a local school.

Recent titles by the same author:

AN ANGEL'S TOUCH
HIDDEN FLAME

SEVENTH HEAVEN

Elizabeth Bailey

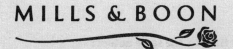

MILLS & BOON LIMITED
ETON HOUSE, 18–24 PARADISE ROAD
RICHMOND, SURREY, TW9 1SR

*First published in Great Britain 1994
by Mills & Boon Limited*

© Elizabeth Bailey 1994

*Australian copyright 1994
Philippine copyright 1994
This edition 1994*

ISBN 0 263 78247 6

*Set in 10½ on 12 pt Linotron Times
04-9403-76574*

*Typeset in Great Britain by Centracet, Cambridge
Made and printed in Great Britain*

CHAPTER ONE

IN A garret room kissed by a weak late winter sun sat a solitary figure. Mr Septimus Berowne, poet, wrestling with his muse. One shapely set of fingers supported his frowning brow, while the other held a quill pen poised over a sheet of paper on the table. The exact phrase with which to complete the rhyme of the final verse eluded him.

To judge by the many crossings-out and the scribbles that adorned the discarded sheets, several of which had been screwed into balls by a frustrated hand and flung against the opposite wall, the muse this chill March morning was proving recalcitrant.

Not that Mr Berowne was troubled by the cold. Oh, no. The place in which 'he suffered for his art', as he so eloquently phrased it, was in fact a very pleasant roomy apartment — known by common consent among his well-trained siblings as 'Setty's garret' — which was situated on the second floor of the massive Grosvenor Square mansion, in which the three remaining stay-at-home offspring of the beautiful Dolly Berowne rattled around, in the poet's words, like chained ghosts in a deserted castle.

In truth, however, they all basked, as he did, in lavish comfort, quite regardless of expense — and much to the chagrin of innumerable disgruntled tradesmen who would have been very happy to receive even a modest sum on account! — with a substantial fire blazing in the grate. It was thus possible for Septimus Berowne to exercise his literary talents in the dishabille of shirt-sleeves — of silk, naturally, with costly lace at the wrists — and, in defiance of fashion, his own long brown hair loosely tied and falling down his back.

He looked excessively romantic, which, he was prone to argue, was essential for a poet. He was also excessively handsome, which, he asserted with equal fervour, was not. 'It is hardly the business of a poet,' he maintained, 'to be concerned with his physical appearance.'

A numerous following of adoring ladies would not have agreed with him. For the light brown eyes typical of his family, the full sensual lower lip and that fatal charm of manner, combined with the voice of honey with which he recited his verses, were more than enough to cause many a heart to flutter painfully, and not one of the damsels so afflicted could have been brought to condemn his careless habit of dress, even were his fond sisters to inform them that it was quite deliberate. In keeping, so he maintained, with his Bohemian calling!

His 'garret' room, which adjoined a handsome bedchamber, was attractively furnished with an elegant day-bed — essential to the poetic dreamer, he said — in addition to several comfortable chairs, a tallboy, and the large table by the window at which he sat overlooking the comings and goings in the square below. The walls were papered in old brocade of faded green with a yellow print which, said the poet, was restful, reminding him suitably of meadows and buttercups.

But he gazed unseeingly upon them this morning, his mind busily searching out that elusive rhyming phrase. All at once his eye brightened and he smiled. Dipping his pen in the inkpot, he drew a fresh sheet of paper towards him and began to write.

Then the door burst rudely open and an explosive male voice called out, 'Setty, the most dreadful thing!'

Septimus flung out a hand. 'Hush! Not a sound! Not a breath!'

In the doorway, a slight young gentleman hovered uncertainly, obediently silent, watching the bent head and the busy quill travelling rapidly across the paper. Decimus, at eighteen the youngest of the Berownes, was big with news and fairly aching to unburden his woes. But he knew from long experience that he could never hope to hold his brother's attention unless he permitted him to complete the lines that evidently had him in their grip.

But in a moment Septimus looked up, satisfied, and, seeing who had entered his sanctum, laid aside his pen. 'Oh, it's you, Dess. Back already? How did you fare? Come inside, my babe, and tell me all!'

Shutting the door with alacrity, young Decimus Browne made his announcement. 'Setty, she *refused* me!'

Septimus tutted sympathetically. 'Did she so? My poor Dess!' He raised an admonitory finger. 'Mind, I did warn you how it would be if you offered for a woman named Shittlehope.'

'Her name has nothing to do with it,' said Decimus irritably, coming forward into the room and kicking moodily at the carpet.

'It has everything to do with it,' argued his brother, rising from his chair and crossing to the mantelpiece to collect a long clay pipe. 'She was not born to such an abomination, I presume?'

'Of course she was not,' Decimus said impatiently. 'She is a widow, as you very well know.'

'Exactly. A widow,' agreed Septimus, facing his brother as he began to fill his pipe. 'Now I ask you, what kind of woman would wantonly marry and adopt such a name? *Shittlehope*. It does not bear thinking of! At least the wretched fellow had the grace to die before he passed on such a label to some unfortunate boy. At least. . .' He broke off, gazing at Decimus in some anxiety. 'I do trust that I am not mistaken in this. She has no children?'

'Not that I know of,' Decimus told him frowningly. 'There is, I gather, a dependent female — a poor little dab of a thing. I caught a glimpse of her on the doorstep as I left. She was with that dreadful battle-axe, Lady Pyrland.'

'Never mind Lady Pyrland,' Septimus said sternly. 'You must not sneer at the "poor little dabs", Dess! It is precisely such colourless, downtrodden females into whose drab lives I am endeavouring to bring a little colour and light.'

'Oh, be damned to you, Setty!' exploded his brother. 'My heart is broken and all you can do is prate of your confounded poetry!'

'"Confounded"?' echoed Septimus, insulted.

'Well, you know what I mean.'

A gleam entered the elder brother's eye. 'It *would* have been "confounded" if this abominable widow had accepted you. Only conceive of trying to find a suitable rhyme for Shittlehope!'

Decimus could not suppress a grin, but he grumbled nevertheless, 'I wish you would not harp on about her name.'

'I *must* do so,' protested his brother, selecting a taper and putting it to the fire. 'It shows her to be a woman of no sensitivity whatsoever. I utterly forbid you to have a broken heart on her account!'

Decimus threw himself down on a chair before the fire, rumpling the sober blue cloth suit he had thought proper to wear for the solemn occasion, and causing his elegant powdered tie-wig to lie a little askew.

'It is too late. Lady Louisa has blighted my life! Do you know that she did not even remember me? She asked me who I was. And that was *after* I proposed!'

Septimus appeared to choke on his pipe, which he happened at that precise moment to be lighting. When he could speak again, he said, 'No doubt she felt it to be an important point. One can't go about accepting marriage proposals from total strangers.'

'But we were not strangers! She *had* met me.'

'Once, my babe. Only once.'

'It was enough for me!' declared young Decimus. 'Besides, it was only a day or so ago. Why, I knew as soon as she looked at me. Such *eyes*, Setty!'

Mr Septimus Berowne, having been indisposed with a slight chill this past week — 'Bed, my babes, is the only sensible course, lest it should fatally descend upon my lungs, and I sink into my grave, thereby depriving the world of my talent!' — had not been privileged to see the Lady Louisa Shittlehope. But he had heard of her in detail, for all the Berownes were naturally disposed to take an interest in a new arrival in town whose late spouse was whispered to have left her in extremely comfortable circumstances.

Mr Shittlehope had been, it was rumoured, a considerable merchant with manufactories somewhere in the north. Notwithstanding this agreeably interesting circumstance, the taint of trade would have closed all doors against his widow, were it not for the fact that she had been born Lady Louisa Lidbrook, daughter of the Marquis of Sedbergh. As it was, her status, her wealth and, as it now seemed, her eyes were everything for which an impecunious youngest son might wish. But Decimus, as he vehemently insisted, had fallen in love.

'At least,' he amended sullenly, 'I *was* in love with her.'

'Oh?' queried his brother, removing the pipe from his mouth. 'What cured you?'

'I'm *not* cured. Only she said such things, and I am not at all sure. . .'

'What things? She suspected you of fortune-hunting, I dare say.'

'Not at all!' stated Decimus indignantly. 'In fact she actually said that she perfectly understood that I was *quite* unmoved by considerations of fortune.'

'Did she indeed?' murmured Septimus appreciatively, seating himself on the day-bed opposite.

'Yes, and that it was not inconceivable that I might have fallen in love with her at sight.'

'A woman of rare tolerance, I perceive,' commented his brother wryly.

'Well, I don't know about that, but she was quite

kindly. Only she brought up the difference in our ages,' disclosed Decimus miserably.

'Well, it is a consideration. How old is she?'

'I don't know. Not more than thirty, I'd have said. Indeed I did say so.'

'*What*?' gasped Septimus. He bit his lip on a laugh. 'And this was the point at which she called the butler to show you out, I suppose.'

'Nothing of the sort. Why, do you think she might have been offended?'

'I think you are remarkably lucky to have escaped without a scratched face!' said the poet frankly, laying aside his clay pipe on a convenient little table.

Decimus blinked. 'All she said was that she must remember to consult her mirror.'

'Oh, is *that* all?'

'Well, but she *then* said it only strengthened her argument.'

'What argument?' demanded Septimus.

'That she is too old for me,' Decimus said sadly. 'She said I could not wish for a wife who would be past all pleasure and riddled with gout while I was still in my prime.'

'Gout!' Septimus closed his eyes as if in anguish and shuddered. 'Gout, he says calmly!'

'Yes, but it shocked me at the time, I confess.'

'The wonder is you did not run incontinently from the house! Had it been I ——'

'I did not. I said I was sure she could not have gout. But *then* she said I should live under the cat's foot, for she is no meek little mouse.'

'So it would appear,' Septimus assented, but with an irresistibly quivering lip.

'And she said,' pursued Decimus, determined to purge his soul, 'that, on top of being impossible to live with, she would almost certainly grow fat.'

Septimus regarded him for a brief moment in mute horror. Then he sank back against the cushions of the day-bed, closing his eyes and throwing a hand across his brow.

'Sal volatile!' he begged in a faint voice. 'Burnt feathers! A gouty Shittlehope — and *fat*. I can bear no more!'

But Decimus did not run for the smelling-salts. Instead he rose up menacingly from his seat, saying crossly, 'Do stop play-acting, Setty! She is *not* fat. At least, not yet. Though she *is* well-padded.'

Septimus jerked upright, his eyes flying open. 'Dess, you are incorrigible! "Well-padded" indeed! I declare, my heart is positively wrung.'

'For me? I should hope so.'

'No, clodpole! For *her*,' said his brother scornfully, and no trace of a swoon was visible in his deportment. 'I do sincerely hope that you did not employ that appalling phrase in her presence.'

'Of course I did not,' indignantly rejoined Decimus. 'I admitted that she might not be the girl of my dreams, but ——'

'Leave me!' uttered Septimus, closing his eyes again. 'Heaven send I may never encounter this female! I should not know where to look. Oh, callow, callow youth!'

Decimus frowned. 'I don't see why ——'

'I know,' interrupted his brother, opening his eyes. '*That* is why. Go away, do! Complain of your broken heart elsewhere, while I attempt to recover my lost dignity. Oh, woe to us all!' he added, casting a glance to heaven. 'A changeling, Lord. He is most definitely a changeling.'

'Don't start that again!' snapped Decimus, rising at once to the bait. '*I* don't claim a different father, even if the rest of you do.'

'And how right you are not to do so,' said Septimus with an instant change of face. 'It is not you, but *I* who was born of some other man. This marquis, perhaps. Who knows?' He frowned. 'No, I think not. I am far too sensitive ever to have been *her* brother. No power on earth would persuade *me* to wed someone of the name of Shittlehope!'

Decimus sighed. 'You are teasing again.'

'Teasing? I was never more serious!'

'I wish you would not, Setty,' pleaded his brother, unheeding. 'I am not in the mood. And it is no use wishing you will not meet Lady Louisa, because you are bound to.'

'Lord have mercy! For God's sake, take yourself off, Dess, so that I may compose a suitable poem in order to placate the lady.'

'The very thing!' exclaimed Decimus eagerly. 'Write an ode to her enormous eyes, Setty. Then I may read it to her.'

'Go away!' begged his brother again, a mock-sob in his voice. 'Go away, before I use you as you so richly deserve and compose you a sonnet to her girth and her gout!'

Decimus went reluctantly to the door. 'Very well, I'm going. But I warn you, I haven't given up hope.'

'Your hopes, my babe,' returned his brother sapiently, abandoning his affectations, 'are blasted! You

had much better go after the "poor little dab". I dare
say she may come in for a share of the substance you
crave.'

This base aspersion on his motives—after all he
had said, what was more!—so incensed Decimus that
he flung out of the room without another word.

The 'poor little dab', meanwhile, having encountered
Mr Decimus Berowne on the doorstep as she entered
the little house in Brook Street in company with Lady
Pyrland, had gone upstairs to her bedchamber to
deposit her purchases with a faint fluttering in her
heart. Mr Berowne might scarcely have taken her
into his notice, but Miss Millicent Lidbrook had most
certainly noticed him!

So had Lady Pyrland, but with far different
emotions. 'What was that Berowne boy doing here?'
she demanded of her niece the instant she walked
through the door of the little first floor parlour.

Lady Louisa Shittlehope hardly turned her head
from contemplation of the heavy account books
which lay open on the desk before her.

'Back so soon, Aunt Hebe? I have scarcely had a
chance to begin!'

Lady Pyrland marched up to the desk and rapped
smartly on its polished walnut surface. 'Attend to me,
Louisa!'

A pair of large, misty blue orbs came up, a lurking
twinkle at the back of them. 'Aunt, you are not about
to ring a peal over me, are you? I promise you I
refused him.'

'*What*?' gasped Lady Pyrland. 'Do you mean to say

that wretched boy had the effrontery to offer for you?'

Lady Louisa smiled. 'Why not? He is desperately in love with me. Though to be sure I cannot be more than thirty, you know, even if I am not quite the woman of his dreams!'

From under her modish round feathered hat, her aunt could only blink at her. She had not even considered the fact that, with her six or seven years' seniority to her suitor, Louisa might not find him to her taste. She had simply reacted to the fact of his being a Berowne. Now that she thought about it, it was ridiculous to suppose that a stick of a boy, as handsome as he was — as were they all, drat them! — could appeal to a tall lady of positively buxom mien.

In fact Lady Louisa's voluptuous figure was remarkably well-suited to the prevailing mode with its emphasis on bosom and posterior, false rumps having largely replaced hoops. A chintz open robe cut low over full breasts concealed under a muslin buffon, and worn over a plain petticoat flaring out a little to contrast with the narrow waist and long tight sleeves, was the more flattering to a 'well-padded' form.

But above it were the smoky orbs of blue, so large that they seemed to blot out the rest of her features, so that she appeared all eyes under a mass of fashionably frizzed and curling hair of deep brown. The soulful impression they gave, however, was misleading. No one could have been more matter-of-fact than Lady Louisa Shittlehope.

'I am glad you sent him about his business,'

observed Lady Pyrland more calmly. 'Nothing could be worse than a connection with *that* set.'

Lady Louisa, recognising that she was not going to be permitted to continue with her work, philosophically laid aside her pen and rose from her chair.

'What set is that?' she enquired.

'Why, the Berownes, to be sure,' said her aunt, rustling over in her silk petticoats to seat herself on the elegant Chippendale sofa that faced the fire. 'Wild to a fault, all of them. And quite penniless.'

'But young Berowne — now what was his name? Decimus? Yes, I rather think that was it.'

'Yes, it probably was,' agreed her aunt, 'for he is the youngest of them, and the *last*, thank the lord!'

'Well, he *assured* me that my circumstances had no bearing on the case,' Lady Louisa told her mildly, coming to stand before the fire and resting one hand on the mantelpiece.

'Pho!' snorted Lady Pyrland. 'I wish I might believe him! You will have the lot of them beating at your door.'

The blue eyes widened. 'How many of them are there?'

'Ten. At least, there are six boys, and two of them are married — at least *one* is. The other — thank heaven! — is safe out of the country, and is rumoured to have taken a wife. Though how in the world any mother could be so idiotic as to allow her daughter to tie herself up —— '

'Ten?' interrrupted her niece blankly. 'Ah, I see. *Decimus*, being the youngest, is the tenth child, yes?'

'Exactly. And there in a nutshell, you have the Berownes.'

A faint puzzled frown creased Louisa's brow. 'I don't understand you.'

'So little did Dolly Berowne — and that poor excuse for a man she married — care about their children that they could not even take the trouble to think of names for them!'

Lady Louisa shrugged helplessly. 'Tush, ma'am, your conversation is beyond me! I gather this Dolly Berowne is the mother of these ten children, but ——'

'They are named for *numbers*, Louisa. One, two, three and so on, as each appeared. But in Latin.'

For a moment her niece stared at her in mute disbelief. Then she broke into laughter. Lady Pyrland glared at her.

'I fail to see the humour in it.'

But Louisa was in stitches, holding on to the mantelpiece for support. Her aunt waited in ominous silence for her mirth to abate, her strong face with its jutting Roman nose pinched in disapproval, and purpling to match her gown. She was a gaunt female, tall and thin like her brother, the late Marquis of Sedbergh. Louisa was fashioned more after her long-deceased mother, but for her height, and her warmth had nothing to do with the Lidbrook side of the family.

Controlling her amusement, Louisa joined her aunt on the sofa, which was almost the only large piece of furniture the little parlour afforded, except for a couple of occasional tables. For apart from the big desk in the window embrasure — a handsome piece, its myriad drawers exquisitely ornamented with rich ivory inlay to the walnut — there was but a pianoforte and stool. Lady Louisa had appropriated it for her study, despite Lady Pyrland's objections about its inadequate size, placating her with a reminder that the drapes and light brocade wallpaper in a muted stripe were of the latest fashion — and extremely expensive.

'Tell me all about these terrible Berownes, Aunt,' Louisa invited coaxingly, patting the elder lady's hand.

'Certainly not! They are not a fit subject for discussion.'

'But if I am to understand why I must have nothing to do with them, Aunt Hebe, it is your *duty* to tell me,' said her niece persuasively.

But Lady Pyrland was not to be caught. 'If we are to talk of duty, Louisa, your own is clear. So far from throwing away your substance on such a wasteful spendthrift as Decimus Berowne —— '

'You would have me throw it away on my cousin Philip instead!' finished Lady Louisa, shifting away a little.

'It would not be thrown away,' declared Lady Pyrland. 'Your father left the estates in a worse case than ever, and poor Philip is burdened with the task of repairing them.'

'My dear ma'am,' Louisa said, in the tones of one who had been over this argument many times, 'my father obliged me to sell myself once for the advantages it would bring him. I am not going to do so a second time.'

'But Philip is *family*, and you have a duty to your name!'

'My name, Aunt Hebe, is neither Sedbergh nor Lidbrook, but Shittlehope,' insisted Louisa. 'And my duty, as I see it, is to make sure my late husband is not choused out of his pennies by another Lord Sedbergh.'

'If by that vulgar expression you mean to imply that Shittlehope was *cheated*, I can assure you it was no such thing. Not that I approved of my brother's marrying you into that class, for I never did. But Shittlehope paid handsomely for the privilege of being admitted to our ranks — and so he should have done!'

'He paid, Aunt, for a marquis' daughter, and he got me.' Louisa sighed. 'Poor Mr Shittlehope! He little knew what he was letting himself in for.'

'Pho! He was amply rewarded,' insisted Lady Pyrland.

'*He* did not think so,' said his widow with a tiny giggle. 'It was what he used to say of me over and over again: "Choused out of my pennies for a pert little chit who does nothing but tell me my business!"'

Her aunt fairly gaped at her. 'You told him his business?'

'Certainly I did,' Louisa assented. 'I was far more frequently in the right than he, let me tell you. I have an excellent head for business. Since I have been keeping the accounts, we have never had a day's incorrect balance.'

'*Louisa*,' gasped her aunt, quite appalled. 'Never tell me *you* had a hand in the running of that cit's affairs?'

There was a twinkle in the large misty eyes. 'It is a pity you never met Mr Shittlehope, Aunt. He felt very much as you do!'

'Louisa,' said Lady Pyrland earnestly, 'I do *beg* of

you never, but *never*, to mention this to another soul! Bad enough to have been married into trade, but to be *engaged* in it!' She shuddered.

'But I *am* engaged in it, Aunt Hebe,' protested Louisa, and almost laughed out loud at Lady Pyrland's horrified face. 'Oh, not directly, I grant you. There is a board to administer the various businesses. But I cast an eye over the accounts, and receive their reports from time to time.' Her eyes danced. 'I have even been known to descend upon one of the manufactories unexpectedly, just to make sure that they *know* I am still in command.'

Lady Pyrland buried her brow in her hands and moaned. 'If this should ever get out! Oh, Louisa, how *could* you?'

Her niece laughed. 'Very easily, ma'am, I assure you. What, would you have had me sit at home being a decorative addition to Mr Shittlehope's parlour?' She paused and sighed. 'Yes, I see you would. Mr Shittlehope would also have preferred it. But I should have been heartily bored. Besides, I was most usefully employed, and, even if some did not like my proposed reforms, I was always able to bring Mr Shittlehope around my thumb.'

Fascinated in spite of herself, Lady Pyrland had lowered her hands and was gazing at her niece in some surprise. 'I had thought you to have been *unhappy* in your married life, Louisa. And you speak of having *sold* yourself.'

'I did sell myself,' Louisa said flatly. 'I was unhappy. At first, that is. What would you, ma'am? Mr Shittlehope was more than sixty when we married, and I was scarce seventeen.'

'I know. Oh, I know!' said her aunt, all the earlier horror vanishing from her voice and giving way to pity. 'I remonstrated with your father, but to no avail.'

'So did I!' Louisa said grimly. 'Also to no avail.' Then she smiled radiantly. 'But he did me a favour, you know, little though I supposed it at the time. Mr Shittlehope and I contrived to rub along together. I found a means of employing my time — to both our advantages, in spite of my husband's complaints! — and since poor Mr Shittlehope had the misfortune to be carried off by his apoplexy, and was so obliging as to leave me everything, I now find myself free while I am still reasonably young, and able to take my pleasures as I see fit.'

'Louisa!' uttered the matron, affronted. 'Do I understand you to mean that you do not intend to seek the protection of a gentleman's *name*?'

'Not unless I fall in love,' Louisa told her tranquilly. Then the implication sank in and she giggled. 'Oh, did you think I meant to become someone's *mistress*? For shame, Aunt! The *merchant* class, you know, is by far more respectable than the aristocracy.'

Lady Pyrland heaved a sigh of relief. 'You have such odd ideas, Louisa, that I would not be surprised at anything!'

Privately though she doubted this, Lady Louisa let it pass. 'I am merely bent on enjoying myself, Aunt, so you may as well stop trying to palm me off on Philip — or anyone else! Instead of wasting your time on me, you may exercise your matchmaking talents on Millie, which would be much more to the purpose.

After all, it is really for her sake that I have come to town.'

'Millie,' repeated her aunt in a disgruntled tone. 'Yes, I thought we should come to that bread-and-butter miss of yours. Why in the world you must needs——'

She broke off as the door opened and Miss Millicent Lidbrook herself tripped into the room. She was, in comparison with the two older ladies, a petite girl, quite pretty in a sprigged chemise gown of muslin tied with a broad green sash, but of a sufficiently retiring and diffident disposition to justify to some extent Lady Pyrland's unkind comment. She had removed her hat to reveal a head of sandy hair, piled into modish rolls and ringlets, and a pair of trustful, green kitten eyes sought out Lady Louisa.

'Am I disturbing you?' she asked in a soft little voice.

'Not in the least,' said Lady Louisa at once, rising from the sofa and coming to put an arm briefly about her charge's shoulders in a warm hug. 'I was wondering where you had got to. Trying on all your new finery?'

'Oh, yes,' admitted the girl with a gush of red to her cheeks. 'But oh, dearest Louisa, I *do* hope you will not be angry! We have spent *ever* so much money.'

'Don't be a goose, Millie!' admonished her guardian caressingly. 'You know very well I want you to spend money. *Lots* of it!'

'But it seems so *extravagant*,' protested Millie, 'when I *have* gowns already.'

'My good child,' interpolated Lady Pyrland, 'as I

have told you I don't know how many times, what may have been acceptable in your northern retreat will not do *here*.'

'But I have not been in the north, ma'am. At least, not lately. I have been at school in Bath.'

'It is all the same!' stated Lady Pyrland, waving the fashionable watering place aside with one dismissive hand. 'You are in *London* now, Millicent, and if I am to sponsor you I will have you decked out in the proper mode, like a *real* débutante.'

'She *is* a real débutante,' said Louisa rather sharply. While she might tolerate animadversions on her own altered status, she would hear no criticism of her favourite. 'You are forgetting, Aunt Hebe, that Millie comes from *our* side of the family.'

Lady Pyrland had the grace to cough in a little embarrassment. 'To be sure. I meant nothing by it.'

But Millicent Lidbrook was too much aware of her own position to take offence. 'I—I think Lady Pyrland is right, Louisa. You know I would *never* have come out in the ordinary way. It is only *your* kindness and generosity that have brought it about.'

'Tush, what nonsense!' said Louisa almost roughly. 'Your father most unfortunately died young, but there was nothing in his lineage to render you ineligible.'

'I know, but, even had he lived, I hardly think we would come to London just for me,' said Millie sapiently, 'for I should not think my papa would *ever* have had any money.'

'Any more than mine!' agreed Louisa grimly. 'A more wasteful pair of profligates I hope I may never meet!'

'*Louisa*! How dare you speak in that disrespectful fashion of your father? You, too, Millicent. Outrageous!'

Millie blushed at this rebuke, but Louisa merely shrugged.

'It is only the truth, ma'am. *My* father gambled away his inheritance, and Millie's father could think of nothing better to do than to get himself killed in a duel and leave his wife and child destitute! Are we to respect them after *that*? Why, you were yourself animadverting to me only a moment ago on the undesirability of these Berownes. I am sure they can be no worse than our respective papas!'

'On the contrary, they are a good deal worse!' declared Lady Pyrland roundly. 'And if that boy does not come around haunting your doorstep, you may call me a Dutchwoman!'

'Oh, I don't think he will,' said Louisa unconcernedly. 'Believe me, after more than a year of wealthy widowhood, I have become adept at discouraging young men.' She twinkled. 'Though I dare say my methods might seem to you a trifle unorthodox.'

She noted all at once that Millicent was gazing at her in mingled doubt and dismay. 'What is the matter, Millie, darling?'

'Nothing,' said her charge hastily. 'I. . .I only wondered if you were speaking of—of that gentleman whom we met on the doorstep.'

Louisa raised her brows. 'Oh, you noticed him, did you? Well, I warn you, Millie, not to lose your heart to him! As my aunt will be only too ready to tell you, he is shockingly ineligible.' She glanced mischievously at her aunt. 'Besides apparently having in his train a family of much *worse* profligacy than our fathers.'

'Well, they are!' insisted Lady Pyrland defensively. 'Gambling and duelling are the least of their faults. If you only knew the half of the follies they have committed! They are drunken, brawling ne'er-do-wells, the lot of them!' She paused a moment, considering. 'Except perhaps Septimus. He may be extravagant and quite tediously affected, but to be fair I never heard any other ill of him. But one can scarcely consider eligible a younger son with nothing to recommend him but a turn for verse.'

'A turn for verse?' echoed Lady Louisa Shittlehope. 'You call that a recommendation?'

'Oh, yes, indeed,' asserted Lady Pyrland quite seriously. 'He is a very fine poet.'

CHAPTER TWO

THE voice was like liquid velvet, and it stopped Louisa in her tracks.

'". . .endless days in ecstasy
Of love, and hearts in harmony. . ."'

She paused in the doorway to the smaller of the two adjoining saloons, thrown open to accommodate the guests attending Mrs Wavertree's soirée.

'"In vain, and hoping endlessly,
The knight in vigil ceaselessly. . ."'

Behind her, in the long room, with its ornate gilded ceiling, and the Wavertree gallery of ancestors decorating its inner wall, the hum of meaningless chatter droned on. The atmosphere was oppressive with the many windows closed, what with the heat from the three huge chandeliers and the overpowering scents from many powdered and pomaded heads of hair.

Leaving Millie to the protection of her aunt, Louisa had escaped, slipping through several groups of people, most of whom were still mercifully unknown to her after her so far brief sojourn in the metropolis, intending to seek for some relief in the next room.

But it appeared that the smaller saloon afforded no asylum. Louisa peeped through the doorway. The owner of those velvety tones was standing outside her line of vision. But a bevy of females, apparently

26

facing him, stood or sat rapt and dewy-eyed, in attitudes of drooping adoration.

'". . .and donned his armour daringly,
And rode — upon his death rode he!"'

Lady Louisa Shittlehope viewed the moonstruck auditors of this nauseously sentimental verse with astonishment, her eyes dancing and a bubble of mirth quivering in her throat. She was just wondering who the reciter of this appalling doggerel might be, when a voice spoke in her immediate rear.

'I trust, Cousin, you are not about to succumb to the vaunted allure of young Berowne, and his idiotic versifying.'

Lady Louisa turned to confront the Marquis of Sedbergh. He was a tall, gaunt widower of some forty years, with two children in need of a stepmother. Thus he was extremely eligible — and even more anxious to partake of the late Mr Shittlehope's wealth than his predecessor had been. He was, unfortunately, also a proud, cold man with fixed ideas of women and their allotted place. Louisa loathed him.

'Idiotic?' she said at once. 'Have you listened to them, then? Or read them?'

'I would not waste my time on such frippery nonsense,' said the Marquis austerely. He had no patience with frivolity, as his conservative suit of dark hue indicated.

'Then you have no business to criticise it,' declared Louisa.

Sedbergh raised his brows and smiled thinly. 'I should have imagined you, Louisa, to have had more sense than to be taken in by such ——'

'I have not been taken in, Philip,' she interrupted flatly, moving away from the door and into the long room. Conveniently ignoring her dismissal of the verses as doggerel, she continued defiantly, 'I have barely heard a line or two. But I would certainly not presume to pronounce judgement upon something that I had not taken the trouble to study.'

The Marquis chose to bypass the challenge in her eye. 'Well, well, no doubt you will fall victim in due course, like many other young ladies.' He continued as Louisa opened her mouth, 'But I have not sought you out to quarrel with you, my dear. Rather to drop a hint in your ear.'

'Oh, yes?' said Louisa dangerously.

'Being so new to town, you cannot possibly be conversant with who is, or is not, a desirable acquaintance,' he went on smoothly, apparently unconscious of the volcano beginning to simmer beside him. 'I am concerned by what Hebe tells me.'

'*What* does my aunt tell you, Philip?' asked Louisa, in a deceptively mild tone.

'This matter of that *Berowne* boy, daring to press his suit upon you,' uttered Sedbergh, so much disgust in the emphasis he placed on the name that Louisa almost visibly bristled.

'Are you, Philip,' she queried coolly, 'being so obliging as to warn me against these Berownes?'

'You must understand that I feel in some sort responsible,' he began stiffly, something of her hostility beginning to penetrate. 'And when I saw you evidently about to enter here where that wretched poet is holding court ——!'

'Oh, so that is who he is!' exclaimed Louisa. 'Aunt Hebe did mention him. Which one is he?'

'Never mind which one he is!' said her cousin sternly. 'Understand me, Louisa. Acquaintance with any one of that family can only destroy your credit. You must not — '

'I *must* not?' echoed Louisa wrathfully. 'By what right, Philip, do you dare to tell me what I must not do?'

The Marquis glanced about them, fearful that her rising tones might attract attention. But they were in a clear space at one end of the long room, and seemed to have been temporarily left alone.

'I beg of you to lower your voice, Cousin,' he said anxiously. 'If I seem to you to be outside my role, let me assure you that it is only my regard for our family that — '

'Poppycock!' snapped Louisa, borrowing from her late husband's vocabulary. 'It is regard for your own interests, Philip. Let me tell you that I will choose my own acquaintances, sir, be they Berowne, green, scarlet, or — or anything else! *You* have nothing to say in the matter.'

'I am shocked — I may say *appalled* — to hear you speak in such a fashion, cousin. If you are to reject the mildest offer of advice — '

'I am in need of no advice from you, Cousin,' Louisa said, the large blue orbs flashing magnificently, 'and if you persist I will almost certainly run counter and go out of my way to make friends of these dissolute Berownes!'

'Bravo!' applauded a jovial new voice, and a pair of hands clapped.

Turning, Louisa beheld a portly individual, richly apparelled in green brocade over black silk breeches, with plump cheeks and merry brown eyes, brimful of mischief.

'Good God, another of them!' ejaculated Lord Sedbergh disgustedly, and, turning on his heel, he left his cousin flat.

'Good riddance!' said the newcomer, laughing. 'Allow me to assist you in your laudable ambition, Lady Louisa. I am Quarto Berowne, number four of the *dissolute* gang your cousin so heartily despises.'

Louisa held out her hand with automatic grace, the fire dying out of her eyes, to be replaced by an answering twinkle. 'You know me, then, Mr Berowne?'

'Oh, not *Mr*,' he begged, retaining her gloved hand in his pudgy one. 'You will never manage us all if you insist on formality. *Quarto* will do very well.'

Louisa found herself smiling. 'Must I manage you all, Quarto?'

'Undoubtedly. You are, after all, a lady of legendary wealth, and we are all as poor as church mice. You are bound to be plagued by every Berowne under the sun!'

'Oh, indeed? I suppose I may look next to hear *you* avowing devotion of no common order.'

'Decimus!' said his elder brother instantly. 'I little thought the infant would manage to steal a march on me! Yes, yes, I will be as devoted as you please,' he agreed gracelessly, 'if only you will scatter coin in my direction.'

'You are outrageous, Quarto,' scolded Louisa,

trying not to giggle. 'A refreshing approach, though, I grant you.'

They were interrupted by their hostess, a large, jolly woman, with an unbecoming head of hair of astonishing luxuriance, covered over in the very latest mode with bright red powder. There were several such heads in evidence tonight, as the fashion rapidly caught on, but it was still new enough to be startling.

'Quarto, you abominable boy!' she cooed, rapping the gentleman smartly on the knuckles with her folded fan so that he let go Louisa's hand at last. 'Playing off your tricks, are you?' She turned to Louisa. 'Your poor aunt is like a cat on hot bricks! She sent me over to break up your little tête-à-tête.'

'Did she indeed?' said Louisa, her eye kindling again.

'Don't tell her that, ma'am, for God's sake! I have only just succeeded in smoothing her feathers after that clod Sedbergh ruffled them so high.'

'Tush, don't fear me, Quarto!' Louisa told him. 'I can manage my aunt.'

'I don't doubt it,' said the gentleman with a jovial grin. 'I've only known you a moment or two, but I'm pretty sure already that you could manage anyone.'

'Go away, Quarto!' ordered Mrs Wavertree. '*I* can't manage Hebe. She frightens me to death. And I have endured enough of a scold for inviting you Berownes at all!'

'Surely, ma'am,' protested Louisa vehemently, 'you don't allow anyone to dictate to you about your guest list?'

'Good God, Lady Louisa,' Quarto burst in, 'it is

plain you are new to town! Four out of five hostesses
will bar us from their doors if they can.'

'It does not seem to bother you overmuch,'
observed Louisa, raising her brows.

'Not in the least. We have ways of getting around
them, you see.'

'Oh? Such as what?'

He laid a finger to the side of his nose. 'Ah, that
would be giving away a secret.'

'Pish, Quarto!' interrupted Mrs Wavertree. 'As if
we were not all very well aware of your "secret"!
They play off rival hostesses one against the other,
my dear, by telling one that her arch enemy will be
upset by their presence. Why, you may ask? Because,
if you please, her husband is the real father of one of
the Berownes!'

Even Louisa's matter-of-factness was shaken by
this revelation. 'You are not serious!'

'I see we *do* shock you, Lady Louisa,' said Quarto
in a voice of mock-sadness.

'Frankly, yes,' agreed Louisa. 'I hope I may never
learn anything else of what you may do, or I shall find
myself in agreement with my aunt and cousin!'

Quarto laughed. 'In that case I shall reserve the
more grisly items.'

Which, reflected Louisa, was just as well, for Lady
Pyrland joined them at that moment, in company
with Millie. However much she might fly in the face
of convention on her own account, she would be
obliged to be a little circumspect on Millie's behalf. It
would be grossly unfair to jeopardise her darling's
chances merely because she chose herself to defy her
relatives.

So she turned to Quarto with an air of dismissal, holding out her hand, and speaking with deliberate hauteur. 'No doubt we shall meet on some future occasion. Good evening.'

Quarto Berowne, twinklingly appreciative of her methods, had nothing to do but to kiss her gloved hand with a bow and take himself off.

Lady Pyrland watched his retreat with a minatory eye, and then turned to her niece. 'I am glad you sent him packing. Though to be sure, he is not as bad as Quintus.'

'I don't know that,' objected Mrs Wavertree. 'Only today the two of them were engaged in the most absurd race against some of their cronies.'

'What was that?' demanded Louisa at once, forgetting her vow to protect Millie from the Berownes' bad influence.

'Oh, it was their phaetons, as usual,' Mrs Wavertree told her, and her enjoyment in the story was patent. 'You see, they are both of them very able whips, Quarto and Quintus, and so it seems the other gentlemen would not race against them unless they were suitably handicapped.'

'And so?'

'Well, they decided to run their carriages *backwards*.'

Louisa's eyes danced. 'No, did they indeed? Were the rivals similarly hobbled?'

'*One* was. Decimus told me all about it. The brothers engaged to drive over half the distance each, going backwards, with one taking over from the other. Whereas their competitors were permitted to drive one backwards for the first half, and the other forwards for the second half in the normal way. Did you ever hear of anything more ridiculous?'

'Utter folly!' snorted Lady Pyrland disgustedly. 'I wish they had broken their necks!'

'Oh, *no*, Lady Pyrland!' piped up Millie's soft voice. 'How tragic that would have been!'

'Pho! Society has been prophesying—nay, hoping!—forever that they will come to grief in some violent fashion over their exploits, for we will not get rid of them by other means.'

'Very true,' agreed Mrs Wavertree, nodding. '*All* the Berownes are distressingly healthy.'

'Did they win?' asked Louisa interestedly. 'Today, I mean.'

'I neither know nor care!' stated her aunt.

'Indeed, I was so amazed by the story,' said Mrs Wavertree, shaking her head, 'that I quite forgot to ask.'

'*Lady Louisa*!' came a cry from their right.

All four ladies looked towards the doorway leading to the smaller saloon to see Decimus Berowne, very smart in blue velvet, evidently having just come out. Behind him was emerging the troop of poetry lovers—still sighing and simpering, Louisa noted with amusement.

Decimus came bounding up to the group, quite failing to notice Lady Pyrland's baleful glare, or Miss Millicent Lidbrook's dilating glance. He had eyes only for his inamorata.

'Lady Louisa, I did not expect to see you here! How do you go on?'

Louisa greeted him with a friendly smile. 'How do

you do, Mr Berowne? Oh, no. Decimus, is it not? I have been talking with one of your brothers.'

'Oh, pray don't!' begged the young man impulsively. 'I couldn't bear to be in competition with *them*.'

'Decimus Berowne!' said Lady Pyrland awfully. 'As regards Lady Louisa, *you* are in competition with no one!'

'Do you mind, Aunt?' Louisa said in an undervoice, as the unfortunate boy's head whipped round and his cheeks flooded with colour.

'Oh — er — Lady P-Pyrland,' he stuttered. 'I d-didn't see you.'

'You see me now,' stated the matron. 'I would as lief, however, that I did not see you!'

Mrs Wavertree, as acutely embarrassed as the young man himself, edged quietly away, quite unable to bring herself to intervene as a good hostess should. She need not have been concerned. Louisa was more than a match for her aunt.

'Wait, Decimus!' she called out, as he began to back away. 'I have something to ask you.'

Lady Pyrland's eagle glance swept back to her niece's face in outrage, but it was ignored as Decimus came a step closer.

'Tell me. Your brothers' race. Did they win?'

'I beg your p-pardon?' asked Decimus, too flustered to comprehend her question.

'The *backward* race. Did they win?'

'Oh! Oh, yes.' He grinned suddenly. 'Poor Mindrum — who was the first man of the other team, you know, and had engaged also to back his phaeton—ran straight into the ditch! By the time they had got him out, Quint was already at the winning-post.'

'Excellent!' laughed Louisa. 'How I wish I had seen it!'

'Well, I do not!' It was the aunt again, pale with annoyance. 'Nor do I wish to hear another word on the subject.'

Decimus, once more brought to a sense of his peril if he remained, bowed, again backing away. Unfortunately, Millie had somehow got herself behind him. She had been hovering in the background, torn between her hope that someone might remember to present her, and her dread that Decimus Berowne would speak to her, which would, she was certain, render her stupid and tongue-tied.

In her anxiety to get out of his path, she moved hastily aside, only to bump into one of the ladies who had come out of the other saloon and were now crowding this end of the long room. With a small gasp, Millie leapt back and cannoned straight into Decimus as he turned. In her flutter, as she tried to twist away, she trod on her own dove pearl gown, missed her footing, and fell her length to the floor.

'Millie!' cried Louisa, darting forward.

She had been a helpless spectator of the little drama, which had happened too quickly to be prevented. Unaware of the heads that turned, or of Decimus staring blankly at the girl lying at his feet, Louisa came to kneel beside the prone figure.

'Millie, are you all right?' she asked anxiously, her hands going down to grasp the girl's shoulders as she raised herself on her elbow.

The girl's cheeks brightened with shame at the

spectacle she had made of herself. 'I'm s-sorry,' she stammered. 'So c-careless!'

'Never mind that! Are you hurt, my darling?'

Millie tried to sit up, and her pink cheeks whitened again. 'My ankle!'

'Oh, no!' uttered Louisa, distressed. 'Is it very painful?'

She looked towards Millie's feet, and saw that a gentleman unknown to her was already on his knee, taking the ankle gently in his hands — seemingly unmoved by the immodesty of such a proceeding — and removing her buckled shoe.

'Is it bad?' Louisa asked, hardly noticing anything but the slender fingers going over the stockinged ankle.

'Does this pain you?' said the gentleman, in a voice that was only vaguely familiar in Louisa's preoccupied state.

Millie had quivered slightly at the pressure exerted on the joint. 'A — a very little,' she admitted, her colour fluctuating as she glanced up at the sea of interested faces above her.

'It does not seem to be swelling much,' announced the gentleman. 'I think it is only a slight sprain. If you will rest it awhile I think there will be no lasting damage. Come, let me carry you to a sofa.'

He made a move to lift Millie, but was forestalled.

'I'll do that, Setty,' Decimus announced, dropping to his knee beside the fallen girl. 'After all, it was my fault.'

'No, oh, no!' fluttered Millie, her heart beginning to pound as she was lifted into the alarming embrace of two strong arms. 'It was n-not your f-fault. It was *mine.*'

'Put your arm about my neck,' said Decimus, unheeding, and moved with his burden towards the door to the smaller saloon. 'There is a sofa in here. You may rest there.'

The immediate throng about them gave way, watching them go. But the interesting episode formed but a brief interlude in the festivities, and, after chattering for a moment on the matter, they went about their business much as before.

Louisa, her worst alarms already allayed, was beginning to rise when she found one slender hand held out to her.

'Allow me to assist you to your feet, ma'am.'

'Oh, thank you,' she said, and, taking the hand, she came up to find herself staring into a pair of pleasantly smiling brown eyes in quite the most attractive face she had yet seen in London. All of a sudden recognition snapped into her mind.

'The velvet voice!' she exclaimed. 'You are the poet!'

His eye gleamed. 'The enormous eyes! You are the Lady Louisa Shittlehope!'

She laughed. 'Yes, I am. How do you do? You are a Berowne, of course—I seem to be fated with Berownes tonight!—but I can't recall which one.'

'Easily remedied, ma'am.' He bowed with rare grace. 'Septimus Berowne, poet. Entirely at your service.'

'Like your brothers Decimus and Quarto, no doubt,' commented Louisa.

She looked him over with interest, taking in the

florid nature of his attire: silvered silk grey jacket over a crimson and cream striped waistcoat, only half buttoned, breeches of cream brocade, the whole somehow turned awry by the unbuttoned cuffs, the carelessly knotted fringed cravat and the unpowdered brown locks with strands escaping confinement and drifting on to the cheeks.

'*Very* poetic!' Louisa remarked, twinkling at him, and then realised that his glance was travelling with equal interest over her own person, clad in sky-blue that brought out her eyes even more than usual.

'Very *youthful*,' returned Septimus smoothly, 'for a lady riddled with gout, past thirty and verging on obesity!'

Louisa broke into laughter, that irrepressible merry jig in her eyes. So full of warmth were they, lighting up her face, that Septimus caught his breath. He thought her whole personality to be captured in that instant, and knew a moment of intense desire. Well-padded? Why, the woman had a magnificent figure! Rarely had he seen the new chemise gown worn to better effect, its low *décolletage* amply rewarding, with a sash drawn in over a gratifyingly narrow waist, and then flaring out with the promise of soft round flesh beneath. It was with difficulty that the poet brought himself to concentrate on what the lady was saying.

'Poor Decimus! He was in a regular quake by the time I had finished with him. I think it will not be long before he abandons any pursuit of me.' She twinkled at him. 'Well, Septimus Berowne, poet, I have to thank you for your assistance with my ward. Perhaps you would be kind enough to tell me where your brother has taken her.'

'I shall do better than that,' said Septimus, offering her his arm. 'I shall lead you there myself.'

Louisa cast a brief look over her shoulder, discovered that Lady Pyrland had melted away somewhere — no doubt too angered to stay! — and put her hand on his arm.

But she said ruefully, 'If it weren't for my anxiety over Millie, I don't think I should come with you. I am far from wishing to please my aunt and cousin, but I suppose I ought, in common charity, to save them from apoplexy.'

Septimus choked. 'Do they stand in danger of it, do you think?'

'I should not be at all surprised,' Louisa told him frankly. 'My aunt is fairly tearing her hair already, and Philip — Lord Sedbergh, my cousin, you know — has already tried to warn me against you all.'

'Ah, the impossible Berownes! Of course, I understand now,' Septimus said as he steered her towards the smaller saloon. 'You cannot blame them, Lady Louisa. Anyone who had your best interests at heart must needs object to the Berownes.' He smiled. 'Not to *me*, naturally. Being a poet, I am *expected* to live dangerously.'

Louisa looked round at him, unconsciously pausing in the doorway. She was so tall that he topped her only by inches, so that her mobile eyes easily met his own bland ones.

'You take care to live up to expectation, I collect?'

'Certainly,' agreed Septimus. 'I am, of all things, a conformist.'

'So you conform to the popular idea of a poet?'

Septimus sighed. 'You are by far too shrewd, Lady Louisa. Pray don't consort with my admirers. You would ruin me!'

Louisa laughed. 'There is not much fear of that.'

Septimus threw back his head, dramatically laying the back of his hand against his brow. 'Ah, me! A blow to end all blows! Have you *read* my work?'

'I heard you, Septimus Berowne, poet, reciting a few of your lines. That is all.'

'Worse than that you could not have said!' uttered the poet brokenly.

Louisa giggled as she moved into the other saloon. 'Is this your idea of a poet's manner, Septimus Berowne? I should rather have expected you to lounge in dark humour in some corner, frowning at the world.'

Septimus stepped back and stared at her. 'Do you know, Lady Louisa, you have a point. It is an idea. Decidedly it is an idea. I may well take your excellent advice.'

'If you take my advice,' Louisa said tartly, catching sight of Millie in a swooning attitude on a sofa on the far side of the room, with her rescuer kneeling beside her and clasping both her hands, 'you will remove to the other room and take your brother with you. At once, if you please. Before you ruin both our reputations!'

'Madam,' Septimus said gravely, 'your word is law. Decimus!' He beckoned briefly to his brother as that young man looked up. 'But allow me to point out, Lady Louisa,' he added, turning his bland gaze once more upon her, 'that *nothing* could ruin the reputation of anyone saddled with a name like Shittlehope!'

Bowing, he left Louisa staring, and passed out of the room in company with his brother.

The Berowne clan, being not unnaturally blackballed from membership of the exclusive precincts of White's Club, chose to frequent Boodles. Quintus was therefore to be found almost every evening — whenever the luck was in and he was in funds — hard at play at one of the gaming tables. He was frequently accompanied by his brother Quarto, less frequently by Decimus and, with reluctance, by Septimus, whose main purpose was to prevent his young brother from coming too much under the influence of the elder. Quint was not an example for a fledgling to follow!

His very attitude, as he lounged at the table, with Quarto looking on behind him, was redolent of his decadent habits. An expensive waistcoat of flowered satin hung open, and he had removed both his coat and his wig, revealing his shaven pate, which gave him a sinister air. For his once comely visage, with the proverbial Berowne features, had been flawed by debauchery.

His skin had a greyish tinge, that below his eyes sagging puffily, and his cheeks were sunken. Lines ran deeply from mouth to chin and his lips had acquired a permanent sneer. Oddly, this dissipated look rather enhanced than detracted from his appeal to the opposite sex, many of whom sighed a little in his sight.

'Confound it!' he growled as the dice ran against

him for the third time. 'Thought Dame Fortune was on my side after this morning.'

'It wasn't Dame Fortune, Brother,' observed Quarto sapiently. 'It was Mindrum's poor judgement.'

'A pox on the bones!' exclaimed Quintus, rising from his chair. 'Your pardon, gentlemen. I'll try the cards again.'

'As you please,' said one of the gamesters indifferently, too intent on his own luck to care.

'Hold hard, Quint!' protested another, who happened to be winning. 'The night's young yet. Time for the luck to change.'

'I intend it to,' said Quintus, reaching for the half-full bottle of burgundy that stood on a stand at his elbow. 'But not at this table.'

'Have it your own way, then,' rejoined his colleague a trifle sulkily, and turned back to the game.

Quarto retrieved his bother's coat and wig for him, slipping the latter carelessly over the bald dome so that it lay askew. Without bothering to correct this, Quintus took the coat and slung it over one shoulder as they wandered away.

'This constant living on the edge of poverty sickens me,' he complained in a surly tone. 'Why the devil can't a man have an easy time of it for a change?'

'What you need, Brother, is a wealthy widow,' Quarto told him, slapping him on the back. 'But I warn you, I'll fight you for her tooth and nail.'

There was a speculative gleam in the other's eye as he looked round at him. 'The Shittlehope? You've met her? What is she like?'

'Met her at Wavertree's this very evening. She's a

merry piece, full of fun and gig, I'll wager. But shrewd, mark you! Not easily taken in. The managing sort, what's more. Too damned inconvenient, I dare say, if she hadn't so much brass.'

Quintus looked thoughtful, pausing in his way to one of the large table where cards were in use instead of dice and a little skill might tip the luck in one's favour.

'How much brass?'

'God knows! The fellow was a merchant, that's all anyone has heard. The house is hired, but furnished, so Dess says, in the first style of elegance.'

'Hmm.' Quintus was frowning, an idea revolving in his head. He might set Sexta on to find out more. She would do anything for him, that he knew — if he went the right way to work with her. But if Quarto was also in the running, he would do better to keep his scheme to himself. He cocked an eyebrow at his brother.

'Don't tell me Dess is hanging out for a rich wife already?'

Quarto laughed. 'At eighteen? Use your head! Silly nodcock thinks he's in love.'

The sneer on the other's mouth became more marked. 'Young fool!' The noise of fresh arrivals at the main door attracted his attention. 'And here he is. Oh, the devil!'

Quarto looked round to find not only Decimus, but Septimus also, coming their way, and understood at once his brother's dissatisfaction. Verbal duels between poet and reprobate were frequent.

'That was a capital race, Quint!' said Decimus enthusiastically as they came up. 'I wish you will show me the trick of backing my horses.'

'Some day, infant, some day,' Quintus drawled carelessly, 'if you can find me awake and sober enough to demonstrate.'

'You'd do better to have Quarto teach you, then, my babe,' put in Septimus, 'else you'll wait til Domesday.'

There was an instant of frozen tension as their eyes met.

'Ever tried to compose verse with a broken head, Brother?' enquired Quintus meaningfully.

'I've no fancy for it, Quint,' the poet said blandly. 'Nor for the sentence imposed for fratricide. But I could always flee the country and join Tertius, I dare say.'

Tertius, the third Berowne, had — as a desperate measure imposed by his own father, fearful of finding himself liable for his lamentable offspring's debts as well as his own! — been shipped off to the West Indies, and was by all accounts settled there in style and comfort, himself the father of a rapidly growing family of dubious heritage.

'By all means let us try it,' Quintus drawled. His contemptuous glance encompassed his other two brothers. 'Would either of you care to bet on the outcome?'

'No!' snapped Decimus, who hated to see his brothers at outs.

'*They* can't lose, Quint,' Septimus said, his light brown eyes glittering with a dangerous light. 'Either way they gain. For if you send me to the devil instead, it will be *you* who joins Tertius in exile.'

'Which is the more likely, milksop!' began Quintus angrily, squaring up.

'Hey! Hey!' interposed Quarto, calling them to order. 'Close ranks, my boys, close ranks! We're in a public place.'

It was the practice of the clannish Berownes, regardless of their personal feelings, to present a united front to the world at large. For the world's odium had been earned principally on account of their parents' indifference, and their only defence was to stand firm together.

Quintus sank back, shrugging. 'It's all one to me. I'm for the cards.'

He went off, and his youngest brother, casting a reproachful glance at Septimus, followed him. 'I'm with you, Quint.'

'That was blunderheaded, my boy,' commented Quarto when they were out of earshot.

'I know it,' admitted the poet with a wry grimace. 'I can't stand to see Dess hero-worshipping him, that's all. Remember how Quint himself was with Original?'

Septimus was firmly of the opinion that Quintus's own character had been ruined by copying the antics of their eldest brother, Original, now mercifully under restraint at the hands of his formidable father-in-law. Having married, out of hand, an heiress, he had reaped an unexpected reward when the girl's papa placed him under virtual house arrest. It was rarely that he escaped to town, and of late years — so reported their sister Secunda, who happened to live in the same vicinity — he had grown so gross and indolent that he was unlikely to make the effort, a prophesy that the rest of his siblings greeted with unalloyed relief.

Quarto patted his younger brother gently on the shoulder. 'Don't vex yourself, Setty. Dess is as unlike Quint in character as he could be. Damned if I can fathom *who* Quint's father might have been!'

'Or yours, Quarto!' retorted Septimus, grinning suddenly, and digging his brother significantly in his growing paunch. 'Personally, I'm thinking of laying claim to Fielding, after all.'

'Henry Fielding?' frowned Quarto in a puzzled voice. 'Thought he wrote prose.'

'He did. But he also had a hand in setting up the Bow Street Runners. He must have had an acute sense of the decline of modern morals, and I can't otherwise account for my presence in this hideously immoral family!'

CHAPTER THREE

QUINTUS BEROWNE'S immorality was never in doubt. At his lodging in Clarges Street, awaiting him as usual that evening, was his current mistress, sometime actress Lily Levant, snug in his bed and ready to welcome him suitably. Drunk or sober, he was always in need of her services. This evening, having continued to lose, even at cards, he was not only drunk, but in a foul mood. Lily was halfway to assuaging these evils, when a violent knocking sounded on his outer door.

'Hell and the devil confound it!' Quintus cursed furiously, as the noise penetrated the whirling pleasurable sensations in his brain.

'Don't heed it!' begged Lily, so much in the throes herself that the thought of his leaving was torture.

'Must heed it,' growled the man, struggling out of the bed. 'Can't do anything against that confounded racket.'

Indeed, the knocking had not ceased, the loud rat-a-tat-tat continually sounding, with only the briefest of intervals in between. Throwing on a robe, Quintus staggered out through the living-room and undid the bolt. At once the knocking stopped. He flung open the door.

'What the devil——?' he began, and stopped as he saw the cloaked figure of a woman standing there. 'Sexta!'

'I *had* to see you, Quint,' pleaded his sister in her rather high-pitched voice.

'At this time of night? Are you mad?'

'No one knows I am not in my bed,' she explained quickly. 'Please let me in!'

He stepped back automatically, and shut the door behind her as she slipped quickly inside. She put back the hood of her cloak and watched her brother with anxious eyes as he went to the table and re-lit the recently snuffed candles that had been left alight for him. Then he turned to face his sister, his features set and hard.

She was a thin woman, the least attractive of the Berowne girls, and the only one left single. She lived in a state of perpetual high-strung tension, anxiety for her favourite brother gnawing at her. They were but ten months apart in age, and very close. At twenty-seven, Sexta's complexion had already turned sallow, and her eyes had a tendency to bulge. Coupled with their darting nervous movement, this gave her an air of slight insanity.

'You've no business coming here at all, Sexta,' scolded her brother, 'let alone at this hour. Dolly may be lax, but by God she'd lock you in your room if she knew of this!'

'She wouldn't care,' uttered Sexta sulkily. 'And I'd still have come if she locked me in for a week!'

Quintus shrugged. 'On your own head be it. What do you want?'

She came up to him then, her eyes round with distress. 'Oh, Quint! Dess told me how you quarrelled with Setty tonight. I wish you would not! You know — you *know* he is not the "milksop" you call him. Oh, he affects that silly pose of his, his "poet's manner", but indeed, indeed. . .'

'He is a fine swordsman,' finished Quintus on a drawl. 'Yes, you have told me so many times, and I am perfectly aware of it. We have fenced together at Angelo's often enough. What of it?'

Sexta's mouth quivered. 'You think he is not in earnest when he says these things to you, Quint, but he *is*. He hates you!'

'Gammon!' said Quintus with a sneer. 'Hate his own brother? Why, Setty is no more capable of such an emotion than Quarto. Don't you know him better than that?'

'I know him better than *you*, it seems,' Sexta said desperately. 'It is not you he cares for, but Dess. As they all do. As even I do, for he is the baby, after all. But Setty has a *special* feeling for him.'

'I can't conceive why you should imagine such a fairy-tale,' Quintus drawled. 'If my brother has a special feeling for anything other than his trumpery verses——'

'My God, but you are *blind*!' Sexta screeched suddenly, her overwrought nerves flying into temper, as they often did.

'Don't throw a tantrum with me, Sexta!' warned her brother, his eyes narrowing.

With difficulty, she pulled herself together. 'I'm not in a tantrum,' she said stiffly. 'I would not have come here but for my care of you. But if you will have none of it, it is all the same to me.'

'I'm glad to hear it,' drawled Quintus. 'Though I don't believe it for a moment.'

'Beast!' she threw at him, and, gathering her cloak about her, prepared to leave.

'Wait!' called her brother imperatively.

She turned her head at the door, half eager, hoping for a change of mood. In truth he had only to crook a finger and she would come running, so strong was her love for him. Quintus, well aware of it, and, deep down, fond of her in his fashion, nevertheless made use of it to suit his own purposes.

He smiled, a lop-sided smile, oddly attractive in a countenance so ravaged. Sexta melted, coming slowly back.

'I need your help, Sexta.'

Her heart sank. She was always afraid of what he might ask, for she knew that however intolerable to her the doing of it might be she would force herself to it — although not always without a show of defiance.

'Sexta, my sweet, there is a new money-bags come to town.'

Her lip quivered dangerously. She was always difficult, Quintus recollected, when it came to the subject of his possible marriage, which would inevitably separate them.

'Lady Louisa Shittlehope,' Sexta said in a subdued tone. 'Dess told me about her.'

Quintus came close, and, putting his arm around her, he drew his fingers across her cheek and chin, and held her so that she was forced to look up into his face. He could feel her uneven pulse-beat against his chest.

'You will make a friend of this Louisa, Sexta.' And for all the caress in his voice, there was an underlying threat. It was an order. 'You will find out all about her late merchant husband, and you will give me an account of it. I want to know just what she is worth.'

Her lips were open, trembling on a yes, when from the doorway behind them came Lily Levant's plaintive cockney voice.

'Quint, love, ain't you coming back to bed? I'm getting cold.'

Sexta wrenched herself from her brother's embrace. Quivering with temper, she stamped her foot at him. 'How dare you? I am at fault, am I, to come here so late? Or is it only because your *whore* is here with you? Well, you need not think I'll *spy* for you, Brother! I wouldn't *speak* to this Louisa if you were to pay me a thousand pounds!'

Then she ran to the door, flung it wide so that it crashed against the wall, and was gone from the room even as her brother called out, 'Sexta! Come back!'

He strode to the door and looked after her as she raced down the stairs. Then he slammed the door shut in his turn and fixed menacing eyes on Lily Levant.

She was backing away, her hands over her mouth as if to push back her foolish interruption. For she knew his temper. The last time the bruises had remained for days.

'You stupid bitch!' he drawled softly, starting forward. 'Get back in bed before I. . .'

Lily fled.

'But this is enchanting!' Louisa said in delight, looking about the gardens, where long walks were interspersed with arbours and wooden benches under flowering gazebos.

'It is very pretty,' conceded Lady Pyrland, unbending a trifle from the stiff disapproval that had been visible in her face up to this moment.

'It is far less crowded than Vauxhall,' Millie ventured, addressing her hostess's daughter.

Charlotte Childrey trilled with laughter. 'That is because Mama has hired the full use of it for the day.'

'I should think so!' uttered Lady Pyrland with hauteur. 'Had she not done so, Augusta would have found her party very thin of company.'

'Oh, why?' asked Millie innocently. 'It is so nice here!'

'Because in the ordinary way,' Charlotte explained kindly, 'these particular gardens are frequented only by cits.'

'Like my late husband, you mean,' observed Louisa with a glint in her eye.

Her aunt cast her a dagger look, but Charlotte Childrey's pretty cheeks went pink.

'Oh, I do beg your pardon, Lady Louisa! I intended no offence.'

'Of course you did not.' Louisa smiled. 'Yet I cannot see why there is this stupid prejudice against our solid citizens here at St Pancras Wells, when the *bon ton* mingle quite happily at Vauxhall and Ranelagh with all sorts and conditions of men.'

'Oh, but Ranelagh is *passé*, Louisa,' Millie told her with a new-found wisdom. She had gained in confidence these few days, having met a number of people and made friends with some her own age. 'Charlotte told me. Remember, Charlotte?' she said, turning to her hostess. 'When you came to visit me the other day when I was laid up with my ankle.'

'Indeed, no one who is anyone would be seen at Ranelagh now.'

'Dreadful place!' said Lady Pyrland. 'Given over entirely to demireps and——'

'And gentlemen, no doubt,' Louisa suggested sapiently.

'Gentlemen will go *anywhere*,' returned her aunt resignedly, 'where they may indulge themselves in liquor. I dare say you will find them doing so here, for I know they serve punch and claret at these places.'

'Well, most of them have gone to the bowling green, or to play skittles and quoits,' Charlotte offered in a palliative tone.

'Skittles!' squeaked Millie. 'Oh, how I should love to play! I was used to be a dab hand at skittles.'

Louisa laughed indulgently. 'Yes, it was your chief accomplishment at school, wasn't it, Millie? Do show her where they are playing, Miss Childrey,' she said coaxingly, anxious that Millie should enjoy herself.

Charlotte needed no urging, and the two girls sped away in the direction of the buildings that housed the indoor attractions of the pleasure grounds. In fact it was still rather chilly for a party such as this, and most of the elder members of the company had chosen to remain inside, enjoying coffee or tea and slices from the hot fresh-baked loaves that were so much a feature of tea gardens. Maids brought to them the traditional syllabubs and junkets, the fresh cream and the warm milk straight from the cow, rather than — as was customary, particularly in summer — the guests enjoying the novel game of going to see the cows in the meadows hard by to sample these rural delicacies direct.

The young people, however, in general hardier than their seniors and intent upon enjoying the unusual entertainment, were outside having fun, even the damsels ignoring the cold, despite the little protection afforded by their fashionable pastel cotton overdresses and white muslin petticoats.

Louisa had taken the precaution of dressing suitably in a demi-riding coat of blue wool cloth, over heavy petticoats in a lighter shade of the same hue. A cravat and dashing feathered hat completed her toilette, and she was quite warm under the weak sun filtering a little through the clouds.

'I wonder you should let the girl out of your sight in a place of this kind!' remarked Lady Pyrland disapprovingly as the two younger ladies vanished along a walk.

'Whyever not, Aunt? She will scarcely get into the wrong company. All the "cits" have been excluded!'

The matron stiffened alarmingly, her stiff purple silks crackling. 'Are you having the temerity to laugh at me, Louisa?'

'I should not dream of it!' Louisa saw the colour heighten either side of the elder woman's Roman nose, and smiled. 'Come, Aunt Hebe, let us cry a truce. I will refrain from cheap gibes if only you will cease to lament a circumstance which is no fault of my own.'

Lady Pyrland seemed to struggle with herself for a moment. 'Very well. I am sure I do not wish to quarrel with you over what cannot be mended. Millicent, however, is another matter.'

'Tush, what harm can she come to in the company of Charlotte Childrey?'

'None, if she remain in her company. But Charlotte is bound to mingle in order to assist her mother, and I cannot think that she will find it convenient to keep Millicent in tow.'

Louisa sighed. 'Shall we stroll in the same direction, then? I dare say we will come upon the skittles and find her happily engaged.'

'By all means,' agreed Lady Pyrland in more amiable tones.

She would in fact have preferred to seek the company of some of her cronies inside the house, but she had not yet given up hope of a union between Louisa and her cousin Philip. If only her niece were not so preoccupied with the chit Millicent Lidbrook! Yet another example of her brother's folly. He had taken the girl's widowed mother into his home only because he needed a housekeeper, of course! But what in the world had possessed him to hand over guardianship of the daughter to Shittlehope?

Lady Pyrland was not to know that Louisa, her heart wrung by the sorry plight of a bewildered little girl, and her affection caught by the kitten eyes that responded so trustfully to her overtures of friendship, had made it a condition of her marriage that her husband be named Millie's guardian. On his death this had passed—along with everything else, and at Louisa's instigation—to his widow. Consequently Millie's future was assured.

As the two ladies made their way through the walks, discussing, of necessity, not Louisa's own future, but where the games might be taking place, their ears were assailed by flying feet coming down

one of the parallel walks, and feminine voices like a
pair of twittering magpies.

'Quickly, quickly, Tavey!'

'I'm coming as fast as I can, Nonie! Drat these
petticoats!'

'I only hope Setty is not surrounded by his usual
court, that is all.'

'It's not Setty we need, but Quarto. Setty will only
quarrel with Quint and make everything worse.'

'How *can* it be worse, Tavey?' And a distinct sob
accompanied the words. 'Quint may be *killed*.'

Louisa halted, staring at her aunt with a frown in
her eyes. 'Someone is in trouble!'

'Quickly!' came the other voice. 'Heaven help
Wherwell, say I. He is far more likely to be killed
than Quint!'

Louisa seized her stunned aunt's arm and began to
hurry forwards, calling out loudly, 'Who are you?
Can you hear me? Do you need help?'

The feet stopped dead, and there was a sudden
silence.

'Hello!' Louisa called again. 'Who is it? Where are
you?'

'*Louisa*,' hissed Lady Pyrland. 'You cannot interfere! I fancy I know those voices.'

Louisa hardly heard her. The feet had begun to run
again, and so did she. All of a sudden the walk ended
in a square, and beyond it could be clearly seen the
house and the green beside it, where the young
people were at play.

But Louisa looked towards the other walks, and at
once saw two young ladies hurrying down one of
them. She went quickly forward.

'Was it you in such distress?' she asked urgently. 'Let me assist you if I can. Forgive me, but I could not help but overhear something of what you said. What has occurred?'

The two girls stopped so suddenly that they almost cannoned into her, grasping instinctively at each other for support. They were remarkably alike, with pretty features characterised by light brown pansy eyes and full mouths that seemed strangely familiar.

'Oh!' uttered one blankly. 'You are Lady Louisa, aren't you?'

'I am. I have not the pleasure of knowing you, I believe.'

'I am Nona Fullands, and this is ——'

'Never mind presentations now, Nonie,' uttered the other one breathlessly, casting an apologetic glance at Louisa. 'I'm sorry, but we have no time for punctilio.'

'No, of course you have not,' Louisa agreed quickly. 'You need to find someone, don't you?'

'Yes, Quarto Berowne,' she agreed. 'Have you seen him at all?'

Louisa shook her head.

'Or Setty?' chimed in the one who had introduced herself as Nona Fullands. 'I mean Septimus Berowne. The poet, you know.'

'I am afraid not. But perhaps I can be of assistance?'

'*Louisa*!' came angrily from behind her.

'Oh, Lady Pyrland, have *you* seen Quarto or Setty?' begged Nona prettily.

'I have not. And I suggest that you both find your *husbands* if you are in need of assistance. Louisa, you are not to mix yourself up in this affair, whatever it might be!'

'Oh, be quiet, Aunt Hebe!' snapped Louisa impatiently.

Not only Lady Pyrland, her mouth at half-cock, but both young ladies obeyed this behest, staring at one another in amazement.

'Perhaps you *can* help us,' began the second one, eyeing Louisa in awe.

At the same instant her companion, who had caught sight of someone over on the green, cried out, 'There is Dess! He may have seen them.'

All three pairs of eyes glanced round, and Lady Pyrland, forgetting her niece's extraordinary rudeness, gasped with outrage. Because not only was Decimus Berowne clearly visible among the company on the green, but beside him was Miss Millicent Lidbrook, apparently in laughing conversation with him as they stood over a set of fallen skittles.

'There, now, you see, Louisa! What did I tell you? You will have to go and get her away.'

'All in good time, Aunt,' Louisa said, and caught Nona as she began to move. 'Do you go and search for Quarto, while I go with — your sister, I imagine?' Two heads nodded, and she went on, 'Let us run back to the scene of this distressing occurrence and you may tell me the details on the way. Perhaps we may be able to accomplish something.'

'Louisa! I forbid you —— '

'Aunt Hebe, why don't *you* go and rescue Millie? I am otherwise engaged at this present.'

'Certainly I will,' announced her aunt, eyes snapping. 'But if you choose to entangle yourself in the

affairs of these wretched Berownes, Louisa, I wash
my hands of you!'

Louisa barely heard the words as her aunt stalked
off after Nona Fullands, who had darted away, for
she was already on the move with the other girl,
turning back down the walk.

'It is very kind of you, Lady Louisa,' the girl said. 'I
am Octavia Kilgetty, by the by.'

'I am happy to meet you—though not in such sad
circumstances. Tell me what happened, if you
please.'

'Oh, it was dreadful!' uttered Octavia in distressed
tones. 'Sexta and Quint have not been speaking for
days, and they have just had the most terrible
quarrel! They always *do* quarrel, of course. I think it
is just *because* they care so much for each other.'

'I don't quite understand,' Louisa said frowningly
as they hurried along. 'Are they married?'

'Married!' Octavia gasped, pausing and glancing
round with a stunned expression on her face. 'Heavens, no! They are brother and sister, of course.'

'Oh, I see. I beg your pardon,' Louisa said, but
with a little gesture urged her new-found protégée
on. 'It was just that you said they cared for each
other.'

'Well, it is more Sexta who cares for him, I think.
Indeed, it's my belief that is why she never married.
She is a great deal older than me, even. But then
Nonie and I were both married almost out of the
schoolroom.'

Already in the distance could be heard the sound
of raised voices.

'Oh, dear, they are still at it,' uttered Octavia.

'Drat Quint! He cares for nobody, I believe. And if poor Lord Wherwell is to come out of this wounded — or even dead! — it will be a great deal too bad.'

Louisa had met Lord Wherwell, and she vaguely recalled an innocuous-looking man of middle height and mild manners.

'I would not have supposed Lord Wherwell to have been one to become drawn into a fight,' she observed.

'Of course he is not, poor man! His mistake lay in dangling after Sexta. Mind, she probably encouraged him only to annoy Quint. He cannot *bear* her to pay attention to any other man.'

'But what in the world *happened*?' demanded Louisa.

'I'm not even certain myself, though I saw it all,' said Octavia. 'I was so shocked I could hardly take it in. Then Nonie and I decided to run for Quarto.'

'But what can he do?' asked Louisa, still at sea.

'Why, stop the duel.'

'Duel?'

'*Yes*,' said Octavia breathlessly. 'Wherwell has called Quint out — and of course Quint has accepted!'

'Wherwell called him out?' echoed Louisa in disbelieving tones, although the commotion to be heard ahead of them seemed to bear it out.

'Yes, because Quint threw a pot of junket in his face.'

Louisa was breathless herself, but a burst of laughter escaped her at this. '*What*?'

'I know. It is perfectly absurd!' Octavia agreed crossly.

They had reached the end of the walk and came

out into a clearing beside a fenced meadow. Here an extraordinary — and extremely noisy — scene was in progress.

Two gentleman stood a little apart, glaring at each other, and before one of them was a thin girl, her features distraught, her hands locked on the man's arms as if she was holding him back. She appeared to be trying to shake him as she shouted into his face. All three were talking at once, voices angrily raised, so that it was impossible to make out a word.

In a meadow beyond the fence, a pair of interested milkmaids and a cowman — together with several milch cows still chewing cud — gazed upon the scene with mouths wide open. In the clearing a long table, on which were placed various jugs and dishes filled with creamy substances, was attended by an equally interested serving wench, who appeared to be more concerned over the spectacle before her than the depredations that had been made upon her wares. Several dishes lay scattered and broken on the ground, and the remains of their contents littered both the grass and the waistcoats of the two warring gentlemen. Lord Wherwell, indeed, had a face and wig quite festooned with creamy slops.

Louisa, gazing upon this last manifestation, felt an unseemly fit of giggling threaten. But she knew that the situation was still too desperate for laughter. Only drastic measures would serve!

In the voice of an outraged nurse coming upon a scene of disorder among her charges, she demanded, 'What, may I ask, is the meaning of all this?'

Coming in under the high pitch of the battle, the alien sound penetrated. All three combatants stopped speaking almost as one, their eyes flying to find the source of the intrusion.

'Only look at yourselves!' went on Louisa before they had a chance to gather their wits. 'Have you any idea what you look like? A pair of gentlemen behaving like a couple of squabbling schoolboys! At a party, too. You should be ashamed of yourselves. And you, madam, should certainly have more conduct than to remain in the presence of a fight between members of the other sex!'

'Who the devil are you?' demanded Quintus rudely, scowling at her.

'If it is any business of yours,' returned Louisa smoothly, 'I am Lady Louisa Shittlehope.'

Quintus was so surprised that the fury died out of his face. 'The devil you are!' He shot a glance at his sister, who had let go his arms and was staring in mute resentment not at Louisa, but at Octavia Kilgetty.

'Sexta, this is Lady Louisa,' said Quintus with meaning. 'You might at least say, '"How do you do?"'

Sexta turned on him. 'Don't you tell me what to say,' she began shrilly.

'*Enough*!'

The sharp command arrested her. She blinked at Louisa, who nodded. 'Quite enough, madam. Don't you realise that there are many persons within earshot? I am sure you cannot wish to disturb your hostess with this *appalling* conduct.' Without pausing for a reply, she turned to Wherwell. 'I understand that a duel is proposed here over this nonsense, and that you are the author of it.'

'What would you have had me do?' asked his lordship in a disgruntled manner. 'Am I to stand by and see a man strike a lady, be she never so much his sister?'

Louisa's glance went instantly to Sexta again, and her face softened. 'Oh, my dear, is that true?'

It was Quintus who answered, his tone one of drawling sarcasm. '*If* it is any business of yours, Lady Louisa, yes, it is true. But if having a dish of syllabub emptied over my person is not provocation enough, I don't know what is!'

Louisa threw up her eyes. 'You do realise that you have all been behaving like children, and that to be fighting a duel over such a matter can only serve to make you ridiculous?'

'What do you think I care for the world's opinion?' sneered Quintus.

'There is something in that, Lady Louisa,' Octavia said judiciously, intervening at last. 'The world's opinion is so bad of us all already that I cannot think this will make much difference.'

Louisa looked from Octavia to Quintus and Sexta, a quick frown creasing her forehead, and was just about to speak when another party erupted on to the scene.

'What the devil's to do, Quint?' called out Quarto Berowne, puffing into the clearing.

Close behind him came Decimus, with Nona Fullands at his heels. Dashing in, he made directly for Sexta, putting a protective arm about her. 'Are you all right?' He glanced at his elder brother. 'What did you want to hit her for, you villain?'

Louisa's eyes, following him, flew back to Nona

and found Septimus Berowne. He was standing just inside the clearing, his arms folded, running an eye over the tableau before him, and nodding his head as much as to say that he had known how it would be.

'Why, you are *all* Berownes!' Louisa exclaimed.

'Did I not say so?' asked Octavia beside her.

'No, Tavey, you silly!' Nona said, coming up to her. 'I told her my *married* name. How was she to guess?'

Septimus, a twinkle at the back of his eye as he watched Louisa's astonishment grow, her eyes travelling over the members of his family, stepped forward.

'Allow me to clarify it for you, ma'am.' He pointed to Quarto. 'As the three eldest are no longer in town, you have there Quarto, number four, who is senior among us.'

Grinning, Quarto bowed. 'She knows me.'

The poet's hand moved. 'Next you have number five, Quintus, followed by number six, Sexta.'

Although Quintus inclined his head, the sneer on his lips pronounced, Sexta greeted her identification with a toss of the head and a defiant flash of eyes at Septimus. Unheeding, her brother tapped his own chest.

'You are number seven, of course,' Louisa put in, smiling. 'I had deduced that for myself.'

'You would have, naturally.' He drew his younger sisters forward. 'Now, after rather a longish gap, you have the babes. Here is Mrs Kilgetty.'

The girl smiled. 'I am Octavia, number eight, and —'

'Do you mind, Tavey?' Septimus said, pushing her gently away. 'I am doing this. And here is —'

'I can do myself, I thank you, Setty!' chimed in his last sister.

'This,' said Septimus firmly, ignoring her, 'is Nona, Mrs Fullands, who is number nine. Decimus, the last of us, and the tenth, you already know.'

'My aunt was right!' Louisa exclaimed, her eyes dancing. 'There is no quarrel here at all, is there? It has all been a plot to draw me into the devilish Berowne snare!'

An answering gleam came into the poet's eye, but Nona at once demurred.

'No such thing! I *assure* you, Tavey and I saw the whole thing. And Lord Wherwell is not one of us!'

'Quite right, Nonie,' broke in Quarto, coming forward. 'Wish we had thought of it, though. What a famous lark it would have been!'

'May I suggest, ma'am,' Septimus said, 'that you withdraw with our sisters, and let us settle this affair as gentlemen?'

'We're not going anywhere,' said Octavia firmly. 'And I think you are most unkind to tell Lady Louisa to go! She was managing beautifully until you arrived.'

Septimus glanced back at Louisa, his brows raised. 'Oh?'

Louisa shrugged slightly, ridiculously feeling for the first time as if she had thrust herself into this affair unnecessarily. 'I was about to suggest, when I distracted myself by the realisation that you all come of the same family, that Lord Wherwell and your brother should remove their coats, repair to the meadow, and settle their differences with a bout of fisticuffs.'

'Fisticuffs?' echoed Quintus in disbelief.

Quarto broke into laughter. 'All among the cow pats! I wish I may see you, Quint!'

'A highly practical suggestion, Lady Louisa,' said Septimus calmly, 'but unlikely, I fear, to find favour with my brother.'

'So I see,' said Louisa, looking at the sneer of contempt on the face of Quintus.

She glanced across to where Lord Wherwell, who had reverted, now that all passion was past, to his normal reticent manner, was standing a little apart. By the appalled look on his face, it was obvious that he had come sufficiently to his senses to be now fully aware of his invidious position and the danger in which he stood. Compassion stirred in Louisa's breast. Poor man, why should he be the scapegoat in the quarrel between brother and sister? It was apparent that only chivalry—in this case undoubtedly misplaced!—had caused him so disastrously to intervene.

'Very well, Messieurs and Mesdames Berowne,' she said in her matter-of-fact way, 'if there is to be no sensible manner of handling this affair, I am afraid that I have no choice but to lay the matter before a magistrate.'

A hush descended upon the scene as the Berownes glanced one to the other in mute consternation. *That*, their eyes said, was not an outcome any of them relished.

'You have nothing to say?' Louisa asked, and paused.

Everyone hesitated.

'Very well,' Louisa said flatly, and turned to go.

Quintus spoke, menace in his tone. 'I don't think you would be wise to proceed to the extreme you suggest, Lady Louisa.'

In a flash she turned on him, her large eyes afire. 'Are you threatening me, sir?'

CHAPTER FOUR

AFTER the briefest of tense pauses, almost everyone began to speak at once.

'Stuff and nonsense, Lady Louisa!' came from Quarto. 'Quint wouldn't dream of such a thing!'

'Lady Louisa, don't *think* of it!' uttered Decimus in distressed tones.

'Oh, no!' cried out Nona.

'How *could* you, Quint?' demanded Octavia.

'Quiet, my babes, quiet!' begged Septimus, topping them all. 'One at a time.'

Quintus, recognising belatedly that he was shoving a spoke in his own wheel, cast his best smile over his dissipated features and came forward to bow deeply before her.

'Lady Louisa, forgive me! I am too much impassioned today to be capable of moderation.' His eyes gazed limpidly into hers. 'Your intervention, little though I cared for it, I admit, has been more successful than you know.'

Unmoved by his smile, for she felt no warmth in it, Louisa asked, 'Has it, sir?'

'Indeed it has.' He spread a hand over his heart, but the sneer belied him. 'I am smitten with remorse.'

Louisa merely met his eyes, waiting for him to continue.

'There is no need to take the course you intend.

There will be no—er—repercussions from this matter.'

'Are you saying there will be no duel?' demanded Louisa evenly.

He bowed, as if in acquiescence. Louisa, keeping her eyes on him, did not see the swift glance that passed between Quarto and Septimus, nor catch the worried look the latter then cast at the unfortunate Lord Wherwell.

Louisa eyed the man before her uncertainly. She could not believe him sincere. Yet what more could she do?

'I must accept your assurance, I suppose,' she said slowly. She turned to Septimus, who met her eyes quite blandly, not a trace in them of the real fears he had. 'I may trust you to see all right?'

He bowed. 'You may safely leave the matter in our hands.'

'Yours and Quarto's, I dare say.'

'Precisely.'

'Well, I hope you are to be relied upon!' she said roundly.

'Of course, of course,' cried Quarto, bustling foward jovially, and pushing past his brother Quintus, who gave place and moved back. 'Come, now, Lady Louisa. This is supposed to be a party of pleasure. We won't allow these fellows to spoil it.'

'Good God, yes!' ejaculated Decimus, catching the poet's eye. 'At any moment someone may come along. Nonie and Tavey, come on! Let us all go with Lady Louisa. Our absence will be remarked, you know.'

There was a concerted movement towards the

walk, and Louisa turned to go with the crowd. How it happened, she did not know, but she found herself walking not with any of the younger set, but with Sexta, words pouring from her lips in a torrent.

'Oh, Lady Louisa, I have to thank you. How good you are! So *kind* of you to come and take my part when you are not even acquainted with me.'

'Not at all, I ——' began Louisa, but the woman's tongue ran on.

'It was the stupidest thing, after all. I don't know *how* we came to attach so much significance to it.' She tittered, a high-pitched brittle sound. 'I mean, for Quint and I to be so much at outs. As a rule, we *never* quarrel.'

'Oh, indeed? I thought ——'

'We *had* to be close, you see, with so *miserable* a childhood! Small wonder we all grew up wild! And Quint, poor lamb. . .' She broke off, sighing so soulfully that Louisa was startled.

The others had already outstripped them, but Louisa had perforce to dawdle along the walk, for Sexta was clinging to her arm and dragging back. But although she sighed, as with Quintus there was no warmth there, and Louisa, glancing down, thought that the bulging, darting eyes held a calculating look. Why should Sexta confide in her?

'What about your brother Quintus?' she asked warily.

'He does not *mean* to behave badly,' Sexta said sadly.

Louisa almost snorted her disbelief. 'How can you take his part after he has offered you violence?'

'That is just it!' Sexta uttered mournfully, her grasp

still firm on Louisa's arm as they came out into the square before the house and green. 'I *know* he did not mean it. And I began it, you know. We have been at outs for some days.'

'Why?' asked Louisa, pausing, and noted that the colour came and went in Sexta's sunken cheeks.

'Oh, for such a silly reason that it is not worth recounting. He—he asked me to do something for him and I refused. That is all.'

'What has all this to do with me, Sexta?' Louisa asked, spitting the precise point with uncanny accuracy.

A rather hysterical little laugh was surprised out of the woman, and she plucked unconsciously at Louisa's sleeve. 'I only wanted you to *understand*. For he made you angry, I could see that.'

'What if he did? It was momentary, and it is nothing to me. I merely wished to help poor Lord Wherwell, if you want the truth.'

'Wherwell?' echoed Sexta. 'Who cares for him?'

Louisa's eyes narrowed. 'I thought you did. Was not that the original cause of the fight today?'

Sexta tittered. 'No, indeed! How came you to think so? He happened merely to be my escort, and when I began to quarrel with Quint he very stupidly intervened.'

Louisa was so much disgusted by this callous attitude that she wrenched her arm out of Sexta's nervous grasp.

'Excuse me, if you please. I have to go and find my ward. I have neglected her for long enough.'

Sexta tried to detain her. 'Oh, no, pray! Stay with me a little.'

'I have stayed a sufficient time,' Louisa said firmly. 'Good day, Sexta.'

She walked quickly away. Perhaps Society was not so much to be blamed for denouncing the Berownes! Her enjoyment of the day was seriously impaired. Then, as if she did not feel bad enough, Lady Pyrland pounced on her from nowhere as she approached the green.

'There you are at last! I declare, you are the most unnatural guardian, Louisa! You leave your ward to attend to something that is in no way your concern. And then you have the stupidity to *encourage* acquaintance between an innocent child and the most notorious family in the *ton*.'

Louisa stared at her blankly. 'Tush, Aunt! In what way have I done so?'

'Look there!' An accusing finger pointed to the skittle lane.

Millie, still indulging in her favourite pastime, was just throwing a ball, which sailed down the grass and scattered all nine pins in one fell swoop. A burst of clapping greeted this triumph, and, among several onlookers, Louisa saw both the young Berowne girls, Mrs Fullands and Mrs Kilgetty, leaping up and down next to her ward, whose flushed cheeks and sparkling eyes were turned to Decimus beside her, cheering madly and throwing his hat in the air.

'*That*,' said Lady Pyrland in disgust, 'is a direct result of your careless neglect.'

Louisa felt a pang of conscience. There was nothing more natural than for Decimus to introduce his sisters to Millie, for they were all in the same age group, and her own willingness to consort with the

Berownes would certainly be taken as tacit consent
that this might extend to her ward. Now what was she
to do?

Lady Pyrland had no doubts on that score. 'You
must go and bring her away, Louisa.'

'I thought you were going to do so before,' Louisa
said evenly.

'She would not come with me,' her aunt disclosed.
'At least, I could not get her to abandon those stupid
ninepins.'

'You had better leave it to me, then.'

'That is just what it seems to me I cannot do,'
complained the matron. 'Ten to one you will become
involved in the wretched game yourself, or something
of the sort, and you will *both* be seen to be on friendly
terms with the Berownes.'

'The Berownes! The Berownes!' Louisa repeated,
exasperated. 'I have had enough of the Berownes
today!'

'I am delighted to hear it. You have come to your
senses, it seems.'

Louisa cast up her eyes. 'Oh, go away, Aunt Hebe,
do! You will drive me *demented*.'

'You are the oddest girl, Louisa,' commented Lady
Pyrland, apparently unmoved by her remarks. 'I am
sure your marriage to Shittlehope must have turned
your brain.'

'On the contrary,' sighed Louisa. 'Mr Shittlehope
was the sanest man I know. It is your *bon ton* who
live in so unreal a world that everything to me seems
topsy-turvy. Give me the cits in preference any day!'

Lady Pyrland was so much affronted by this remark

that she stalked off to the house without another word.

Louisa took a step or two in the direction of the green, and halted. Why *should* she intervene? They were all so happy! There now was young Nona trying her skill — not very successfully, poor love, much to the amusement of the company! And here was Decimus, evidently offering to show her the trick of it, only to have Millie intervene. Oh, let them alone! She *could* not spoil their pleasure.

About to turn in the direction of the house, she perceived her cousin Sedbergh in a group of men standing just outside the front door. Almost without thought, she turned quickly away, instead making for the walks she had left, and took a path she had not trodden before. A few moments' strolling brought her into a deserted glade, in the centre of which a swing had been erected, owing much to the presence of a large oak, a strong branch of which ran fortuitously into the glade.

Making for this, Louisa sat on the swing, pushing herself with a desultory foot, so that she swayed gently to and fro. The motion was relaxing, and her ruffled temper began to cool. She sat for some time, her hands on the ropes either side, dreamily surveying the scene from under her feathered hat, lost in thoughts of the past.

Something impinged on her consciousness. She blinked, as if to focus her attention. A tiny gasp escaped her.

Standing at the entrance to the glade, leaning negligently against the hedge, and heedless of staining his elegant salmon-coloured frock-coat, one foot crossed over the other to support his weight, and scribbling with a pencil in a pocketbook, was Septimus Berowne.

'Oh, it's you!' she uttered foolishly, feeling unaccountably flustered as he looked up. 'What are you doing here?'

The poet smiled. 'Writing verse. What else?'

'About *me*?' Louisa asked, surprised.

'You look so charmingly there that I was instantly inspired.' He glanced at his pocketbook. 'Do you care to hear it?' And without waiting for a reply, he began to recite.

'"In sylvan glade upon a swing embowered
Sate Loulou, over hearts empowered . . ."'

'Loulou!' interrupted Louisa in a stunned tone.

'Yes, I thought it rather suited you,' said the poet blandly. 'Besides, I mean to go on to compare your habit of blue with the blue of your eyes, and I can do with the rhyme.'

'"Blue" and "Loulou"!' Louisa exclaimed, nauseated.

'Well, you couldn't expect me to addle my brain with "Shittlehope". That would be quite unreasonable.'

'Pray don't "addle your brain" with *anything* concerning me!' begged Louisa.

'Mind you,' mused Septimus, unheeding, 'it would be a challenge. Let me see now; rope, Pope, cope, mope.' He struck his forehead. 'Aha! *Mope*. Listen.

"Upon the swing she sits to mope
That melancholy Shittlehope."'

'You abominable creature!' cried Louisa, breaking into laughter. 'Let me tell you I am neither melancholy nor moping!'

'Ah, but are you Shittle*hoping*?' riposted Septimus, quick as a flash.

Louisa giggled. 'How can you? My poor Mr Shittlehope must be turning in his grave!'

Septimus grinned. 'You see my difficulty, then? I think we had better confine ourselves to "Loulou" and be thankful.'

'You may confine yourself to some other female, I thank you, Septimus Berowne, poet, and leave me quite out of your fatuous doggerel.'

'Doggerel!'

'Yes, doggerel,' Louisa said firmly. 'If *that* sample is anything to go by!'

Septimus opened his mouth and flung his hands in the air, and then paused, scratching his head and setting on his hip the hand which held his pocketbook. In a musing tone he uttered, 'Now would it better become me to rail against her heartless criticism, or should I march away in a dudgeon?'

As he paused, staring into her face with a look of profound concentration, as if he seriously considered the question, Louisa's eyes began to dance.

'Neither! You must draw yourself up, put away your pocketbook in a marked manner, and inform me that I shall eat my words.'

Septimus looked struck. 'You are a positive mine of brilliant ideas, Loulou. Like this?'

And to Louisa's deep delight he drew himself up with a haughty expression, flourished his pocketbook and carefully replaced it in an inner recess of his coat, and then spoke in a tone of bitter hurt.

'Madam, you shall eat those words 'ere long, I promise you. And may they taste of wormwood and gall!'

'Excellent!' Louisa cried, clapping her hands. 'What a pity you did not choose the stage instead of poetry!'

The poet's pose collapsed and he shook a fist. 'And *those* words may well choke you, Loulou the cruel!'

A crow of mirth escaped her, and without thought she let go the ropes of the swing and held out her hands to him. 'Cry friends, poet! I will engage not to say another word until I have thoroughly studied what you have written.'

He came forward at once and grasped both hands, encased in their blue kid gloves, pulling her up from the swing, his eyes smiling into hers. 'A generous concession, Loulou!'

As he drew her close Louisa became aware of an odd warmth sweeping through her body. For a moment she was mesmerised by the sparkle of the light brown eyes. Then sanity returned. What was she *doing*? Encouraging liberties from a personable young man — a Berowne at that! And she a *widow*. Was she mad? What could be more compromising?

Dragging back a little, she said sharply, 'Beware, poet! I said *friends*, nothing more.'

A frown came into his face and he dropped her hands abruptly. 'How wise of you to warn me! I was about to throw you to the turf and do my worst.'

Louisa met the grimness of his glance with her wide stare, although a faint flush stained her cheeks.

'Indeed? I thought you meant only to kiss me. It just shows how wrong one can be!'

It was his turn to redden a little. Apology gleamed in his eye and a smile quivered at the corners of his mouth. 'Forgive me! You are perfectly correct. Will you believe me when I say that there was no premeditation? Or is my family connection too much against me?'

Louisa's eyes softened. 'I hope I am not so prejudiced.' Her glance became speculative. 'But I confess I am wary. Why did you come here?'

'I followed you,' he admitted, and then flung up a hand at her challenging look. 'Only because it occurred to me that we had none of us thanked you for your intervention in our stupid affairs.'

'Oh, that,' Louisa uttered, surprised to discover that she had almost forgotten the episode. 'Is all well?'

Septimus shrugged. 'As well as might have been expected. Don't concern yourself over the matter, I beg.'

Louisa looked him over, suspicion kindling in her breast. She did not trust that bland expression of his! 'You did not manage to stop it, did you?'

'I repeat,' he said evasively, 'don't concern yourself, Lady Louisa. We are not worth it.'

'*You* may not be,' Louisa said tartly, 'but what of poor Lord Wherwell?' He did not answer, and Louisa sighed. 'How I despise this stupid practice of duelling!'

'I think I may safely say——' the poet smiled '——that you are at one there with most of your sex.'

'Yes, but I have a cogent reason,' Louisa said, her

large orbs full of such distress that Septimus had
much ado not to seize hold of her hands again. 'I shall
never forget my first sight of that poor little mite
when she came to us. Bereft at one stroke of all hope
of happiness — and all because her father had got into
just such a foolish quarrel.'

'Of whom are you speaking? Not the young girl
who resides with you?'

'Millie, yes.' She drew a breath. 'Why do gentlemen hold life so cheap? And don't tell me faradiddles
about *honour*.'

'I should not dare!' he returned lightly. 'Though in
defence of many of my own sex, I would say it is
rather because we hold life so dear that we would risk
it on account of our honour — or a lady's, perhaps.'

'That is sillier than anything!' declared Louisa. 'Of
what use, pray, is your lifeless body to the lady who
loves you, now that honour is satisfied?'

'You don't feel that there are considerations more
important than life?' he asked diffidently, and then
twinkled. 'No, I see you don't.'

'Being a poet, you would, of course,' Louisa said,
goaded. 'Martyrdom is so *romantic*.'

'Naturally,' he agreed, grinning. 'But tell me. What
were you dreaming about on the swing there? Or is it
secret?'

Louisa shrugged. 'My thoughts are my own, of
course. Why do you want to know?'

'It will help my poem,' he said quite seriously.

She eyed him. 'I see. Well, I am afraid you will be
disappointed, poet. I was thinking of my marriage,
and nothing could have been less romantic than *that*.'

A quirk at the corner of his mouth betrayed

Septimus, although his expression was bland. 'That does not altogether surprise me. The name itself——'

'Don't start that again!' warned Louisa, trying not to laugh. 'My poor husband had less choice in the matter than I. He was born to the name.'

Septimus frowned, attacked by an odd sensation of tightness in his chest. 'You had no choice?'

'None at all,' Louisa said calmly. 'At seventeen, females don't.'

'I have never before had reason to think that my sisters were fortunate,' he commented.

Louisa opened her eyes at him. 'Are you imagining me to have been unhappy? No such thing. To be sure, my lamentable parent used me shockingly, marrying me off to a merchant more than forty years my senior, but——'

'*What*?' exclaimed the poet, horrified.

'I know,' Louisa said, rather amused. 'Dreadful, wasn't it? I assure you Mr Shittlehope was fully as conscious of it as I.'

'Then how could he have consented to such an unequal alliance?' exploded Septimus in a tone of strong censure.

'Don't distress yourself,' begged Louisa. 'He had a fancy to better himself. Afterwards, of course, he recognised how foolish he had been, for it was rather I who came down than he who came up.'

'A somewhat belated recognition,' the poet said grimly.

Louisa smiled. 'Yes, but in the end it all turned out for the best. It was a most successful marriage in many ways.'

The poet stared at her, the indignation dying out of

his face. What a valiant female she was! To triumph so cheerfully over an intolerable situation.

'You have certainly earned your reward,' he said.

'Reward?' Louisa repeated, her eyes clouding a little.

'You are a rich woman, are you not?'

'Oh, *that*.' Her eyes cleared and she broke into laughter. 'It is not all for me, you know. I control the finances, yes, but they. . .' She broke off, on the point of mentioning her involvement in business, suddenly recalling her promise to her aunt. For all she knew, this poet might spread it about.

But Septimus had rememberd what must be another call on her purse. 'Ah, yes, the girl. Millie, you said. What is she to you? Are you related?'

'We are cousins only. But she is my ward,' Louisa told him, wondering now at his interest.

'Unusual,' he commented.

'Oh, yes. But then I managed it myself.'

Septimus's lip quivered. 'Of course I should have guessed that you did so.'

'Why?' demanded Louisa suspiciously.

'Does *anything* happen in your life that you have not specifically arranged?' he countered.

'Yes. Poets waylay me in "sylvan glades" and plague me with versifying!'

'Which reminds me!' exclaimed Septimus, digging into his costume for his pocketbook. 'You have not heard it all.'

'Pray don't trouble to recite me any more,' begged Louisa, making for the walk.

'But Loulou ——'

'And *don't* call me Loulou!' she ordered, turning on him.

He broke back with exaggerated fear, throwing up an arm as if to ward off a blow. 'A slip of the tongue,' he said in placatory tones, adding in a noisy aside, 'Good God, next she will be calling me out!'

'She will box your ears rather!' Louisa said crossly, trying not to laugh. 'And if you really wish to ingratiate yourself with me ——'

'I *never* ingratiate,' Septimus protested, drawing himself up.

'Very well, if you wish to *please* me ——'

'But I don't! What in the world gave you such a ridiculous notion?'

The big eyes glared at him in some frustration. 'Septimus Berowne, you are fast approaching "romantic martyrdom", do you know that?'

The poet clapped both hands to his heart. 'And she dares to rail at honour.' He fell on one knee, spreading wide his arms. 'Very well, slay me! But remember that my talent dies with me.'

'In that case I'll borrow your sword,' Louisa returned, twinkling. 'I wish you will cease play-acting; this is *serious*.'

He rose to his feet at once, his mouth solemnly pursed, but with so much mischief in his eyes that Louisa could not help laughing.

'How is anyone ever to know when you are in earnest?' she demanded.

The mischief vanished and his glance seemed to lock with hers. 'Believe me, Loulou, when I *am* in earnest you will know it.'

Louisa felt breathless all at once, that warm glow

once more invading her breast. The look in his eyes
was more intimate than a caress. The colour rushed
up into her face. 'You are being absurd, Mr
Berowne.'

'Septimus,' he corrected, and released her — or that
was how she felt it. 'Or Setty, if you prefer. It ought
to be *Sette* —— ' giving the word for 'seven' its correct
Italian pronunciation ' — but my distressingly ignor-
ant family cannot manage it.'

'I think your family is delightful,' Louisa said
impulsively. 'But that does not mean that your young
brother will be permitted to dangle after my ward.
Tell him so, if you please.'

Septimus looked at her rather enigmatically. 'Why
don't you tell him so?'

'I will, if need be. But the poor boy has been
embarrassed enough on my account. A word from
you in due season might spare him.'

'You have a warm heart, Lady Louisa Shittlehope,'
he said gently. 'Don't allow the worthless Berownes
to impose upon it!'

Two mornings later Louisa was shaken into consciousness at an unseasonable hour by her maid.

'I'm sorry to wake you, m'lady,' apologised
Goodeth Shawford, the plump, bluff countrywoman
who had been promoted from the parlour on Louisa's
marriage to wait upon her, Mr Shittlehope despising
what he termed 'them fancy French pieces'.

'What is it, Goody?' Louisa asked sleepily, leaning
up on her elbow and peering into the gloom of early
dawn.

'Visitors, m'lady. I told them it was a daft hour to

be calling, but they insisted. Ladies they are. All of a
doodah, too!'

'Who are they, Goody?' Louisa demanded, a cold
apprehension creeping down her spine.

'A Mrs Fullands and a Mrs Kilgetty, m'lady.'

'Nona and Octavia!' exclaimed Louisa, throwing
off the covers hastily and getting out of bed. 'What
can have happened? Give me a robe, Goody,
quickly!'

Throwing on the dressing-robe handed to her by
the maid, Louisa thrust her feet into a pair of slippers
and ran quickly down the stairs to the big saloon
where Goody had left the visitors. She could hear
their voices as she threw open the door and found
them both pacing. They turned as one and ran
towards her.

'Oh, Lady Louisa, thank goodness!' said Octavia.

'Please help us, Lady Louisa!' begged Nona.

'What has happened?' demanded Louisa. 'Why are
you up at this hour?'

'We have been up all night!' said Nona dramatically, clutching about her a warm pelisse.

'Not quite,' amended her sister, rubbing gloved
hands together against the numbing early morning
cold. 'But I stayed with Nonie last night, for we
agreed to come here this morning together. We did
not want to wake you in the middle of the night.'

'No, and besides we would have been *too* early
then,' put in Nona.

'Too early for what?' asked Louisa bewildered.
'What *is* it?'

'Why, the duel, of course. It is set for six o'clock.'

'*What*? But I thought. . .' She paused, remember-

ing how Septimus had evaded her when she had
questioned him about the duel. She looked at the
anxious sisters. 'How do you come to know of it?'

'We had it from Sexta,' Octavia told her, 'who had
it from Quint himself.'

'So we *knew* it had to be true,' chimed in Nona.
'And in any event, both Quarto and Setty warned us
not to interfere, so that made it *certain*.'

'Of course we paid no attention to *that*,' Octavia
put in. 'We threatened to call in a magistrate as you
did, but we don't know how to set about it.'

'So then I suggested we should come to *you*,' Nona
added brightly.

'Yes, but it is far too late for a magistrate now,'
Louisa protested worriedly.

'Then what is to be done?' asked Nona, crestfallen.

'We *cannot* allow Quint to harm that poor man!'
Octavia said determinedly.

'And Sexta said positively there was no moving
Quint!' Nona wailed. 'He is quite *determined* to fight
Wherwell.'

'Of course we cannot allow it,' Louisa said at once.
'What is the time now?'

'Close on five,' Octavia said.

'How did you come here? In one of your
carriages?'

Nona's laugh trilled. 'Heavens, we don't have
carriages! We came in a hackney.'

'Very well, then I shall order mine,' Louisa
decided. 'Come upstairs with me while I dress.'

She led the way out, asking, 'Did neither of you
think to ask your husbands to intervene?'

Again there came a trill of laughter from Nona.

'Why, what could *they* do? Captain Kilgetty is away with his regiment, in any event. And my darling Jamie is very likely under the table in some tavern by now.'

'Hush, Nonie!' whispered her sister admonishingly. 'You will give Lady Louisa a very odd idea of Mr Fullands!'

An odd idea indeed! thought Louisa, affecting not to hear. It began to seem as if the hints she had received of the Berownes' lack of parental guidance were true. She was ready to bet that Captain Kilgetty would prove to be a half-pay officer. It was obvious that the girls had married the most undesirable of *partis*, and probably thought the world well lost for love!

'I wish you will drop formality,' she said as they reached her bedchamber. 'I feel we are already on far too friendly terms to have any further need of "Lady". "Louisa" will do.'

Both girls thanked her prettily, eyeing the elegant appointments of her chamber with evident admiration. Goodeth Shawford had waited for her mistress's return, shrewdly guessing that she might be needed.

'Did you find out where this duel is to take place?' Louisa asked, as with her maid's help she began rapidly to dress.

'Oh, yes, it is at Chalk Farm. They *always* go there,' Nona volunteered.

'Always?'

Octavia laughed. 'Well, we have six brothers, and they have all been out, you know.'

'Even Septimus?' Louisa found herself asking, with an unexpected hollowness in her chest.

'Oh, well, Setty is usually shut up in his garret,' Nona said airily. 'But *has* he been out, Tavey? I never heard of it.'

'Yes, you did. He went over that stupid man's spitting his book of poems with a sword.'

'Lord Ulceby!' shrieked Nona with her musical laugh. 'I had forgot. Yes, it was just after they were published. And Setty said he would spit *him* with a sword——'

'And the wretched man said, "By all means try it——"'

'And so Setty *did*.'

Louisa felt the inevitable question burning on her lips, but there was no need to ask it.

'And he won!' Octavia finished. 'I will say for Setty, though, that he was satisfied with first blood.'

'Which Quint certainly *won't* be,' Nona said warningly.

'What in the world is "first blood"?' Louisa asked over her shoulder, feeling quite sick, and thankful that her back was turned as her maid tied her laces.

'It means that he who draws blood the first on his opponent may consider his honour satisfied,' Octavia explained. 'A scratch is all that is necessary. Only far too many gentlemen feel the insult deserves a more bitter punishment, and——'

'And they won't stop until one of them is *really* wounded,' Nona uttered ghoulishly. 'And if it is to the death, then——'

'Be quiet, Nonie!' ordered her sister, noting in the candlelight as Louisa turned round that her features had whitened. 'Don't be alarmed. It is not as bad as pistols. A sword fight will give an opponent more than one chance at least.'

'How far do you suppose Quintus will take *this* matter?' Louisa asked rather shakily.

'There is no saying,' Nona began. 'He is quite capable of——'

'Quint won't kill him, I believe,' interrupted Octavia.

'*None* of them would go that far,' Nona put in comfortingly. 'That is why they never choose pistols, you see, which would be *fatal*, for both Quarto and Quint are crack shots. But a sword wound can be *very* nasty, and may result in a death if it is not properly cared for.'

'Or if the sword point should enter some vital spot,' corroborated Octavia. 'And Quint, I regret to say——'

'Will go further than "first blood",' Louisa finished flatly. She drew a breath. 'Then we had better *hurry*.'

The journey to Chalk Farm did not take very long in Louisa's town coach and four, the locality being only a mile from town, but by the time they arrived she felt as if she had been acquainted with the Berownes forever.

Nona and Octavia chattered ceaselessly, speaking with artless innocence of their various brothers' dissipations, and with unbecoming freedom of their mother's *affaires*. They appeared to regard drinking and gaming simply as agreeable pastimes, and faithlessness as natural. Nona showed scant interest in her baby boy—who was mentioned only by her sister—

and both saw their wholly ineligible husbands in the light of romantic heroes.

It was too bad, Louisa thought, as she listened. Someone ought to take these wretched Berownes in hand!

But before she could think of a suitable candidate for the task, the coach stopped. Louisa and the girls leapt out and found themselves by a large coppice which lay on the edge of the wilderness of Marylebone Fields. The White House tavern was well out of sight some distance up the lane, and the whole place seemed eerily silent in the cold grey light of a frosty morning in early April. But they were not alone in this solitary place, for two other conveyances were to be seen close by.

'Oh, there is our family coach!' exclaimed Octavia, seeing the heavy old vehicle waiting under the trees ahead.

'And that must be Wherwell's,' Nona said, pointing to another, sheltering a little further back.

'Then we have not a moment to lose!' Louisa said urgently, feeling her heart beginning to pound with fear.

Running into the wood, they darted through the trees, holding up their long skirts against the dewy grass. In a moment they were guided by the faint echo of voices, and a short distance brought them to a clearing, the obvious scene of the duel.

All three ladies stopped short at the sight before them.

'We are too late!' cried Nona.

'It looks to be all over, certainly,' Octavia agreed.

On one side was Wherwell, in his shirt-sleeves,

seated on a convenient tree-trunk, lying back, and held against one man behind him, while another — from his physical wig obviously a doctor — appeared to be tending a wound on his upper arm. A third man near by was putting up a wicked-looking rapier in a long sheath.

Opposite, just replacing his coat and wig, was Quintus Berowne. Louisa's kindling gaze took in the two other men who flanked him: Quarto Berowne, his bulk wrapped in a huge greatcoat, and his younger brother Septimus, at once unfashionable and romantic, swathed in a swirling grey cloak, on his head a large-brimmed grey hat with a pink cockade.

CHAPTER FIVE

'WELL, really!' Louisa ejaculated, drawing upon herself every eye from the scene of the late battle.

'Good God!' came from Quarto.

'What the devil is *she* doing here?' roared Quintus.

'I imagine she was brought by our little sisters,' Septimus replied, a smile glimmering on his lips.

'Yes, she was,' said Louisa, marching purposefully into the arena, her gaze fixed on the poet. 'And if there was one person I did not expect to find mixed up in this deplorable affair it was you, Septimus Berowne.'

All four of his siblings looked at him in amazement, being wholly unaware that the two were more than barely acquainted.

'Altruism, Lady Louisa,' he pleaded, coming forward to meet her, removing his hat and throwing his cloak back over his shoulders as he made a gallant leg. 'Sheer altruism.'

Octavia and Nona exchanged glances of mute question. Had Setty set up one of his flirtations with Lady Louisa, of all people? But her response did not bear out the suspicion.

'Indeed? No doubt you have some glib explanation hovering on your tongue.'

'Not glib, ma'am,' he murmured meekly. 'Quite reasonable, in fact.'

'Don't even try me with it!' Louisa snapped, her

gaze moving on to his brothers behind him. 'According to your sisters, Mr Berowne,' she went on, moving to address Quintus, 'we may consider ourselves thankful that you are not in the habit of choosing pistols. But you, sir, let me tell you, may be thankful that I knew nothing of this until a bare hour ago, or I should undoubtedly have brought with me constables to hale you off to Bow Street!'

'I can't conceive what the devil you're doing here at all,' returned Quintus rudely. 'My silly little sisters are scarcely a surprise, for their conduct is always doubtful——'

'How dare you, Quint?' burst from Octavia, and Nona uttered a shriek of rage.

'But as they very well know,' went on their brother, ignoring the interruption, 'this is no place for a lady. Though considering your recent history, perhaps I should not be entirely surprised at you either.'

'That'll do, Brother, that'll do!' put in Quarto, pushing forward. 'Don't heed him, ma'am! Not himself this morning.'

Louisa raised her brows. 'Oh? When *is* he himself? It is not, apparently, when he is brawling or attacking his sister. Nor yet, I presume, when he is racing backwards or playing at cards or sinking his wits in liquor. Indeed I should be astonished to learn that he has any time to discover himself at all!'

'By God, ma'am, if you were but a man——' began Quintus.

'Gently, my boy, gently!' intervened Quarto.

'If I were a man, sir,' Louisa answered, eyes flashing, 'I should very much prefer to be one of a class with my late husband, who for all his despised status was worth a dozen of any member of our high-born gentry!'

Turning her back on the man, she crossed swiftly over to his late combatant to find out how he did, leaving the Berownes to gather in a quarrelsome huddle.

'I wish you would not antagonise the lady, Quint,' grumbled Quarto. 'How can any of us make headway with her if you can't control that devilish sharp tongue of yours?'

'So that's what is in the wind,' muttered Septimus.

'I should dashed well think it is! Be damned fools to let all that glistening gold slip through our fingers.'

'Well, what the devil did these two have to fetch her here for?' demanded Quintus, indicating his sisters, as he seized his own greatcoat from Quarto's grasp and slung it carelessly across his shoulders.

'That's right!' Quarto agreed, glaring at them. 'What do you mean by it, the pair of you?'

'We *had* to, Quarto,' Nona protested, 'didn't we, Tavey?'

'It is no use turning on us, Quarto,' Octavia said crossly, squaring up to her brother. 'You and Setty were supposed to settle this whole affair the other day at St Pancras. What *could* we do but try and stop it?'

'Yes, but what did you want to drag in Lady Louisa for?' demanded their elder brother in a harassed way. 'Now I shall have all to do to placate the woman. Don't you realise what she is worth?'

'Oh, I'm so sorry, Quarto!' Nona exclaimed. 'I had no idea you meant to *marry* her. Shall we tell her what a catch you are?'

'No, you keep out of it, Nonie,' replied her brother ungratefully. 'You'll only make bad worse.'

Septimus, bearing no further part in the discussion as his sisters responded and fierce argument broke out, glanced from his brother's face to Louisa where she stood talking to Wherwell, who had got to his feet at her approach. She would not marry Quarto, would she? Surely not! And Quint was certainly out of the running. But a covert search of that brother's face made him immediately suspicious. He was looking after the widow himself, a speculative glint in his eye. Heaven help Loulou! Should he warn her? No, she was perfectly capable of handling Quint for herself, as she had already demonstrated.

More than capable! he decided as he recalled how she had all too swiftly nipped his own impromptu overtures in the bud. She was certainly desirable, and a refreshing change from the generality of females. But she was much too *managing* for his taste. Good God, she would drive a fellow demented, ruling the roost! *His* ideal was far other than Lady Louisa Shittlehope. Something more clinging, and adoring. Someone more suited to a poet—who *liked* his verse, what was more, instead of continually poking fun at it!

Then Lady Louisa was moving back towards them and he lost his train of thought as he watched her, for under her furred pelisse, which hung open, the petticoats of the yellow gown she had chosen to wear swayed with the motion of her hips like waving daffodils against the green. He did not even notice that the conversation beside him had ceased, and was about to speak when he was forestalled by Quarto.

'Lady Louisa, allow me to make reparation for my sisters' ill-advised interference. I will drive back to town with you, and Setty will escort the girls to their homes.'

'Well, they certainly should be at home,' Louisa agreed. 'Especially you, Nona. Only conceive of your husband's consternation if he should find you absent!'

'Oh, he's probably snoring in bed,' Nona said unconcernedly.

'Nevertheless, your place is beside him,' Louisa said firmly, and turned to Octavia. 'When does your husband return, my dear?'

'Not for a month yet,' replied the girl, sighing.

'That must be dull work for you. Why do you not remain at your sister's? You might with advantage help her to take care of her little boy and learn something in preparation for your own turn at motherhood in due time.'

It was plain from the blank expressions on the pretty faces before her that neither one of the two sisters had ever considered such a thing.

'Don't know much about the Berownes yet, do you?' said Quintus sneeringly. 'Nonie and Tavey dance attendance on an infant? I wish I may see it!'

Louisa ignored him, but Octavia said suddenly, 'Yes, it *is* a good idea!' She linked her arm in Nona's. 'Come on, Nonie. Let us go home and visit little Jimmy in his nursery.'

Nona was clearly unconvinced, but she obediently turned to accompany her sister, and they went off in the direction of the road, calling to Septimus to hurry.

The poet hesitated. 'You are full of sound advice,

Lady Louisa. Are you quite certain that you wish to take on the management of this family?'

'Don't be so absurd,' Louisa began, and paused, eyeing him suspiciously. 'I suppose you mean to tease me, do you? You will not soften me by such tactics, Septimus Berowne. I am very much displeased with you!'

'Alas!' he said mournfully. 'I shall retire discomfited for the present. But——' with a mischievous twinkle ' — I shall come about, see if I don't!'

'Yes, when the moon turns to green cheese!' retorted Louisa, unable to help herself.

Septimus laughed, and, bowing, turned away with a swirl of his cloak and followed his sisters. As Louisa gave her hand into Quarto's waiting arm, she glanced back at the duelling ground to see that, although Wherwell and his party were making their way out of the coppice the cause of the fracas was standing where they had left him, calmly unbuckling his sword — for as fashion was moving to cut away the skirts of gentlemen's coats, a sword was becoming a less essential part of their dress.

'What of your brother Quintus?' she asked.

'He'll go with Setty, of course. They will wait the coach for him.'

Arrived in the lane, Louisa entered her own coach with Quarto, and the vehicle set off towards town. In the dim interior of the coach, the silhouette of Quarto's face gave him the look of an oversized, pouting baby. Amusement drove away the ill humour into which Louisa had been thrown by this morning's events.

'Well, Quarto Berowne,' she said conversationally,

'I confess I expected more serious consequences than I found. Lord Wherwell appeared little the worse for his wound.'

'Oh, he's all right now,' Quarto said unconcernedly. 'Was in the deuce of a quake at the outset, though he made a good show of courage, I'll say that for him.'

'Yes, I rather gathered that Quintus is a formidable opponent.'

Quarto grinned. 'Gammon, Wherwell's a poor one! Not Quint's weapon, the foil. Nor mine either, come to that.'

'Indeed? Your sisters gave me to understand that you were both crack shots with a pistol, however,' Louisa said.

'Not me. Pay no attention to Tavey and Nonie. They don't know what they're talking about. *My* skill lies in driving. I'm an able shot, perhaps, but Quint can't miss.'

'Then why in the world did he choose swords?' demanded Louisa, quite at sea.

'Ah, that's a matter of pride,' Quarto told her, laughing. 'Quint has always to prove his mettle — handicap himself and *still* will. Not that Wherwell is any match for him. Even I could beat the fellow!'

'Poor man,' Louisa said, her sympathy stirred. 'He told me that the fight was over very quickly, I must admit.'

'Dashed tame!' Quarto grumbled, forgetting his company for a moment in recalling a grievance. 'That was Setty's fault. Quint would have given the fellow a damned good run for his money, only Setty spoilt it. He called out "First blood, first blood!" when Quint had barely pinked the fellow! Of course the man's seconds leapt straight in and demanded if we were satisfied. I was about to refute the case hotly, for I never saw a more humdrum fight, when Setty ups and tells them, "Naturally, gentlemen, we are perfectly satisfied. Let that be the end of it". I swear I was ready to seize the fellow's sword and clash with my own brother. And I would have done, only Setty is such a devilish fine swordsman that I know I'd get the worst of it!'

Louisa, quite spellbound by this extraordinary story, was struck by a wave of remorse. So that was why Septimus had been present! He must have chosen to support his brother only in order that he could be at hand to intervene and prevent any serious hurt to Lord Wherwell. And she had lashed out at him! Then Quarto's last comment impinged.

'*Septimus* is a fine swordsman?' she echoed faintly.

'Gad, yes, he's a nonpareil!' Quarto asserted. 'Even at Dess's age he was skilled. He's six-and-twenty now, and few can touch him! Angelo says he is one of the best fencers he's ever trained.'

'Who is Angelo?' Louisa demanded.

'Little Italian fellow. Runs an academy at the Opera House. His father's place, in fact, but rumour has it the old man may retire soon.'

Slightly stunned by the revelation that the seemingly innocuous poet was master of a weapon of potentially lethal destruction, Louisa sat silent for a few moments. With very different feelings did she now recall his really mild response to her condemnation of duelling. What had he said? Something about there being more important considerations than life. . .such as a lady's honour. Her heart seemed to swell within her. Lucky the lady whose honour was upheld by such a man! For he would not lightly risk his life. Oh, no, not he.

'Beg pardon, Lady Louisa!' Quarto said, interrupting her thoughts. 'Not fit for a lady's ear, all that. Too *Berowne* of me, eh? Ha, ha! But you'll forgive it?'

'Readily,' responded Louisa in a friendly tone. 'You need not stand upon ceremony with me, Quarto. Your brother Quintus was quite right. My own conduct has been scarcely ladylike, and I shudder to think what my aunt would say if she knew of my activities this day! Not that I care for that.'

'That is what I like so much about you, Lady Louisa,' declared Quarto, laughing. 'You're just like us, ain't you, for all your fortune and position? Care-for-nobody, that's what we are. And I believe you're the same.'

'I suppose there is *some* similarity,' Louisa conceded reluctantly, 'in as much as I am a trifle unconventional.'

'There you are!' said Quarto in tones of triumph. 'Both unconventional. What could be better than to join forces? Come, what do you say?'

Louisa eyed him in the uncertain light. 'I'm not sure I follow you, Quarto. Join forces how?'

'Why, by marriage, ma'am, what else?' he uttered, surprised. 'I'm sure I could do no better than to have you to wife. And though I don't pretend that there are not better men than I, you must agree at least that I'm your man for fun and jollification!'

'Is that your recipe for a successful marriage, Quarto?' Louisa asked. 'Fun and jollification?'

'Why not? It's what life's about, ain't it? Don't see any reason why we shouldn't deal extremely.'

'Don't you? Well, I'm afraid I do!' Louisa said roundly. 'In the first place, I am not hanging out for a husband.'

'That needn't concern us. I'm not hanging out for a wife!' declared her suitor ingenuously.

'Yet you will sink your scruples in favour of my charms, I suppose. Oh, have no fear! I am aware that my chief charm lies in the size of my balance in the bank.'

'There you have me,' admitted Quarto. 'No use trying to conceal my motives. A woman as sharp as you would be bound to see through me.'

'Quarto, is this a serious proposal?' demanded Louisa. 'Because if so, you are going a very strange way to work!'

A podgy hand reached out and seized one of her gloved ones. 'Ah, but I've intrigued you, confess! And I've another method up my sleeve, if you wish for it.' He squeezed the hand he held and moved closer, reaching out as if he would clasp her to him.

'Quarto, unhand me at once!' Louisa ordered, pulling at her imprisoned fingers and warding him off.

'But I want to kiss you!' he insisted, holding her hand tightly and grabbing at the round flesh of her hip.

A ringing slap caught him in the face, and he let her go, putting fingers to his plump cheek and staring at his assailant with popping eyes. 'What did you do that for?' he asked in an injured tone.

'Need you ask?' Louisa said crossly. 'I don't want

your amorous advances, Quarto. And I *don't* want to marry you!'

'Well, you had only to say so,' he grumbled, aggrieved.

'I have said so. Besides, you have only offered for me to steal a march on your brothers. You know very well you don't really want to marry me.'

'No, but I'd be a fool not to, wouldn't I?' he said frankly.

Louisa burst out laughing. 'It is well I have no pretensions to be admired for myself alone! First Decimus, giving me five additional years, and now you, Quarto. When may I expect Quintus to offer, do you suppose, or have I made myself too objectionable to him?'

'He won't give a fig for that,' predicted Quarto, rapidly regaining his usual good humour. 'But I can't in all charity advise you to marry him. Fond of the old fellow myself, of course, because he's my brother. But I'd be sinking too low if I pretended he'd make you a suitable husband.'

'Whereas you would, I suppose.'

'No, but there's no *harm* in me.'

'I don't know about that, but you are at least *honest*,' Louisa said warmly, 'which counts for a good deal.'

'Enough to marry me?'

'*No*. Let me tell you there is not the smallest likelihood of my marrying *any* Berowne, so you may as well give it up now. And while you are at it, tell Quintus to do the same, for I won't marry him either.'

Quarto sighed. 'Very well, if you say so.'

'I do say so.'

'Yes, yes, I hear you. Seems such a *waste*. Pity, but there it is, I suppose.'

'Yes, there it is,' Louisa agreed, thankful that she had got through to him at last. Looking out of the window as the horses slowed, she saw that they had reached Brook Street.

'And here we are at home! After all this excitement, I shall be heartily glad of my breakfast.'

Miss Millicent Lidbrook, partaking of an early repast alone in the downstairs parlour, was wondering idly where her guardian might have gone off to so early in the morning, when the sound of knocking on the front door startled her.

She glanced at the clock over the mantel and found it to be just a little after seven. Who could be calling at such an hour? As she heard heavy footsteps passing the parlour, curiosity drove her out of her chair to peek out down the hall. The butler was just opening the door.

'Yes, sir?' Millie heard him say to the visitor outside. Then a most disturbing voice smote her ears.

'Oh—er—is Lady Louisa at home?' asked Decimus Berowne.

'Her ladyship is out, sir.'

'So early? I mean—is she. . .?' He stopped.

'Sir?' said the butler politely.

In a rush then the burning question came. 'Can you tell me, did she have any visitors? Before she went out, I mean. Did two ladies call here?'

'I cannot take it upon myself to say,' began Mortehoe austerely.

But Millie, propelled both by her already roused

curiosity and a burning need, was suddenly behind him. 'It's all right, Mortehoe. Pray come in, Mr Berowne.'

'Miss Lidbrook!' uttered Decimus, a smile lighting up his features as the butler held the door wide for him to enter. He removed his three-cornered hat and executed a neat bow. 'I'm sorry to disturb you at such a moment.'

'Oh, you are not disturbing me,' Millie said, a blush suffusing her cheeks. 'What is it? I can tell something is wrong.'

'Very much so, I am afraid,' Decimus said, casting a doubtful glance at the servant who still stood by the closed door, disapproval writ large in his face.

Miss Lidbrook took his glance, saying at once, 'You may go, Mortehoe. Mr Berowne has come to — to deliver a message.'

'Of course, yes. A *message*,' corroborated Decimus eagerly.

It was doubtful whether Mortehoe was taken in by this hasty improvisation, but it was not his place to censure his betters, particularly these northern persons who had invaded the Brook Street house for the season. Mortehoe would much have preferred to retire with the owners to the country, but the party hiring the house had insisted on some resident help. Sniffing, he departed to the nether regions to impart this latest instalment of the peculiar Goings-On to the cook. But Millie was perfectly aware of the compromising nature of her actions.

'I know I ought not to receive you like this,' she apologised, leading the way back down the hall. 'But

I have guessed there is trouble of some kind, and perhaps I may be excused this time.'

'I am sure you may be excused *anything*, Miss Lidbrook,' uttered Decimus fervently, 'as innocent as you are.'

She paused on the threshold of the breakfast parlour and looked round at him. 'I am not innocent, Mr Berowne, if you mean to imply that I do not know this is wrong.'

He smiled at her. 'That is not what I meant, Millie — I mean, *Miss Lidbrook*.'

She blushed. 'Pray call me Millie.' She went into the parlour. 'I was only at breakfast, and if we leave the door open perhaps Louisa will not mind so very much.'

'Forgive me, Miss — I mean, Millie,' Decimus began, reminded of his mission, 'but do you know whether my sisters came here this morning?'

'Nonie and Tavey, you mean?' she asked, for she had lost no time in getting upon very friendly terms with the girls. 'I have not seen them.' She started. 'But stay! There *was* some sort of commotion. From Louisa's bedchamber, I believe. But you see we are on separate sides of the hall, and I was half asleep, so I thought perhaps I was dreaming.'

'Then they did come here!' exclaimed Decimus, laying his hat on the table.

'I cannot be *sure*,' Millie said carefully. 'I gave up trying to sleep, and when I asked for breakfast to be put forward I was told that Louisa had gone out very early. But, pray, what has happened?'

'I cannot tell you,' Decimus said.

Millie's face fell, and the kitten eyes showed

sudden hurt. Decimus took a step towards her and grasped her hands.

'Millie, don't look like that! It is not that I do not trust you, indeed it isn't! But I am sure Lady Louisa would never forgive me if I sullied your innocent ears with such a tale. Indeed, I could scarce forgive myself!'

Millie could not forbear returning the pressure of his hands, her trustful eyes smiling up at him. 'Pray don't tell me, if it will give you distress. I should *hate* to be the cause of that, dear Dess.'

'Oh, Millie!' he sighed, lifting her hands to his lips.

A voice from the doorway arrested him. 'Have you come to breakfast, Decimus Berowne?'

Millie snatched her hands from his and pressed them to her burning cheeks. Decimus whirled to face Lady Louisa, his own complexion darkening.

'Oh, lord!' he ejaculated ruefully, like a schoolboy caught out in some misdemeanour.

Louisa compressed her lips to conceal a smile and raised her brows at him. 'You are seeking your sisters, I dare say.'

'Yes, that is it!' he said gratefully, and cast a worried glance at Millie, who had hidden her face in her hands. 'Don't blame Millie, Lady Louisa. She — she heard me, I believe, outside the door, and ——'

'I am sure Millie can speak for herself, Decimus,' Louisa said calmly, coming forward into the room and stripping off her gloves. 'As for your sisters, you will, I think, find them safe at Nona's home, where your brother Septimus has taken them.'

'Oh,' he said blankly. 'Is all well, then?'

'Yes, I am thankful to say.'

'Yes, indeed! I—er—I have not said anything to Miss Lidbrook. I thought you would wish me to keep silent.'

'Not as silent as I found you, Decimus,' Louisa said wryly, 'if *action* is to be the substitute!'

He flushed fierily and Millie turned quickly away, tripping to the far end of the room as if she would escape from him. Decimus took up his hat and began to edge for the door, stuttering in his haste to speak.

'P-pray don't be angry with M-millie, L-lady Louisa! It—it was all my fault. I did not mean anything by it, I assure you. *Pray* don't be angry with her.'

'My dear boy,' Louisa uttered kindly, 'your chivalry does you credit, but it is quite misplaced. I am not a gorgon! However, I think it only fair to point out that a repetition of what I was privileged to witness just now will certainly call down a good deal of recrimination upon your head. Do I make myself clear?'

'Quite clear, Lady Louisa,' Decimus said quietly, as pale now as he was before red. 'I understand you perfectly, and I have nothing to do but to beg your pardon and take my leave.'

Louisa nodded, although she was secretly impressed by this show of dignity. 'You are absolved—this time.'

Throwing one more glance—in which Louisa detected more than a touch of yearning—across the room at Millie, he left the room, closing the door behind him.

Louisa looked at her ward. 'Well, Millie?'

'Oh, Louisa, I am so ashamed!' wailed the girl,

taking her hands from her face to show her preceptress a woebegone countenance, with tears drowning
the kitten eyes.

'Tush, Millie, don't be a goose!' Louisa said bracingly. 'You have not broken the commandments, you
know. I am sure you are quite aware that you should
not receive a man alone.'

'I am, I am!' cried Millie. 'And I would not have,
but that he spoke of his sisters. I wondered then if it
had something to do with your not being here
and——'

'Oh, dear, it is my fault!'' Louisa decided
worriedly.

'No, no,' protested Millie, drying her eyes.

'On the contrary, yes, yes!' She came over to put
an arm about her ward. 'My darling Millie, I am a
poor friend to you. My aunt warned me about the
Berownes, and——'

'But they are so *nice*, Louisa!' Millie burst out.
'Oh, I so much liked Tavey and Nonie! And. . .and
Dess—I mean, Decimus. . .' She broke off, hastily
putting up her handkerchief in pretence of drying her
cheeks to hide the tell-tale pink.

Louisa went to sit at the table. 'My love, it is not
what *we* think of them, unfortunately—and I agree
with you, they are most of them very charming and
amusing—but what the world thinks of them. To be
candid, Millie, if you are to make a favourable match,
you cannot *afford* the Berownes. Do you see?'

Millie stood unconsciously kneading her handkerchief with unsteady fingers. 'I—I don't much care
about making a favourable match, Louisa. I mean, I
have not met anyone—anyone *eligible*, I should

say—whom I could like well enough to think of marrying.'

'There is time enough for that, Millie, darling,' Louisa said kindly. She glanced about the table. 'Ring the bell, will you? We can do with fresh coffee, I think.'

As her ward complied with this request, Louisa added cheerfully. 'Let us forget the Berownes, Millie. From now on I am going to make a determined effort to avoid them.'

The words struck misery into Millie's heart, and she shed tears later as she donned a pastel-green walking dress with long sleeves and swathed a large diaphanous shawl across her elbows, preparatory to a promised morning call she and Louisa were to make on Lady Pyrland. But she fought for calm as she waited in the large saloon for Louisa, who had elected to practise the pianoforte in her little adjoining parlour. Fortunately for her overwrought nerves, the music ended shortly. The interconnecting door opened to admit Louisa, who came in, flexing her fingers.

'I really must put in more time. Mr Shittlehope would be grieved to know how much my playing has deteriorated.'

'I am sure he would understand, Louisa,' Millie offered. 'There are so many demands upon you in town.'

'Yes, frivolous ones!' Louisa said, twinkling. 'If you think Mr Shittlehope would have considered them a sufficient excuse, you have little remembrance of him.'

'I did not know him at all well,' admitted Millie. 'I

was a child, you know. And he seemed so *old*.' Immediately she put up a hand to her mouth in consternation. 'Oh, I *beg* your pardon, Louisa!'

But Louisa was laughing. 'Poor Mr Shittlehope *was* old. But a generous, splendid, *trustworthy* person. And that is what I remember most.'

Millie's eyes filled. Trustworthy! Oh, how *unworthy* was she of the love of one to whom she owed so much!

'Oh, *Louisa*,' she uttered brokenly. 'How I *wish* I. . .' Her voice failed.

'Why, Millie, whatever is the matter?' Louisa asked, crossing quickly over to her.

It was at this inopportune moment that Mortehoe ushered several morning callers into the room.

'Mrs Kilgetty, Mrs Fullands and Mr Berowne, my lady,' he announced, in a voice that clearly indicated his disassociation from any consequences.

'What in the world——?' began Louisa, as Nona and Octavia tripped into the room, breaking into instant speech.

'Oh, Lady Louisa, we have had *such* a time of it!'

'We *had* to come and tell you, for we could not do as you suggested, and Tavey would not have you think us *ungrateful*.'

'Softly, my babes, softly!' chided Septimus, closing in behind them. 'You will deafen the poor woman if you both talk at once.'

They had all three shed their outer garments downstairs, and Louisa unconsciously cast an appreciative eye over the poet's for once plain attire — a light blue frock over buckskin breeches —

which had been concealed by his dramatic cloak earlier in the day.

She had moved forward to conceal her ward and give her a moment to compose herself. Her immediate reaction to the invasion was one of exasperation, but at the poet's comment she laughed.

'Yes, do try for a little *calm*, my dears. What has happened?'

'It is Sexta,' Octavia began.

'Oh, not again!' Louisa uttered, casting up her eyes.

'We have had her in *hysterics*,' Nona announced with relish, 'screaming and tearing her hair—you know the way she does.'

'I am happy to say I do not!' Louisa snapped.

'Of course she does not. Don't be silly, Nonie!' Octavia said crossly.

Nona trilled with laughter. 'Oh, dear, that *was* silly. But it seems, you know, as if we have known you *forever*, Lady Louisa, and so you must be acquainted with *all* our foibles.'

'Yes, it is beginning to seem like that to me, too,' Louisa said, throwing a twinkling glance in the direction of their brother, who was standing to one side, patiently awaiting a break in the conversation. 'Perhaps I shall better understand this if *you* tell me.'

'My dear ma'am,' Septimus said blandly, 'I never attempt explanation when my hog-grubbing sisters are by. It is a waste of energy.'

'How *dare* you, Setty?'

'You are *very* unkind.'

'On the contrary, my babes, I am indulgent in the

extreme. Didn't I escort you here, braving dire consequences?'

'*What* dire consequences?' demanded Octavia.

'Oh, he is teasing, Tavey. Don't heed him!' said Nona dismissively.

But Louisa's glance met the questioning gleam in that of their brother, and held. She smiled. 'None, I promise you. But more of that later. Pray tell me, one of you, what all this is about.'

But by this time the girls had discovered Miss Lidbrook, nestling quietly in the background, her green kitten eyes once more respectably dry.

'Millie!' squeaked Nona. 'You will not *believe* —'

'I didn't see you, Millie,' Octavia interrupted. 'Please forgive us for being so dreadfully rude.'

'Oh, no,' Millie said quickly. 'I know you have some urgent business on hand, for Decimus came looking for you.'

'Millie, we have had the most *dreadful* day!' exclaimed Nona.

'Wait, Nonie,' Octavia said, puzzled. 'We have just seen Dess, and he never mentioned his visit here.'

'Probably because he could not edge in a word,' murmured Septimus, and made an elegant leg. 'How do you do, Miss Lidbrook? I trust your ankle is fully recovered from your unfortunate fall the other night.'

'Oh! Oh, h-how do you do? Oh, yes, it was better directly, Mr Berowne.'

'Septimus, please,' he begged, smiling. 'I gather you are already upon terms with my younger siblings. You may as well add me.'

Millie smiled prettily. 'That is kind.' She cast a doubtful glance at Louisa, who was frowning. 'I — I think perhaps I should leave you, though. Shall I, Louisa?'

'Tush, Millie, don't be a goose!' Louisa said quickly, coming to herself with a start. A faint ruffle of heat disturbed her face, for she had surprised in herself the oddest pang when the poet spoke so kindly to her ward. Shrugging off the feeling, she added, 'I had not meant you to know of any of this, but I see it is useless to try to keep it from you.'

'Oh, have we done wrong, Lady Louisa?' asked Octavia contritely. 'Should we not have come?'

'Don't be absurd; I am very glad to see you both,' Louisa said warmly, quite unable to find it in her heart to repulse them. She twinkled. 'I thought we had agreed on informality, by the by.'

'Yes, but it seems so *odd*, you know, to speak to you as *Louisa*!' exclaimed Nona. 'I don't know how it is, but it seems dreadfully disrespectful, doesn't it, Tavey?'

Octavia's pansy eyes lit unexpectedly. 'Could you tolerate *Aunt* Louisa, perhaps?'

'No, I could *not*. Aunt, indeed! As if I have not had enough to contend with from Decimus and Quarto.' But her eyes were twinkling. 'If that is the alternative, stick to Lady Louisa, I beg of you! But I am still quite in the dark, you know. Do sit down and unburden yourselves about your poor sister.'

The two girls sank gratefully on to a sofa together, looking like a pair of colourful twittering birds as they began their tale, with their expressive brown-pansy eyes, and round hats perched at a jaunty angle on their frizzed coiffures, the flowers and feathers bobbing as they talked.

'It was as we reached Quint's lodging it began,' said Octovia.

'Sexta must have been lying in wait, for she came running out the *moment* the coach stopped,' Nona added.

'She should not have been there at all!' Octavia said austerely.

'For Dolly has told her *over and over* on no account to visit him in Clarges Street.'

'Not that she pays any attention to Dolly.'

'Nor anyone else!' put in Septimus drily.

'Except Quint *himself*,' Octavia pointed out.

'Yes, but on *this* occasion she wouldn't listen to *anybody*,' Nona cried. 'Least of all Quint.'

'That was *his* fault, Nonie, you know it was.' Octavia turned to Lady Louisa. 'He was in such a foul mood because Setty stopped the fight so quickly——'

'And because I intervened, too, I expect,' Louisa interpolated.

'Oh, yes, he was *furious* about that, Louisa,' Nona agreed, suddenly finding no difficulty at all in addressing the lady by name.

Octavia took up the tale again. 'Sexta fell on his neck as he got out of the coach, crying that she was sorry.'

'And Quint just *pushed* her aside, and shouted at her that *he* wasn't wounded, and she had better have gone to Wherwell's lodging instead.'

'In an *instant* they were quarrelling again,' Octavia said in exasperated tones.

'Poor Setty nearly got struck trying to intervene,' laughed Nona.

'Yes, by Sexta,' said the poet aggrievedly.

'Oh, no!' uttered Louisa, eyes dancing. 'And all this out in the open street?'

'How *terrible*!' commented Millie faintly. Her horrified green eyes had jumped from one to the other as she followed the story.

'Oh, it got *much* worse,' Nona told them.

'Yes, for Sexta went into one of her fits, drat her,' Octavia revealed crossly, 'and we had all to do to get her in the coach and take her home.'

'And if you have never driven in a coach with a hysterical female,' Septimus put in acidly, 'plus a couple of shrieking attendants adding to the cacophony, let me beg you by every means in your power to avoid it!'

'Oh, poor poet!' Louisa burst out. 'I can well imagine your sufferings.'

He grinned. 'Yes, it's well for you to laugh. The next time I may bring her here for you to manage.'

'No, pray don't,' Louisa begged. 'Though you should of course have slapped her. A shock is usually effective medicine in such a case.'

'That settles it! I *will* bring her here. You would clearly know exactly how to do.'

'Yes, you would, Louisa,' Octavia agreed, looking at her with approval as she too dropped the formal address with sudden ease. 'Unlike Dolly!'

'Oh, Dolly is *hopeless*,' Nona said, adding her mite. 'All she would do is moan about her "poor nerves" and beg us not to expect *her* to quiet Sexta.'

'As if we would! Sexta would just have screamed all the more if Dolly had come near her.'

'But who is Dolly?' Louisa asked, bewildered.

Both girls stared at her blankly. Then they

exchanged glances, and Nona said in astonished tones, 'You don't know?'

'If she did she wouldn't ask,' Septimus said drily. 'Dolly is our mother.'

'What?' gasped Millie, round-eyed.

Louisa looked them over, all three. 'Of course. Dolly Berowne. I *had* heard it. And you had difficulty calling *me* by name!'

'Well, but we don't *usually* speak so of her to strangers,' Octavia said excusingly.

'It is not *our* fault,' chimed in Nona. 'Dolly will not have us address her as Mama. At least, she does not mind so much us girls doing so.'

'Dolly feels,' explained Septimus kindly, 'that to have a set of hulking great young men addressing her as Mama will very quickly drive her into her grave. Like you, Lady Louisa, she is conscious of the passing years.'

'Septimus Berowne,' Louisa uttered with a kindling eye, 'if it did not accord very ill with something I particularly wish to say to you, I would certainly box your ears!'

'There, now, that is *just* like Dolly!' exclaimed Nona.

'Yes,' giggled Octavia. 'Dolly does box the boys' ears if they *dare* to address her as Mama.'

Louisa rose from her chair. 'Thank you; I have heard enough! Now if you, Nona and Octavia, would care to regale Millie with the full story of today's events — for she is looking quite stunned and bewildered, poor Millie! — your brother and I have something to discuss.' She added, as she passed him on her way to the interconnecting door to her private sanctum, 'Septimus, if you would not mind?'

'I am naturally at your service,' he murmured, following her.

The two sisters exchanged one of their conspiratorial questioning glances, but Millie saw nothing odd.

In her shy voice she said, 'Oh, yes, please *do* tell me it all, dear Tavey. And Nonie. I am *consumed* with curiosity, and it is very kind of Louisa to allow me to enjoy your company.'

'Oh, is *that* why?' Nona exclaimed, looking towards the door through which the other pair had gone. 'I thought——'

'Be quiet, Nonie!' Octavia muttered, digging her in the ribs. 'Millie, when did Dess come here?'

That was enough to silence Nona. Losing immediate interest in the older couple, the three young ladies were very soon enjoying a delightful cose.

Louisa, meanwhile, having stepped into her little parlour, moved to the fireplace and turned to face the poet.

'Lady Louisa, may I say——?' he began.

'No, let me speak first!' Louisa pleaded. 'I have brought you in here to apologise for so *misjudging* you, Septimus.' Her large orbs were warm, their misty look enhanced as she gazed earnestly into his face. 'Quarto told me—though indeed it was not his intention to vindicate you!—how you acted during that regrettable duel. I saw at once that you were there only for that, and oh, I *beg* your pardon! I had no right to jump to a false and *base* conclusion merely because your name is Berowne. Will you forgive me?'

For a moment he stood silent, just staring at her,
bowled over by her candour, bewitched by the
enchantment of those soulful orbs. His lips opened
and stayed so. Then he shrugged helplessly, betrayed
into a self-conscious laugh.

'Lady Louisa, you have taken the wind out of my
sails!'

She smiled. 'Have I?'

'Good God, yes! Here had I come prepared with a
mouthful of explanation and apology on my own
account, only to be met with — with *this*. I don't know
what to say.'

The large eyes twinkled. 'Say I am forgiven.'

His own eyes gleamed. 'Forgiven? Certainly not!'

'What?' exclaimed Louisa.

'Well, not before you have made reparation,' he
amended and the teasing quality was back in his
voice.

'I see,' Louisa said grimly. 'And what have you in
mind?'

'A forfeit, a forfeit!' he cried. 'You shall listen,
without a *word* of interruption, to an entire poem.'

'Yours, I collect.'

'Naturally. Would I offer you Pope?'

Louisa frowned portentously. 'You really feel that
the crime merits so severe a punishment?'

The poet's eyes narrowed, although there was a
tell-tale flicker at the corner of his mouth. 'I really
feel, Lady Louisa, that *that* question merits a more
severe punishment still. You shall listen to one of my
poems about *you*.'

'Oh, no, spare me!' cried Louisa, breaking into

laughter. Then she opened her eyes at him. '*One* of them? How many are there?'

'I've lost count,' Septimus said hastily.

'Have you indeed?' Louisa asked sceptically. 'I fear, Septimus Berowne, that you are not a very truthful person.'

'*Lady Louisa*!' he said, outraged. 'Are you intent upon *another* forfeit?'

'No, no, no, no, *no*!' she uttered, waving her hands frantically. 'I take it back, I take it back! I know,' she added as he laughed, 'I shall play for you instead. Do you like music?' She moved to the pianoforte as she spoke and sat on the stool.

'I like music, yes, but I am not to be put off so,' Septimus told her, following. 'I am determined that you *will* hear my poetry.'

'Another time, perhaps,' Louisa murmured, spreading her fingers over the keys.

She began to play softly, a melodic air by the young genius Mozart. She played from memory, with a gentle touch, and a feel for the music that was at once intuitive and original, so that the listener felt he was hearing the piece for the first time. So effortless and fluent was her performance that she was able to converse at the same time.

'Mr Shittlehope was used to love this piece. He would have me play it for him endlessly.'

Septimus, lost in wonder with her proficiency, and caught by the quality she brought to it, did not answer. He had taken up a negligent stance, leaning on the instrument to watch her, and, since her eyes were on the keys, his gaze roved down. From the tight-laced bodice of her yellow gown rose the swell of her bosom, glimmering palely under the muslin neckerchief she wore, crossed over and tied behind. The music faded in his ears a little as his heartbeat quickened.

When she had finished, and looked up for his response, he spoke with sincerity, his eyes quite serious, but he knew he did not refer entirely to her playing.

'That was a beautiful forfeit, Loulou. You are freely forgiven.'

A faint smile touched her lips, and their glances held.

'Thank you,' she said, hardly aware that her tone had softened. 'But I *will* hear your poems one day.'

From the saloon to which the door was still open there came a most unwelcome interruption.

'Lady Pyrland,' announced Mortehoe in a voice of doom, 'and Lord Sedbergh.'

CHAPTER SIX

'OH, NO,' murmured Louisa, consternation spreading across her features. 'Now we are in trouble.'

'Your aunt?' Septimus muttered, putting out a hand to help her to rise.

'*And* my cousin,' Louisa said, taking his hand and allowing him to help her to her feet.

'Never fear!' he whispered. 'I'll take my sisters away.'

'Thank you, but I dare say the damage is done now.' She crossed to the the door and entered the saloon. 'Aunt Hebe, I beg your pardon. We were supposed to come and see you.'

Lady Pyrland's Roman nose was in the air, her gimlet eye boring into the two pretty faces staring at her with their mouths at half-cock.

'Yes, you were, Louisa,' she said, casting her erring niece a look that spoke volumes, 'but I gather you have been *otherwise* engaged.' Her eyebrows flew up as the poet entered behind her niece, and she bent a glare upon Louisa. 'And what, may I ask, is the meaning of this?'

Louisa's temper began to rise. 'This, Aunt, is, as you very well know, Mr Septimus Berowne, who was kind enough to bring his sisters to visit me.'

'His sisters or *himself*?' demanded another voice.

For the first time Louisa took in her cousin, standing just behind Lady Pyrland, on his face a look of rigid disapproval. She was aware suddenly of Septimus beside her and could almost feel his stiffening. Through her mind flitted the remembrance of Quarto's revelation in the coach that morning. A 'nonpareil' with a sword was Septimus Berowne. Turning to him quickly, she put a restraining hand on his sleeve.

'Pray don't take an affront into your head! I will deal with this.' Swiftly she stepped forward. 'Yes, Philip, Mr Berowne is here to see me, in fact. At *my* request. I wanted to hear some of his poetry.'

'Liar!' Septimus muttered behind her under his breath. Aloud he said, 'Good day, Lord Sedbergh, Lady Pyrland.' Nodding at the matron, he added, 'You need not hesitate to speak your minds. We are all of us quite aware of your emotions. Lady Louisa and I had matters of our own to discuss — *private* matters — but I fail to see that they can in any way concern either of you.'

'I *beg* your pardon!' uttered Lady Pyrland furiously.

'Granted,' said Septimus blandly, and turned to his sisters. 'Nonie and Tavey, we must take our leave. Say your farewells and come.'

With which he bowed briefly to the company at large, and went to hold open the door. His two sisters, quite cowed by the heavy atmosphere, whispered quickly to Millie, thanked Louisa as they passed, and hurried out of the room.

As the door closed behind Septimus, Lady Pyrland turned on her niece. 'Now, then, Louisa!'

But Louisa was not attending. 'In a moment, Aunt. Wait!'

Then she darted to the door and quickly followed the party, who were already halfway down the stairs.

'Septimus!' she called.

He paused on the stairs, turning to look up at her.

'Yes, Lady Louisa?'

'Stay a moment!'

Septimus hesitated. Then he motioned to his sisters to wait for him by the front door, and swiftly ran up the stairs to meet Louisa on the landing.

'What is it?' he asked curtly.

Louisa looked at him and sighed. 'Nothing! Only I — I'm so *sorry*. Forgive me!'

His face softened. 'Again?'

Louisa smiled. 'I know it is asking a lot, but yes, again.'

'There is nothing to forgive, Loulou. *You* are not to blame for the conduct of your relatives.'

'Yet that is precisely what is done to you,' she pointed out.

A short laugh escaped him. 'I am used to it.'

'Don't you care?' Louisa asked, frowning in a little perplexity.

He shrugged. 'It can be a nuisance. But I *care* about my siblings, you see.'

Impulsively Louisa put out a hand to him. 'And you said *I* had a warm heart!'

The poet took her fingers in his and lightly kissed them. 'You have. You need not have done any of the things you did today.' He pressed her hand, smiling. 'You had better go back. Don't forget the "apoplectic" aunt!'

'Would that I could!' laughed Louisa. 'Goodbye, then.'

'Let us say rather *au revoir*. Aunt or no aunt, you do not get rid of me so easily!'

Louisa giggled as he went off down the stairs, and she was still smiling when she re-entered the saloon to find Lady Pyrland stiff with anger and Millie in tears. Her smile faded, giving place to sparkling wrath.

'What have you been saying to my ward, Aunt Hebe?' she demanded, crossing to put a protective arm about the girl.

'Nothing that I would not say to you, be sure,' Lady Pyrland told her defensively.

'Then *say it* to me, but leave Millie alone!'

'Louisa!' called her cousin imperatively. 'How can you take such a tone with your aunt? I am shocked, I may say *disgusted*, by what I have seen here today.'

'In that case, Philip,' Louisa broke in angrily, 'I suggest you leave at once.'

'I shall do no such thing! If your poor father were alive to hear you, I shudder to think of his reaction.'

'And if my poor Mr Shittlehope were alive to hear *you*, Philip,' retorted Louisa, 'he would have shown you the door — as I do!'

Leaving Millie, she marched to the door and opened it, glaring at Sedbergh's stiffly outraged features.

'Are you throwing *me* out, too, Louisa?' demanded Lady Pyrland in tones of bitter hurt.

A sharp rejoinder hovered on Louisa's tongue. But her glance caught Millie's terrified kitten eyes, and all the consequences of a breach with Lady Pyrland came crashing in on her. With a long, shuddering sigh she shut the door.

'No, Aunt Hebe, of course I am not throwing you out.' She looked at her cousin, stiffly forcing out the words. 'I beg your pardon, Philip. That was ill done of me.'

He sniffed. 'It is of no consequence. If you could but bring yourself to see ——'

'Thank you, Philip,' she interrupted quietly, 'but I do see.' She moved to Lady Pyrland and took that matron's hand between both her own. 'Aunt Hebe, I am sorry you had to come and find us here with the Berownes like this. You are quite right. My intervention the other day at St Pancras Wells *has* drawn me a little into the arena of their family affairs. But no one outside of us here knows anything of it, and ——'

'If you think people won't hear of it, then you know little of those Berowne girls,' snapped Lady Pyrland, withdrawing her hand. 'A pair of looser tongues you will never come across!'

'Very well, then, we will do our best not to encourage them,' Louisa said, hanging on to her calm exterior with difficulty.

'It is too late now,' predicted Lord Sedbergh. 'I have seen it happen before. Once they find someone foolish enough to be drawn in, they are like leeches. They will *cling* to you, Louisa.'

Louisa was much inclined to agree with this assessment, but she did not say so. She repeated her assurances that she would do her best to maintain a proper distance, and could only be thankful when her aunt and cousin at length took their leave.

'Well, I *tried*,' she said despairingly to Millie after they had gone.

'Oh, Louisa, you are so brave!' uttered Millie. 'I could *never* answer her as you do.'

'I never answer her as I should,' laughed Louisa ruefully. 'Much as I hate to admit it, I am afraid they are right. We may well be saddled with the Berownes!'

Millie pressed a surreptitious hand to her bosom against the sudden flurry of her heart. 'What are we going to do, Louisa?'

'Do? Why, nothing. What *can* we do?' She smiled. 'Don't concern yourself, Millie. Perhaps we shall find that Aunt Hebe exaggerates the reaction of Society.'

But over the next few days it became abundantly plain that this was not the case. Lady Childrey, catching Louisa in a convenient velvet-curtained alcove at an exclusive rout which did not include the Berownes, issued a kindly warning.

'Everyone is talking of this unsuitable friendship, my dear, and as you met the Berownes at my party at St Pancras I feel palpably to blame.'

'Nonsense!' Louisa said briskly.

'Alas, I wish it were. Though no one blames *you* for not knowing the proper way to go on, with your background.'

'I had better make it my business to thank them,' Louisa murmured drily.

'But young Millicent is another matter,' Lady Childrey went on, apparently impervious to irony. 'I do not mean to be cruel, but the fact is that *she* has no birthright to protect her. If she falls, my dear, there will be no net for her.'

Louisa glanced across to where Millie was chatting animatedly to Charlotte Childrey. There was a leaden feeling in her chest, a weight of oppression for which she could not account. Why *should* she be so unwilling to drop the Berownes? Especially when it was for Millie's sake.

But her conviction that there was a need for such a sacrifice was fostered by an encounter with Mrs Wavertree. That large lady leaned her red-powdered coiffure perilously close to the candelabrum on the wall behind them, and uttered in a confidential tone, 'I saw that Childrey woman beard you. Been warning against this acquaintance you've struck up with the Berownes, I'll wager.'

Louisa sighed. 'She has indeed. Are they so very dreadful, Mrs Wavertree?'

The matron nodded vehemently, setting the plumes on her elaborate headdress aquiver. 'Quite appalling. But they had no guidance, poor things. And the worst possible example!'

'Dolly Berowne, ma'am?' asked Louisa.

'A heartless mother she's been,' sighed Mrs Wavertree, sadly shaking her head. 'But she was always so beautiful, and so charming, that everyone forgave her.'

'Tush, Mrs Wavertree, you speak as if she were dead!'

'She might as well be so far as Society is concerned. They tolerate her children — just! — but scarcely any hostess of the *haut ton* will receive Dolly herself. She contrives to maintain a position among the *lesser* gentry. Especially the *male* sector. As for Berowne himself, I believe he is so badly in the gout — which, from the way he always drank, surprises no one! — that he hardly stirs from the house.'

'But was this Dolly so *very* bad?' Louisa demanded.

'Shocking!' said Mrs Wavertree, not mincing matters. 'Berowne was quite a catch, you know. But he was ever a profligate, diced away his inheritance, except for the house, which is entailed. Dolly spent freely, too, and when Berowne's resources ran out she began to dispense her favours so that she might continue to live as she was accustomed.'

In other words, Louisa thought in disgust, she became little better than a courtesan. She thought of the two younger girls, and a wave of compassion smote her. Small wonder they were so lacking in moral values!

'Poor children!' she said aloud.

'Dolly never wanted children, she was used to say,' Mrs Wavertree explained.

'Nor Mr Berowne, I take it,' Louisa commented drily.

'Well, I truly think,' said the elder lady judiciously, lowering her voice even more, 'that the older ones *are* his. They may *all* be true Berownes, to be fair, for it was a good many years before the parents became completely estranged.'

Louisa found, to her own astonishment, that her eyes were pricking. 'What a sorry life for them both!'

Mrs Wavertree broke into chuckles. 'Dolly would not agree with you. She is anything but sorry!'

'Well, she *should* be,' Louisa said emphatically. 'At least for her children.'

'Ah, you *have* succumbed, haven't you?'

'If I have,' Louisa uttered in a determined way, 'I am perfectly well able to recover, I assure you.' Her

PLAY "LUCKY 7"
AND GET AS MANY AS SIX FREE GIFTS...

HOW TO PLAY:

1 With a coin, carefully scratch away the silver panel opposite. You will now be eligible to receive two or more FREE books, and possibly other gifts, depending on what is revealed beneath the scratch off area.

2 When you return this card, you'll receive specially selected **Mills & Boon Romances**. We'll send you the books and gifts you qualify for absolutely FREE, and at the same time we'll reserve you a subscription to our Reader Service.

3 If we don't hear from you, within 10 days we'll send you six brand new Romances to read and enjoy every month for just £1.90 each, the same price as the books in the shops. There is no extra charge for postage and handling. There are no hidden extras.

4 When you join the Mills & Boon Reader Service, you'll also get our FREE monthly Newsletter, featuring author news, horoscopes, penfriends, competitions.

5 You are under no obligation, and may cancel or suspend your subscription at any time simply by writing to us.

ou'll love your
uddly teddy.
is brown eyes and
ute face are sure to
nake you smile.

Just scratch away the silver panel with a coin.
hen check below to see which gifts you get.

YES! I have scratched away the silver panel. Please send me all the gifts
for which I qualify. I understand that I am under no obligation to
rchase any books, as explained on the opposite page. I am over 18 years of age.

S/MRS/MISS/MR   3A4R

DDRESS

STCODE   SIGNATURE

 WORTH FOUR FREE BOOKS
PLUS A CUDDLY TEDDY AND MYSTERY GIFT

 WORTH FOUR FREE BOOKS
PLUS A MYSTERY GIFT

 WORTH FOUR FREE BOOKS

 WORTH TWO FREE BOOKS

MILLS & BOON 'NO RISK' GUARANTEE

- You're not required to buy a single book!
- You must be completely satisfied or you may cancel at any time simply by writing to us. You will receive no more books; you'll have no further obligation.
- The free books and gifts you receive from this offer remain yours to keep no matter what you decide.

If reply card is missing, write to:
Mills & Boon Reader Service, FREEPOST,
P.O. Box 236, Croydon, Surrey CR9 3RU

Mills & Boon Reader Service
FREEPOST
P.O. Box 236
Croydon
Surrey
CR9 9EL

glance, passing across her ward's face, found the
ladies Pyrland and Childrey in close conversation.
She drew a breath. 'And for Millie's sake, I had
better!'

For more than a week Louisa managed to hold
aloof from the Berownes. Or else they held aloof
from her. She had, although reluctantly, instructed
Mortehoe that she was not at home to them. Whether
this had deterred them, or whether perhaps Septimus
had imposed some sort of barrier, she could not tell.
The latter suspicion entered her mind when she found
that although twice he smiled and waved on seeing
her at some gathering he did not approach her.

Louisa quashed a feeling of disappointment, and
told herself she had no right to suffer pique. She
ought to be glad that the poet had enough consideration to keep his distance. That he had said she
should not get rid of him so easily was neither here
nor there! As for his *au revoir*, well, that had been
merely a spur-of-the-moment challenge thrown in to
tease her. It was not that she missed his teasing, of
course. It was just a trifle *melancholy* that their
budding friendship had to be so abruptly terminated.

As for Millie, she seemed often to be in the
company of Charlotte Childrey. Certainly Louisa's
chaperonage was not always necessary by day, which
left her free to attend to some pressing business
concerning the late Mr Shittlehope's manufactories,
and to work on the ubiquitous accounts.

But some engagements they had to attend
together, including Mrs Wavertree's breakfast party
at the Florida Gardens in Brompton. For Lady

Childrey had set a fashion, and all the hostesses were now vying for the choicest of the smaller tea gardens.

The charming Florida Gardens had recently been purchased by a German horticulturist. His April blooms made a splendid showing, and an innovation in ice-creams assured the younger people's pleasure. Louisa found herself walking around the grounds with her hostess, with whom she had struck up a friendship.

'Oh, dear, I *loathe* playing hostess,' confided Mrs Wavertree, sighing.

'Then why do you do it?' asked Louisa, amused.

'Well, one *has* to, doesn't one? I declare, I could have *killed* Augusta Childrey. I've had the devil's own time of it — if you'll pardon the expression — to get a suitable place.'

'I think you've contrived it splendidly,' Louisa told her, glancing about the pretty arbours with their trailing flowered greenery. It was so much warmer that Louisa had dared to leave off an outer garment, and wore only a long polonaise looped up into puffs behind over an embroidered petticoat.

She breathed deeply of the fresh spring air. 'And you have a gorgeous day for it.'

Mrs Wavertree cast a worried look at the sky, which was almost free from cloud, the sun warmly shining. 'Yes, if only it won't come on to rain later.'

'Poppycock! It is perfect, Mrs Wavertree. Only look how the youngsters are enjoying themselves.'

She pointed to a clear green where a group of youthful enthusiasts were laughingly engaged in a rather inexpert game of battledore and shuttlecock.

'Pish! Don't talk as if you were my age, Louisa!' scolded the matron. 'You're a youngster yourself.'

'I don't feel like one,' laughed Louisa. 'Especially when I see *that* sort of conduct.'

She nodded to where two young ladies, clad in full-skirted diaphanous muslins, with trailing shawls across their elbows, were giggling and putting up their fans, pointing to one of the distant arbours. Then they turned slightly and Louisa recognised them.

'Why, it is Octavia and Nona.'

At the same moment Mrs Fullands caught sight of her and uttered a shriek that brought her sister Mrs Kilgetty's head about. They both waved and came running up, breaking into breathless speech.

'Louisa, isn't it *splendid*?' cried Nona.

'We are *so* delighted, aren't we, Nonie?' uttered Octavia. 'And we never guessed!'

'No, all the time she was with us, we didn't notice a *thing*.'

'Until *now*, of course, when nothing could be more *obvious*.'

Louisa held up her hands, laughing. 'Wait! Wait! I haven't a notion what you are talking about.'

The two girls stared, then looked at each other and back to Louisa, the feathers on their forward-tilting straw hats fluttering with the jerky movements.

'You mean you don't *know*?' Octavia uttered in astonished accents.

'Don't know *what*?' begged Louisa.

'Why, Millie and Dess are in *love*!' announced Nona gleefully.

For a second or two Louisa simply gazed at her, the

colour draining out of her face. The excitement in the animated countenances before her changed visibly to consternation.

'You — you are not pleased?' faltered Octavia.

'Oh, dear! Oh, dear!' uttered Mrs Wavertree faintly, her shocked eyes on Louisa's white face. 'Can I get you anything, my dear?'

But Louisa reached out and gripped Octavia's wrist. Her voice was hollow. 'How do you know this?'

Two popping pairs of eyes searched each other frantically, and came back to the large blue compelling orbs.

'We've just seen them together,' Octavia said. 'They're in the arbour over there.'

Louisa released her wrist and made purposefully for the direction she indicated. Nona and Octavia looked at each other.

'We shouldn't have said anything!' Nona whispered.

Octavia hesitated.

Nona shook her. 'Tavey, what are we going to *do*?'

'We'd better go too,' Octavia decided. 'Come on, Nonie.'

Mrs Wavertree, quite appalled, stood looking after them, a worried frown in her eyes. What should she do? Oh, dear, why did it have to happen *here*, at her party? She glanced about to check if anything had been noticed, and breathed a sigh of relief when no one appeared to be in the least bit interested in anything other than their own activities. Characteristically, Mrs Wavertree crept away to lose herself among her guests. This was not a situation in which she wanted to become involved.

Louisa, her brain reeling, marched towards the arbour, where she could now see a young couple sitting close together on a bench. She was hardly aware of Octavia and Nona hurrying behind her, and barely heard them when they caught her up and began to speak.

'Forgive us, Louisa, pray!' pleaded Octavia. 'If we'd had any *idea* you wouldn't care for it ——'

'We would've *died* before we said a word!' Nona finished.

'And truly we didn't notice anything until today, though we *might* have done these past mornings.'

'Yes, for we have been all together so *often*.'

Louisa halted abruptly, her eyes flying to Nona's face.

'You have been together? *When*?'

Anguished glances were once more exchanged. 'Well, at — at the Royal Academy,' Octavia offered.

'And we met in Bond Street,' Nona put in.

'And again at the Green Park yesterday.'

Louisa's eyes darkened with anger and distress both.

'Are you telling me that you and Millie, *and* Decimus, have been spending time together all *week*?'

'Why — why, *yes*,' Octavia confessed, and the pansy eyes filled suddenly. 'But we — we didn't know you would *object* to it.'

Nona burst into tears. 'Oh, Tavey are we in *trouble*? Oh, Lady Louisa, *pray* don't scold us!'

'We d-didn't *know*,' Octavia said again, biting her lip against hiccuping sobs.

Louisa melted. What a pair of innocent babies they

were! No, it was not their fault. She reached forward and put an arm about each, drawing them close.

'Hush, now! It's all right. I won't scold, I promise.'

'We were so *h-happy*!' wailed Nona.

'I wish I were *dead*!' Octavia uttered miserably.

'Don't be so absurd!' Louisa said, betrayed into a laugh. 'I'm not angry with *you*. Come, now, stop crying, both of you. You will ruin your complexions, and that would be a great pity. Only think how your husbands will complain! Dry your eyes, do!'

Breaking into rather watery giggles, the girls complied with this request, dragging handkerchiefs from their sleeves and sniffing into them.

The commotion had, despite their absorption in each other, attracted the attention of the couple on the bench, who no sooner saw Lady Louisa than they jumped up as one. Pale and trembling, they both stood — suddenly several feet apart! — awaiting the descent of retribution.

But Louisa, having calmed the two excitable young ladies, turned to confront the erring couple with perfect composure. She came towards them with lifted eyebrows, and halted, looking them over.

'I think, Millie, that you have a trifle of explaining to do.'

Millie flushed scarlet and hung her head. Manfully, Decimus stepped forward.

'Lady Louisa ——'

Louisa held up a hand. '*No*, Decimus. Don't say a word. This is hardly the time or the place. You may come and see me tomorrow morning.'

He bowed, unable to help his eyes flickering across

to Millie's averted countenance. 'As you wish, ma'am.'

'Good. Let us say at ten o'clock. For now, please escort your sisters to some other part of these delightful gardens.'

All three young Berownes, accepting their dismissal, withdrew without another word, casting glances from Millie to Louisa, and exchanging apprehensive grimaces.

Louisa went to sit on the bench. 'Millie, come here, please.'

Miss Lidbrook came slowly, eyes still lowered, and sat gingerly beside her guardian, fiddling nervously with her blue tiffany petticoats. There was an awkward silence.

How to handle this? Louisa wondered. She was both hurt and distressed by the deceit Millie had practised upon her, but so much aware of her own part in the tangle of this present crisis was she that she could not unleash her own emotions on the child.

'Millie, darling,' she began tentatively.

A tiny sob greeted this endearment. 'Oh, pray don't!'

'Don't what? I have done nothing yet.'

'Don't call me by so caressing a name,' Millie got out, her face averted. 'It—it makes me feel so *dreadfully*.'

'Would you rather I took a stick and beat you?' asked Louisa, on a light laugh.

The green eyes came round to look at her then. '*Much* rather! For I *deserve* it. I know I do.'

'Well, that I can't deny!' Louisa sighed. 'Oh, Millie, what *am* I to do with you?'

Millie collapsed in tears. 'Oh, Louisa, pray, *pray* don't be *kind* to me! I cannot *bear* it. I have used you so shockingly, I know I have.'

'Well, if you are determined to wear sackcloth and ashes, Millie,' Louisa said tartly, 'then that will excellently serve your turn. It will not, however, help us very much in this present pass.'

But Millie was not to be succoured from the abyss of her guilt. 'I did not *mean* to deceive you, Louisa, pray believe me. Only I. . .I knew how Lady Pyrland would scold, and I thought—I thought if you did not *know* of it you could not be blamed.'

'That is very poor logic, Millie, and I am afraid I don't believe you,' Louisa said candidly. 'Oh, I dare say you *think* that was your reason, but is it not the truth that you knew I would infallibly nip this in the bud had I known of it?'

Millie hung her head again, sniffing dolefully. 'It is true that I knew you would not approve.'

Louisa drew a breath. 'That rather depends. Are we talking of your acquaintance with Nona and Octavia, or your relationship with Decimus?'

Silence. Louisa saw that Millie was trembling violently, jerking her handkerchief between her fingers. Her heart sank. She reached out and quieted the restless fingers with a warm clasp.

'Millie, darling, we must try to keep a proper perspective about this,' she said gently. 'I dare say you think you are in love with him, but—'

'I don't *think*,' Millie said in an unexpectedly fierce voice. 'I *know*.'

Under her hand, Louisa felt the mittened fingers stiffen. She released them, drawing her hand away, as a sharp pang shot through her. Was this her little Millie? In her mind's eye she saw again the child's face in all its pain and bewilderment. Was she to see it all again?

'Millie,' she said quietly, 'I don't want you to be hurt.'

At that Millie's eyes flew round to meet hers, a glow in them that Louisa had never seen before.

'He couldn't hurt me! He *wouldn't*. Oh, Louisa, I know he's a Berowne, and I know he's not the man you envisioned for me, but he's — he's *Dess*.'

'Indeed?' Louisa said drily. 'That doesn't really tell me a great deal.'

'I know what you are thinking,' Millie uttered, a desperate note in her voice. 'You are thinking of what Society will say! You are thinking that I may find myself shunned and — and without friends.'

'As a matter of fact, I had not remembered all that,' Louisa said. What she was remembering was that Decimus Berowne, not much more than a couple of weeks ago, had been professing his undying love for herself! But that she could scarcely mention to Millie.

'Decimus has not, I trust,' she said instead, 'actually offered for you.'

'Oh, no. At least,' amended Millie conscientiously, 'we have talked in a — in a *general* way of — of marriage and — and how it might be in certain circumstances.'

'In other words,' Louisa said flatly, 'you *have* discussed it. Has he said he loves you?'

'Not — not in so many words,' Millie admitted. 'But I *know*, indeed I do, Louisa, what his sentiments are.'

Oddly enough, this forbearance on the part of Millie's lover found favour with Louisa. 'Well, I dare say there may be hope for him yet,' she muttered under her breath.

'What did you say, Louisa?'

'Nothing. Millie, I cannot at this moment allow you to consider this matter seriously.'

The girl's face fell. 'But you said you will see him tomorrow. I thought ——'

'You thought I was giving him the opportunity to request your hand in form,' Louisa guessed. 'No, I'm sorry, Millie. I hate to sound like Aunt Hebe, but I could not be said to be discharging my duty towards you if I were to consent to a betrothal between you.'

Rather to her surprise, Millie took this without a murmur. 'You *have* to say that, of course.'

'I mean it, Millie.'

'I know you do, Louisa,' she said quietly. She smiled rather tremulously up at her guardian. 'But I can always hope, can't I?'

CHAPTER SEVEN

SEPTIMUS BEROWNE, poet, sat at his desk, in shirt-sleeves as was his wont, puffing at his long clay pipe, and leafing through a sheaf of poems. He ran his eye down the final page, and, sighing, flung down the papers with a weary gesture.

'Damn you, Loulou!' he said calmly. 'Must you take over the whole of my muse?'

It seemed as if every theme that entered his head these days led him directly back to Lady Louisa Shittlehope! An ode to the passing of winter brought a mental image of twinkling blue eyes smiling out of the clouds. From spring daffodils grew an hour-glass figure in a yellow gown, and behind the veil of gauze that fluttered in a gentle breeze there blossomed two mounds of enticing mystery, where a man might set his lips to voluptuous exploration.

He brushed a hand across the top page as if he would erase the words he had placed there. For such poems as he had written could never be seen by any other eyes than his own. And certainly not by *those* eyes, the source of his present inspiration. Good God, she would *slaughter* him!

Taking a draw at his pipe, he turned the sheaf of papers face down. He *must* shake her out of his thoughts. As if his other writing commitments were not waste of time enough! Those he *must* fulfil, if he was to live. But his publishers were already gathering a list of subscribers for the second volume of his verses, and here he had still to produce at least a third of the necessary material.

'*Damn* you, Loulou!' he said again. 'Get out of my *head*.'

A knock at the door for once came as a welcome interruption. But he hastily lifted the offending sheaf of papers and stuffed it into a drawer of his desk. Rising, he called to the person without to enter. The door opened to admit his brother Decimus, a dejected figure in a suit of sober brown, bowed down with woe.

'Good God, babe, what is amiss?' demanded Septimus, staring.

Decimus heaved a despairing sigh. 'I have been to see Lady Louisa.'

Oh, damn you, Loulou! thought the poet savagely. *Now* what?

'About Millie, I suppose?' he queried aloud.

Decimus nodded. Coming to the mantel, he gripped its broad edge and rested his head on his knuckles, staring into the empty grate. 'She found us together yesterday, you see.'

'Yes, Tavey told me,' Septimus said.

He had already spoken his mind to his sister. Had he not tried to explain to them all the difficult position into which they were putting Lady Louisa? As well try to explain to a parrot, as to his feather-headed sisters! As Tavey had pointed out, they *had* kept away from Louisa. It was too much to expect them to appreciate that the prohibition extended to Millie as well!

'You didn't seriously expect to be welcomed with

open arms, did you, my babe?' asked Septimus frankly.

Decimus did not move. 'I did not expect to be welcomed at all.'

'Which is why you have been engaging in clandestine meetings.'

That brought the young man's head up. 'I have *not* done so. At least, not *intentionally*. We met by accident at the Royal Academy, and — and it was only because the girls said they would be shopping in Bond Street that Millie thought of going.'

'And I collect it was also by accident that you chose to escort Nonie and Tavey thither?' his brother put in drily.

Decimus glared at him. 'I did not think *you* would take Lady Louisa's part!'

'I have not taken her part,' Septimus replied calmly, seating himself on the day-bed. 'I am merely pointing out the flaw in your reasoning.'

'Damn you, Setty!' said his brother sullenly. 'I suppose you think I have done wrong.'

Septimus gave him a wry smile. 'I think you have done little to promote your own cause. In fact you have behaved very much as people would expect of a Berowne.'

'Yes, that is the *real* reason,' Decimus said bitterly. 'She may say what she chooses, but I know better.'

'I find it difficult to believe, Dess,' his brother said carefully, 'that Lady Louisa said anything at all against you for being a Berowne.'

Decimus kicked moodily at the fireguard. 'Well, she did not. But you cannot deny that being a member of this family *is* against me.'

'I don't deny it. I merely said that I can't believe Lady Louisa would use it against you.'

Decimus was silenced. His elder brother settled himself in comfort, putting his feet up, and puffing at his pipe. This was evidently going to take some time.

'What *did* she say, then?' he asked at length, when his young brother showed no signs of volunteering any further information.

The young man flushed. 'She reminded me that I had said I was in love with her.'

'Ah, now we come to it.'

'Yes, but that was *weeks* ago.'

'Two of three only, I should say. Enough, at any rate, to throw doubt on your constancy.'

'Constancy?' queried Decimus, as if he had never heard the word.

'Yes, you clodpole. Lady Louisa might be pardoned for wondering whether your feeling for Millie may be just as ephemeral. I would wonder myself. After all, you told *me* your heart was broken.'

Decimus had the grace to blush and stammered, 'I kn-know, b-but I *wasn't* in love with her. Oh, I thought so, but I believe I was merely dazzled. I know now it wasn't so, because the way I feel about Millie is quite *different*.'

'How do you feel about the "poor little dab", Dess?' enquired his brother curiously.

'Don't call her that!' snapped Decimus.

'Oh, I beg your pardon,' Septimus said with exaggerated courtesy. 'How very unfair of me it is to remind you of your own first impression!'

A reluctant grin wavered on Decimus's mouth. 'Well, I had only caught a glimpse of her. It was later when I—when she fell at that party. Oh, Setty, she is such an adorable little darling! So innocent, and so *sweet*.' His voice cracked and he threw a hand across his face. 'I don't know how I am to support life without her!'

'Yes, I remember thinking much the same thing at your age,' Septimus began sympathetically.

'It has nothing to do with my age!' Decimus said fiercely. 'Oh, you don't understand! Millie and I are *meant* for each other, you see. We both knew it almost at once, though nothing was *said*. We didn't *need* to say it. We still haven't, if you can believe that.' He stopped abruptly, and the fire died out of his eyes. Crossing to a chair, he slumped into it. 'What's the use? You'll never understand. No one will.'

'Do you mind?' Septimus said, insulted. 'You are talking to a poet!'

A fleeting smile was all his brother accorded this sally. Evidently he was not to be joked out of his dejection. All the sensible arguments rose to Septimus's tongue—they were both young, Dess was not an enviable catch, they should wait and prove their constancy—only to be rejected. He wanted to scoff at the outmoded Romeo and Juliet theme, but he cared too much for his brother to be so cruel. He was somewhat shaken by the strength of the boy's belief. Could one be that certain?

'You must love her very much,' he ventured.

Decimus barely glanced his way. In a weary voice he responded, 'I am not going to be permitted to spend my life with her, am I?'

'I don't know,' Septimus admitted. 'I presume Lady Louisa has forbidden the banns?'

'Banns?' echoed Decimus on a short laugh. 'They are hardly in question! I must not even speak to her, or approach her in public. I am not to go where I think I may meet her. In a word, we have been torn apart!'

Septimus frowned. 'I must say that seems a little drastic. Is this Lady Louisa's dictum?'

'Almost word for word,' Decimus said bitterly. He glanced over to find on his brother's brow a portentous frown. 'Why do you look like that? Do you think I am making it up?'

The frown cleared. 'Of course not, my babe. It just seems very unlike what I would have expected from Lady Louisa, that's all. She struck me as an eminently sensible woman, and *that* programme. . .' He broke off, shrugging. 'Ah, well. It is none of my affair.'

Decimus sat up suddenly, an eager light in his eye. 'But it might be, Setty. She has refused Quarto, for he told me so. But if *you* were to marry her ——'

'Have you taken leave of your senses?' interrupted his brother, swinging his legs to the ground and sitting bolt upright. '*I* marry Lady Louisa?'

'Well, but you could influence her in my favour then. And she could scarcely refuse to let me marry Millie if she was marrying a Berowne herself,' Decimus explained ingeniously.

'I thank you! So I am to tie myself up to the most managing female in the world only so that you may be united with your inamorata. I had rather enter into competition with you for the poor little dab herself!'

'But I thought you *liked* Lady Louisa,' protested Decimus, blinking at him. 'Nonie and Tavey told me that ——'

'Nonie and Tavey talk too much!' Septimus said crossly. 'I may like her, but that does not mean I want to *live* with the woman. Good God, I should be chivvied to death! And she does not even care for verse.'

'But she is wealthy, Setty, and——'

'I,' Septimus said loftily, 'am a poet. I have a soul far above such mundane considerations. Nothing would induce me to sell myself for sordid gold. If you are looking for a champion to support your cause with her, you had better try Quint—he needs managing!'

Louisa was in no mood for martyrs. But Quintus Berowne was not to know that Miss Millicent Lidbrook's conduct was driving her guardian to screaming point.

On the one hand, there was the die-away air she wore when she thought Louisa was not looking. On the other, there was the determined cheerfulness when she knew she was observed, which was enough to send Louisa into the dumps herself. She said nothing only because the latter act fooled everyone else successully. But she was quite ready to murder Decimus Berowne, who had changed an adoring child into a distant stranger.

Consequently, when Quintus Berowne succeeded in gaining admittance to the house in Brook Street— having craftily circumvented the butler in favour of a pert housemaid who was open both to flirtation and bribery—his avowed errand found little favour with Louisa.

'I am come first to make my peace with you,

ma'am,' he announced, with the crooked smile that had charmed more hearts than he could count.

It had no visible effect upon Lady Louisa Shittlehope. She asked candidly, 'Why should you?'

'Because, for one thing, you have been very kind to my little sisters,' Quintus said with a small bow. 'And for another, I have, I confess it, begun with you on quite the wrong foot.'

'Well, I can't deny that,' Louisa agreed. 'But there is no reason I can think of why you should have begun with me at all.'

'I did not,' he reminded her gently. 'It was rather *you* who began with me at St Pancras Wells.'

Louisa was betrayed into a wry smile. 'Very true. By all means, then, let us make peace. I have no wish to be at outs with anyone.'

With a rather gallant gesture — which did him no harm in her eyes — he took her hand and kissed it.

'Thank you.' He smiled. 'May we sit?'

'Certainly.'

With a swirl of her chintz petticoats, Louisa sank down on to a sofa near the fire at one end of the saloon. She indicated a chair opposite and her visitor sat, casually crossing his legs. He was dressed with unusual care in a suit of plain broadcloth over a flowered waistcoat, his brown tie-wig neatly in place.

'Madam, I am come in the guise of an envoy,' he said. 'No. That is the wrong word. An ambassador, an intercessor, you might say.'

'I see,' Louisa said warily. 'Upon whose behalf?'

'My *own*,' he uttered in a tone of sudden intensity. 'And through me, one other.'

'Decimus?'

'Decimus,' he confirmed. He held up a hand as she opened her mouth, and spoke with an emotional throb in his voice that was worthy of Garrick. 'Pray don't be alarmed. I am not about to try to persuade you of his good qualities — though he has many — but to put before you a certain proposition. This proposition might — indeed, I believe it *must* — make you alter your mind.'

Louisa blinked at him. 'Pray don't be so theatrical, Mr Berowne. I have had enough of that from your poet!'

'Heaven defend me from any such comparison! Setty play-acts to quiz us all. I, on the other hand — ' with a burning look in his eyes as they raked her ' — am serious.'

'Oh?' Louisa said evenly, raising her brows. 'Just what is this proposition?'

Quintus met her eyes and tried, with a heavy stare, to hold them. 'I want to marry you, Louisa.'

Louisa stared back at him, almost stunned by his audacity. 'You want to marry me? Are you mad?'

'I may be so if you refuse me!' he uttered, still with that intense regard.

For a moment Louisa just sat there, half fooled by the manner of his proposal that he was in earnest. She drew a breath. 'Mr Berowne — ' she began.

'Quintus, please,' he interrupted with a quick flash of his lop-sided smile.

'Very well, Quintus,' Louisa said impatiently. 'What I call you is immaterial. After both your brothers' attempts, I would have supposed I had made my sentiments clear. I had truly not seriously supposed that *you* would ask for my hand. You are not going to pretend, I hope, that you have fallen in love with me.'

'No,' he agreed baldly.

'Then you must, like Quarto, be in want of my fortune.'

'That, yes,' he agreed, so dismissively that she was puzzled. 'I am a Berowne. My pockets are always to let. Of course a fortune is desirable. But that isn't it.'

'What is "it"?' Louisa demanded, intrigued in spite of herself.

Under her startled gaze his face seemed to change. The eyes appeared to flicker and darken, narrowing a little as they played over her gauze-covered bosom. The mouth took on a lascivious leer, and the tip of his tongue ran over his lips. He leaned forward a little, and his voice was husky and thick.

'It is *you*, Louisa, that I want. You are one of the most desirable women I have ever met. I want to take you to bed.'

Louisa shrank back a little, repelled and disgusted. Did he imagine such a speech to be alluring, such a manner to be attractive? He *must* do so. She felt suddenly nauseous, and the food she had eaten that morning rose up to choke her. She fought down the feeling, clenching her hands in her lap, and looking away from the sickening sight of Quintus Berowne's avowed lust.

'But since I know,' he was continuing in a more normal tone, having apparently no inkling of her reaction, 'that a lady of unimpeachable virtue would never consent to become a man's mistress, since I understand the rules governing the conduct of the merchant class, I have no choice but to ——'

'To offer for me?' finished Louisa, and her voice shook.

'Precisely,' he agreed, and smiled, waiting expectantly.

Louisa pulled herself together. Her palms were damp and she straightened her fingers, fastidiously wiping them on a handkerchief she dragged from her sleeve. She swallowed down her nausea, and forced herself to look at him.

'Quintus Berowne, one does not, I believe, thank a man for such an offer, though I grant you it is an original approach.'

'But I *meant* it,' he said with feeling.

'I sincerely doubt that,' Louisa grated tartly. 'Moreoever, I doubt that anything would have induced you to come here today with this preposterous proposal if you did not believe that you might turn Decimus's preoccupation with my ward to good account.'

His cheeks darkened a little and the lascivious look faded from his face. 'I don't understand you.'

'Oh, I think you do. You hinted as much earlier. Had you met with the success you expected — though I can't imagine why! — you would have gone on to plead his cause, thus making certain that *all* my interests accorded with those of the Berownes, Millie being a favourite with me. Very convenient, Quintus, but I am afraid not very clever.'

Startled out of his role, Quintus demanded hotly, 'Why not?'

'Because I had rather marry a toad!' declared Louisa roundly.

He blinked, shaking his head as if he could not believe his ears. 'You don't mean that!'

'Oh, yes, I do!' She shuddered. 'Come to that, I would rather *kiss* a toad than take one step towards a bedchamber with you. I will go further. If I were obliged to touch you with a ten-foot pole, it would be too close. I find you slimy, deceitful and utterly repulsive!'

'*What*?' he cried, leaping from his seat as the sense of her words sunk in.

'I think you are undoubtedly the *worst* of your family — that I have met, at least — and I can only be sorry for them all that they are obliged to tolerate you.'

'Why, you insulting, patronising little vixen!' Quintus exploded. 'How dare you?'

'And was it not patronising of you to suppose that you could make yourself acceptable to me by such an insulting proposal?' returned Louisa, rising also, and speaking in an even tone that accorded ill with the flare of anger in her eyes. 'What, am I a woman of the streets, to be enticed with a *bedding*? How dared *you*, sir? That may be in keeping with the standards obtaining in your family, but they have nothing to do with those of a Shittlehope!'

'Are you referring to my mother?' he demanded furiously.

'If the cap fits, sir, then let "Dolly" wear it!'

For a moment Quintus glared impotently. Then he strode to the door, turning with his fingers on the handle. 'You have not seen the last of me, madam. Fair means I have now tried. I will not be deterred from attempting foul!'

Wrenching open the door, he almost walked into the same housemaid who had admitted him.

'Beg pardon, sir,' she said hastily, dropping a curtsy.

She cast an apprehensive glance at his murderous face, but Quintus was not looking at her. He was staring at the woman in the corridor behind the maid.

'What the devil are you doing here?' he snapped.

'What is the matter, Quint?' Sexta asked fearfully, her dilating eyes on his. 'Did you not meet with success?'

'You and your schemes!' he hissed furiously. 'I have been subjected only to insult for my pains, and I'll thank you to keep out of the matter from now on!'

Brushing past his sister, he ignored her pleas for him to wait, and ran down the stairs. At her back, Sexta heard the maid's voice announcing her in the saloon.

'Miss Berowne, my lady.'

'Oh, for pity's sake!' exclaimed Louisa as she caught sight of the woman in the doorway. 'What in the world do *you* want, Sexta?'

Sexta Berowne almost ran into the room, clutching her cloak about her and barely waiting for the door to be shut before crying out, 'What have you said to upset him so? Oh, how *could* you?'

Louisa fairly gasped. 'How could *I*? Have you any idea what he came here to say?'

'Of course I have,' Sexta uttered scornfully. 'I suggested he should come. Poor Dess was so distressed when he spoke to me! Something he said gave me the idea that if only you would consent to marry

Quint you *could* not refuse Dess and this girl of yours.'

'Are you telling me,' Louisa demanded in a voice of rigid control, 'that the three of you concocted this scheme among you?'

'Oh, no, no! *Dess* knows nothing of it. It was *my* notion. And,' she went on aggrievedly, 'I thought it a capital one, for we would have killed two birds with one stone, and Quint would then be in a position to help us all. Only you have *ruined* it!'

Louisa was so shocked that she actually laughed. 'Oh, indeed? I suppose you think I should call your hideous brother back here and fall in with your plans!'

'Don't *dare* call him hideous!' shrieked Sexta.

'Don't raise your voice to me!' returned Louisa sharply. 'Unless you have a fancy to be well slapped, you had better come down off your high ropes and attend to me.'

Sexta's defiance collapsed at once. She seemed to see Louisa for the first time, and the sight of that commanding figure with her arms akimbo, large eyes ablaze, sent her scuttling back, her hands flying up to protect her face.

'No, *don't*, please,' she cried. 'Just like Dolly!'

'What?' Louisa gasped, her wrath arrested. 'What did you say about Dolly?'

Sexta's hands came down a little. 'I—I can't help myself, you see. My temper. It. . .it flies so fast—too quick for me. And—and Dolly. . .'

'Dolly *hits* you?'

Sexta nodded miserably. 'Always, *always*. I'm

afraid of her. The others will never let her near me, but — but they are not always by and ——'

'Come and sit down,' Louisa commanded, sailing to a sofa and leading the shrinking woman to a place beside her. 'Now tell me it all.'

The nervous eyes flicked about the room. 'What about?'

'About Dolly, your mother,' Louisa said patiently. Small wonder the girl was a nervous wreck, if she had been subjected to such abuse! 'Has she a temper, is that it?'

'A *temper*?' A hysterical laugh escaped Sexta. 'Where do you imagine I get mine, or Quint his? *All* of them. A more temperamental family you will never meet.'

This did not quite square with what Louisa knew of the younger members, but then she had to admit she did not know them very well. But it was pointless to argue with Sexta.

'Very well,' she said equably, 'Dolly loses her temper. Why?'

'Why?' Sexta's eyes came round to settle for a moment on Louisa's. Her face expressed astonishment. 'Because she *hates* us. She never wanted children; she always said so. Yet here we are, and she can't *abide* any one of us!'

'Sexta, I am sure that cannot be true,' Louisa protested. '*No* mother could be so uncaring towards her own flesh and blood.'

Another of those wild little laughs rang out. 'Ha! You don't *know*. She must hate *me*, for she threw me aside from an infant. She never made the smallest push to find me a husband.'

'But Nona and Octavia ——'

'Oh, she thrust *them* into marriage with the first men who offered, for by then she had *me* on her hands for life and she said she could not face *all* of us remaining at home.'

Her tragic voice caught at Louisa's heart-strings, but she tried to hold on to her common sense. 'Your brothers, however, seem to have fared reasonably well, in spite of your parents' neglect.'

'Fared well?' echoed Sexta. 'When Dess is such a wild young fool, and Setty has no interest outside his stupid poetry? When Quarto is a laughing-stock, and Quint meets everywhere with an unfavourable reception, which he has done *nothing* to deserve?'

'Oh, this is absurd!' Louisa said suddenly, rising from the sofa. 'I have heard quite enough, I thank you! I do not know if I believe the half of what you say, Sexta, but this I *do* know. I am not going to be subjected to any further annoyances from you or your siblings.'

Sexta rose also, staring at her with dilating eyes, her fingers fidgeting with the cloak she still wore. 'What — what are you going to do?'

'How did you come here?' Louisa asked, ignoring her question. 'In a hackney cab, I suppose.' She went across to the fireplace and pulled the bell. 'I am going to take you home in my carriage, Sexta, and then you are going to introduce me to your mama.'

Horrified, Sexta tried by every means within her power to dissuade Lady Louisa from this course. But neither tears nor cajolery daunted her. Leaving a message for Millie, she donned a tippet and hat, and led Sexta inexorably to her carriage, sitting silent throughout the short journey to Grosvenor Square, and refusing to respond to the woman's ravings. At their destination she descended from the carriage and looked up at the enormous mansion.

'Why in the world do they not all remove from this place?' she asked of the air. 'It must cost the earth to keep up.'

Sexta had run ahead up the shallow steps. A servant answered the door, and she slipped inside before Louisa had a chance to stop her. But the servant had seen Louisa, and he held the door with an enquiring look.

'Good day,' Louisa said pleasantly. 'I have brought Miss Berowne home, and I wish to see Mrs Berowne. Is she at home?'

'Always is this time o' day,' answered the man in a surly tone, opening the door for her to enter. 'Only just got up out of her bed.'

Louisa stepped into the wide hall, glancing round at the shabby carpets, the faded curtains and the general air of dilapidation. For the first time the truth of the Berownes' poverty struck her. They always appeared so well turned out that the idea had previously only penetrated in the abstract. The reality was painful to contemplate.

But that made no difference to her mission. She turned back to the servant. 'Kindly take me to Mrs Berowne.'

The footman eyed her warily. 'Who shall I say is calling?'

'Lady Louisa Shittlehope.'

The man's eyes widened in recognition. Her name had evidently been much mentioned in this house.

She followed him up one flight of stairs to a parlour at the back of the house. He opened the door and announced her, and Louisa stepped into the room and stopped short, staring.

On an elegant day-bed, surrounded by branches of lighted candelabra, with the curtains drawn so that the only light in the room fell upon her, reclined a lady in dishabille. She was dressed in a delicate confection of muslin and lace which clung to her slim form, and her brown hair fell about her shoulders in undressed curls. She looked as if she was about to receive a gentlemen caller.

'Oh!' uttered Louisa, taken aback. 'You are Dolly Berowne, aren't you?'

A silvery laugh came from the day-bed, and a languid voice spoke. 'I am. You will have to forgive me, for I never catch these announcements. Who are you?'

'My name is Lady Louisa Shittlehope, Mrs Berowne.'

A delicate hand fluttered towards her. 'Not — I beg you, *not* "Mrs Berowne". I never could *bear* that name.'

Louisa advanced into the room, peering a little in the dim interior. The face on the day-bed, upon which the candlelight played, was startlingly beautiful — the one that characterised all the Berownes, but with soft cherry lips and glowing brown eyes, the piquant face a perfect oval — and remarkably young, although to the velvet sheen of the cheeks had been added by a master hand the faintest touch of colour.

'You won't expect me to rise, I trust,' Dolly said with a sweet smile. 'I am never energetic at this hour.'

She looked as if she was never energetic at any hour, but Louisa did not say so. Instead she said apologetically, 'Forgive me, but I don't think I can converse with you properly in all this gloom.'

As she trod across to one of the windows Dolly called out, 'What are you doing? Not the drapes!'

With a ruthless hand Louisa drew back the curtains. From the day-bed came a shriek, and she turned to find Dolly had sat up with a jerk, throwing a hand across her eyes.

'Oh, how *could* you? It is *far* too bright.'

'Tush, that is nonsense, Dolly!' said Louisa bracingly, coming over to snuff some of the candles. 'You don't need these now. There, that's better.'

She found a straight chair by the wall, picked it up, and brought it across to plonk down before her hostess's astonished eyes. Dolly watched her actitivities with her fingers held to her temples, and blinked when this peculiar visitor sat down before her.

'Now then, Dolly,' Louisa began.

'Who *are* you?' uttered the lady plaintively. 'Why have you *done* this to me?'

'It is time and past that someone did *something*, Dolly,' Louisa declared, looking the woman over with interest.

At close range it was clear why Dolly Berowne chose to receive her visitors by candlelight in the middle of the morning. She was on the shady side of fifty, and daylight crudely emphasised the faded skin, the little wrinkles appearing at the corners of her eyes and about her mouth. Beneath her eyes, too, a light puffy shadow bore witness to a dissipated life.

'Who are you?' Dolly repeated.

'I am Lady Louisa, ma'am. Has none of your children mentioned me?'

The fingers came down from her temples to her breast and a faint frown disturbed the perfection of an alabaster brow. 'Lady Louisa?' She shook her head and fell to smoothing out her ruffled costume. 'I don't recall it. But I don't see them very often, you know, which might account for it.'

'*That* is precisely the point upon which I wish to converse with you, Dolly,' said Louisa, seizing on this. 'You *should* see them. Do you have any idea what habits they have fallen into?'

Instantly Dolly's hand flew to her brow, and she threw back her head. 'Pray don't tell me! I am in no fit state to endure it.'

Louisa had a sudden flash of memory. Just so had Septimus thrown back his head with a hand to his brow on that night she had first met him. Quick suspicion kindled. Was this his inspiration? Her lips quivered as she wondered whether anyone realised that he was poking fun at his mother.

'Dolly,' she said firmly, 'I am sorry if you don't feel up to it, but I am afraid you *must* hear what I have to say.'

'Not, I beg you — *not* if it concerns my lamentable offspring,' she uttered, putting out her hands in a pleading gesture.

'Well, it *does*.'

Dolly fell back upon her day-bed and closed her eyes with a low moan. 'My maid! Where are my smelling-salts?'

'Ask yourself, Dolly,' pursued Louisa determinedly, reaching out to possess herself of one of the

lady's hands, 'why it is that they are so "lamentable".
I beg your pardon but surely you must perceive how
neglectful you have been.'

The eyes flew open, and Dolly snatched her fingers
away. 'Neglectful? What was I supposed to do, fawn
and fuss over them like a mother hen? I thank you,
no! I bore them — and what a *bore* it was! — and there
it ends.'

'But it *can't* end there,' Louisa argued indignantly.
'How are they to grow? How are they to live? Let me
tell you, Nona and Octavia lack even a vestige of
proper conduct. While as for Quintus, he is quite the
most abominable ——'

'Is he the fat one?' interrupted Dolly.

Louisa halted in mid-stride, and stared in disbelief.
Her sense of humour betrayed her, and she bit her lip
on a laugh. 'Don't tell me you don't even know which
one he is!'

'But there are so many of them,' Dolly complained.
Then she threw out a hand. 'Stay! If he is not the fat
one — and he cannot be the poet, for I know him — he
must be the ugly one.' She sighed and pillowed her
cheek on her hand. 'You are right. He *is* bad. I have
often remarked it.'

'Yet you have done nothing to correct it,' Louisa
pointed out.

Dolly looked at her blankly. 'What in the world
could *I* do?'

Nonplussed, Louisa gazed at her. 'But this is
callous beyond belief!'

'Callous?' echoed the lady in disbelieving tones.
'You cannot be *serious*. Why, they had the best
of care.'

'I dare say,' Louisa said sternly, 'but not from *you*. In fact, if Sexta is to be believed, your conduct towards her has been——'

'*Sexta*?' cried Dolly, sitting up again and looking fearfully towards the door. 'You are not going to bring that mad creature in here, I hope! My poor nerves will never stand it!' In a breathless way she added hastily, 'And pray don't dare suggest I should do *anything* for that one. Why, she screams the place down only at sight of me!'

'Is that not because you repeatedly slapped her as a child?'

'Are you *mad*?' Dolly cried. 'I have never been able to get near enough to do so. She is possessed! I wish to heaven she had married and gone away from this house. She is *quite* mad, you know. She never *looked* at any of the gentlemen to whom I introduced her. Well for them!'

Dumbfounded, Louisa could only stare at her. It was evident that she spoke the truth—or at least the truth as it appeared to her. It was equally evident that she was beyond redemption. But Louisa was not ready to give up. She gathered her forces together.

'Be that as it may, Dolly, I insist that you listen to me!'

Dolly looked at her. 'Why? Who *are* you?'

'We have been over all that!' Louisa said impatiently. 'I have come specifically to ask you to exercise some parental control over your sons, for I am quite tired of. . .' She broke off, for Dolly had collapsed against her pillows again, her eyes closed in an attitude of exhaustion. 'Dolly!'

There was a click behind her and she turned her

head to find Septimus Berowne on the threshold. He met her eyes and a wry smile twisted his mouth. 'I thought as much.'

Dolly Berowne's eyes flew open again, and she struggled up. 'The poet! Thank goodness! Do you know this lady?'

'I do, Dolly.'

His mother heaved a relieved sigh. 'Then take her away, I beg of you! For some unfathomable reason she has taken it into her head to make a *mother* of me. Can you believe it?'

'Of Lady Louisa, yes,' he said, grinning. He came forward and held out his hand to Louisa. 'Come along, Loulou. You are wasting your time, you know.'

'Indeed I think so,' Louisa agreed, taking his hand and rising. She looked at Mrs Berowne. 'Dolly, couldn't you —— ?'

'Setty, only *look* at the drapes!' complained Dolly, paying no attention. 'Ruinous to my complexion! *Do* something.'

'I will send your maid in, Dolly,' Septimus said soothingly.

'Oh, yes — and tell her to bring my smelling-salts. *And* my cordial, for I am positively *drained*. Oh, and tell that fool Andrew not to bring anyone else in here, for the love of heaven! I cannot see a soul until I have had time to *recover*.'

'Your wish is my command, Dolly,' Septimus said blandly, drawing Louisa inexorably to the door.

'Goodbye, Dolly,' Louisa called.

The lady waved a languid hand, but a shiver shook her frame and her eyelids fluttered down again.

Outside the closed door Septimus gave Louisa a quizzing look. 'I would have rescued you earlier, but I only heard of your visit a moment ago.'

'Rescued *me*? I thought it was your mother whom you came to succour.'

He grinned. 'Dolly thinks so, naturally.' He began gently to manoeuvre her towards the stairs, a hand at her elbow.

Louisa went willingly enough, but she was hardly aware of her own movement, her mind being almost wholly taken up first with the lady she had just left, and second with the quite extraordinary sense of heat she felt at the touch of the poet's hand on her arm.

'I am sorry to speak so of your mother, Septimus, but Dolly is quite dreadful. Indeed, I am astonished that some of you have turned out so well!'

'We thank you,' Septimus said meekly, but with that mischievous glint in his eye. 'But tell me. What exactly happened to bring you storming in here on the war-path?'

'I was *not* on the war-path!' objected Louisa, but then she twinkled at his lifted eyebrow. 'Well, perhaps I was. Your sister Sexta was the trigger.'

'Ah, then Andrew was right. Our butler,' he explained at her puzzled look. 'In fact he is a sort of general factotum, for he takes care of most things around here. I ran into him on my way out. He said he thought Sexta had been with you.'

'So you came rushing upstairs to drag me away,' Louisa said flatly.

Septimus smiled. 'You are excessively competent, Loulou, but it takes a special knowledge to handle Dolly and her whims.'

'Yes, you obviously succeed there,' observed Louisa.

'On occasion, and provided I do not cross her.'

They had reached the front door, and Septimus held it open for her. Rather to her surprise, he accompanied her out, closing the door behind himself. Then she realised that he was dressed for the street, with a dark hat over a comfortable buff frock and black breeches.

'Is that your carriage?' he asked, pointing to the smart equipage drawn up before the door. He handed her in, and then looked up at her. 'Will you allow me to escort you home?'

'But I thought you were going out. And poor Dolly needs her maid!'

'Don't concern yourself. She will have forgotten all about it by now. Her mind is not tenacious, you know.'

'So I gathered,' Louisa said drily. 'But you are otherwise engaged. I must not keep you.'

'Is that a dismissal?' Septimus enquired on an anxious note.

'*No*,' Louisa uttered, rather more forcefully than she had intended.

'My engagement is of no moment,' he said, bland once more. 'A delivery merely, and it can wait. I had far rather come with you — that is, if you don't object.'

Louisa felt her cheeks grow hot. How foolish! 'How should I object?' she said quickly. 'It is very kind of you.'

The door was shut upon them both, and Septimus

turned, speaking in an authoritative tone which she had never before heard from him.

'Now that we have a little privacy, Loulou, I want the truth! All of it. What has been happening to induce you to try and make Dolly see the error of her ways?'

CHAPTER EIGHT

LADY LOUISA was not accustomed to being spoken to in that tone, but strangely enough it did not strike her either as impertinent or out of place.

'I had just sustained a visit from your brother Quintus,' she replied readily, 'who had conceived the happy notion, he said, of marrying me in order to gain my consent to Decimus marrying Millie.'

'Oh, good God!' Septimus exclaimed. 'That is probably my fault. I said something of the sort to Dess in jest. I *do* beg your pardon, Lady Louisa.'

'Don't be absurd,' Louisa said dismissively. 'One cannot guard every word for fear of some idiot taking it up seriously. I refer, I may mention, to your sister Sexta, who came dashing in as Quintus left to take *me* to task, if you please, for upsetting her brother!'

Septimus began to laugh. 'Do you wish me to stop the carriage and get out now? You must be quite sick of us all.'

'I am glad you find it amusing,' Louisa said tartly. 'For myself, I was so incensed that I was about to scarify Sexta, for she said it had been *her* notion, when she suddenly came out with the most appalling things about your mother *hating* you all and subjecting her to beatings as a child.'

'Never pay any attention to what Sexta says,' Septimus advised calmly. 'She inhabits some world of her own which has nothing to do with the real one.'

165

'So I am beginning to believe,' Louisa agreed. 'Dolly thinks she is mad. Is she?'

In the dim interior of the carriage she saw him shrug. 'If to be high-strung is a form of madness, then yes. But she is quite lucid, if mistaken in her ideas.'

'Poor thing!' Louisa exclaimed, her ready sympathy stirred. 'She must be very unhappy.'

Septimus suddenly sank back in his corner of the coach, flinging a hand to his brow. 'Heaven defend us! Now she will be engaging in *another* crusade.'

'Don't do that!' Louisa ordered sternly, suppressing a giggle. 'Having met Dolly, I am now perfectly aware of what you are about, and it is *outrageous*.'

His hand was instantly slammed to his heart. 'Discovered! Ah, me, I foresee a thundering scold! How shall I bear it?'

'How shall you evade it, you mean,' Louisa corrected, unable to keep from laughing. 'Your luck is in, poet, for we have arrived.'

The coach was indeed slowing, and in a moment drew up before the house in Brook Street.

'Saved!' Septimus exclaimed as the door was opened. He jumped down and turned to assist Louisa to alight.

'Don't think it!' Louisa told him. 'I have not finished with you yet, Septimus Berowne. Come into the house.'

His eye gleamed as he bowed, murmuring, 'What *can* she want? I am all agog, Loulou.'

'Well, it is not to hear one of your poems, if that is what you think,' Louisa told him, entering the house and leading the way upstairs to her little parlour.

She gave her tippet and hat into the hands of the

housemaid, who was still deputising for Mortehoe, and took up her stance beside the fireplace as usual.

'Now then, Septimus,' she said, meeting the expectant look in his eyes, 'since you appear to be the only sensible Berowne, it seems to me that I can do no better than to consult you about the rest of them.'

His lips twitched. 'You are planning some sort of campaign, I take it. Now *why*, Loulou?'

'I am not planning anything at all,' she said crossly. 'But if, as at present seems likely, I am going to end up having to give my consent to a marriage between my ward and your brother, then I may as well know what awaits me.'

'But I thought you were against it.'

'I *am* against it.'

'Then what in *God's* name possessed you to divide them in a manner so thorough that it is almost certain to end in them falling into each other's arms?' he demanded in exasperated accents.

Louisa stared at him. 'You think that is what will happen?'

'I'm quite sure of it. I did not think you such a ninnyhammer, Lady Louisa!'

'I'm *not* a ninnyhammer,' she said indignantly. She bit her lip. 'At least. . .I thought, you see, if Millie was not to see him at all for a time she might forget about him.'

Septimus smiled wryly at the almost pleading note in her voice. 'Out of sight, out of mind, eh? It won't work.'

Louisa sighed. 'It certainly appears not to be doing so at present. Which is why, I suppose, I am preparing myself for. . .' She broke off and her eyes darkened. 'Oh, tush! Why *can't* I manage her right? I don't mean to boast, but I am usually so *good* at knowing how to handle people.'

'Yes, it rather leaps to the eye that your forte lies in that direction,' Septimus said, with a quizzing look.

'Well, it *does*,' Louisa said defensively. 'After all, I managed Mr Shittlehope.'

'I see you did,' he agreed blandly. 'You managed him into his grave!'

To his consternation, Louisa's enormous eyes filled with tears. Huskily she uttered, 'That is cruel! I grew very *fond* of Mr Shittlehope.'

Septimus gazed at her, horrified. Then he started forward. 'Louisa, I didn't mean it! It was a *joke*. Loulou, don't cry!'

Hardly knowing what he did, the poet caught her in his arms and his slender fingers cradled her face.

'I didn't *mean* it, lovely Loulou,' he said tenderly. 'I am certain Mr Shittlehope *adored* being managed by you.'

'I don't know that,' Louisa responded on an odd gurgle, somewhere between a sob and a laugh. She was not aware of any impropriety in this warm embrace, only that she felt safe and comforted. Unconsciously she smiled into his eyes. 'I'm not an "adorable" kind of person.'

'Your eyes are, though,' he said softly, 'all wet and misty like that. *Wholly* adorable.'

His lips found hers then, in a gentle, feather-light kiss. It held so, and for a timeless moment there was nothing more than the sensation of warmth at the point of that tender touch.

Then something seemed to ripple through Louisa's

body — a sliver of heat over which she had no control. Her lips moved with his, and she took in at the edge of her consciousness that Septimus felt it too. His arms tightened, and the pressure of his mouth increased. The heat intensified and, powerless to control herself, Louisa shrank against the body close to hers, unknowingly sliding her hands about its back to draw it closer still.

The response was intoxicating. She was dragged into so tight an embrace that she could scarcely breathe, and the mouth fastened to hers shifted a little, forcing her lips apart. One brief taste of that velvet softness, and Louisa felt an explosion within her that seemed to reverberate through her limbs.

Alarmed and confused, she struggled to be free. At once the hold slackened about her, and she wrenched away, forcing her eyes open by an effort of will. Trembling, she shifted aside, and her glance caught someone in the open doorway.

It was Millie. Shock was in her face, mingled with the stirrings of wrath.

'Oh, no!' uttered Louisa helplessly as the implications of this appalling occurrence flashed across her brain.

She took a step towards the girl, but Millie hurriedly backed out and slammed the door. Her footsteps could be heard at once, flying down the corridor.

Inevitably Louisa turned on Septimus Berowne. Launching into attack, she did not notice that he was looking quite as shaken as she.

'Now look what you've done!' she cried. 'I thought I had endured enough this day from Quintus, but no!

You must take it into your head to make love to me too. Do you seek to wed my fortune as well? Or merely to *bed* my fortune like your brother?'

'It may have been *wrong* of me,' Septimus returned, the apology that had been forming in his mind wiped instantly from his lips, 'but don't, pray, impute such a motive to *me*.'

'What else am I to infer,' Louisa demanded, 'when you grab me and *maul* me as if I were some cheap harlot?'

His eyes narrowed. 'If that is how it seemed to you, then I can only say that your response raises grave doubts in my mind.'

'Don't be insulting!' snapped Louisa.

'I give as good as I get, madam!'

Louisa glared at him. 'You may as well get it over, then. Where is the proposal?'

A flare of anger lit the poet's eye. 'Do you imagine I needs must marry where I kiss? You are hardly the first, Lady Louisa. A romantic poet is expected to indulge his female devotees.'

'I, sir, am *not* a devotee,' stated Louisa, eyes flashing. 'Far from it. Now will you kindly take yourself off? If I never see you again it will be too soon!'

'*Thank* you,' Septimus said savagely. He strode to the door, and hesitated with his fingers on the handle. He looked back at her. 'Louisa, you are both a liar and a fool! And for all your management, you know *nothing* of men.'

Then he was gone. Louisa stood where he had left her, aware only of her violently trembling limbs and the confused tumult of emotion in her breast. How could he speak to her so? She had thought him so kind, so much a friend. Now *this*. Why had he to spoil everything by that terrifying embrace?

The memory of it made her weak at the knees, and she staggered to the sofa and sank down, putting her hands down for support on either side as if she must hold herself upright by this means.

She had liked him so *much*. How could she have known that under the bland exterior he could be so *violent* — both in action and language? Well, she should have known. Wasn't he a Berowne? But at least he had not, like his brother, wanted to marry her. The thought was peculiarly painful somehow.

To her annoyance she discovered tears to be trickling down her cheeks. Dashing them away, she recalled his face when he had seen her weep: his eyes, at first so concerned, then so kind as he held her. . . oh, so *gently*.

Louisa's mind froze on the image. Then a wave of remorse swept through her as the sequence of sub-sequent events flashed by. *She* was in the wrong again, not he! She had been shocked by her own reaction to the kiss, and then she had seen Millie. And Millie's face had jerked her into panic. No self-deceiver, Louisa instantly understood that she had used Septimus Berowne as a whipping-boy for her own rush of guilt. Poor poet! And she had been so *cruel*. Far more so than had been his quizzing comment about poor Mr Shittlehope.

'Oh, Septimus, can you forgive me?' she cried aloud suddenly.

But Septimus was gone. So, too — and *far* more importantly, Louisa told herself — was Millie. With a determined air, she rose a little shakily to her feet. The latter tangle at least she could try to sort out immediately.

Septimus, meanwhile, striding away in a mood of unaccustomed rage, was wrangling with the quite unimportant question of whether he was more furious with Louisa or himself. He had always been aware of his desire for her, and latterly it had taken up far more of his attention than it warranted. But that he would ever have unleashed the force of it upon Louisa herself he had never imagined. He had not intended to, that was certain. Only she had looked so touchingly vulnerable, with those huge eyes full of tears! So fearlessly as she battled through life, it was a shock to discover a chink in her armour.

One moment, a tower of strength, she had been preparing to take on the Berownes single-handed. The next she was standing there, forlorn and quivering, a little girl lost. Good God, how could he *not* have succumbed? And then to have her quiver in his arms, positively *offering* herself to his embrace.

He stopped dead suddenly in the middle of the street. No, that was not it! What a fool *he* was, and he had called her one. She had been married from the schoolroom to an elderly man, poor Loulou. What *could* she know of men? Or of what a man—himself, for instance—might awaken in her. For he could never be brought to believe that she could have performed anything more than her duty in such a marriage. The thought, he found with a sense of shock, revolted him.

All at once the memory of her angry words came back to him—'to bed' her fortune, she had said, 'like your brother'. Something inside him went cold and hard. *What had Quintus intended*?

Five minutes later, entirely forgetting the delivery he had to make of some manuscripts concealed in his coat pocket, he was back in the Grosvenor Square mansion, seeking his sister. He found Sexta partaking of a solitary luncheon in the one small dining parlour that was still in use.

'Sexta,' Septimus demanded without preamble, 'what is Quint playing at?'

She jumped at the sound of his voice, dropping the apple she had been peeling. 'Quint? I don't know what you mean, Setty.'

'Yes, you do,' he said sternly. 'You always know what Quint is about. Besides, you put him up to this business with Lady Louisa; I already know that.'

'I suppose she told you,' Sexta said sullenly.

'She did, yes.' Septimus came around the table and stood menacingly over her. 'What did he say to her?'

'It is no use asking me. I was not there.'

'You were there immediately after. Besides, you planned it with him. What was he *intending* to say?'

'If you must know,' Sexta said sulkily, 'he was to use his charm—for I felt that could *not* fail—and make her think that *she* was more important to him than her fortune. But of course he bungled it somehow.'

'He bungled it by going at all!' Septimus said roundly.

'He was furious, of course, and I don't blame him, for the wretched woman *insulted* him, he said.'

Before Septimus had a chance to enquire further

into this the door opened to admit his two younger sisters.

'Sexta, there you are!' uttered Nona in an exasperated voice. 'How *could* you bring poor Louisa here?'

'Dolly has been *distracted*,' Octavia said crossly, 'and *we* have been blamed.'

'Yes, because she says Louisa mentioned *us*, and it must be our fault.'

'Which it certainly is *not*,' Octavia put in, 'for Andrew told us that *you* brought her.'

Sexta leapt up from her chair, flinging her apple across the room. 'I am sick and tired of Lady Louisa!' she shouted, and flew around the table, making for the door. 'I wish no one will mention her name to me again!'

The door opened almost in her face, and she found her way blocked by Quarto's bulk.

'What's to do?' he asked, pushing in and holding off his sister with one pudgy hand.

Behind him crowded Decimus, demanding, 'Have you all gone mad? Why was Lady Louisa here?'

Sexta hit out at Quarto's chest. 'Let me go! Let me go!'

Her brother seized her wrists. 'Stop that!'

'Let her go, Quarto,' Septimus called.

'Yes, it is no use trying to talk to her,' Octavia agreed.

'I don't *want* to talk to *any* of you!' shrieked Sexta, brushing past Quarto as he released her. She stopped short by Decimus and shouted into his face. 'That is the last time I try to do *you* a good turn, Brother!'

'*Me*?' uttered Dess, startled, as his sister flounced out of the room, slamming the door violently.

Both her younger sisters covered their ears, wincing, and Quarto shook a fist in the air, muttering uncouth threats.

'What have I to do with it?' pursued Decimus, coming into the room, a worried expression on his face.

'I'm afraid you have been prating rather too openly of your disappointed love-affair, my babe,' Septimus told him.

'Dess, you *didn't* mention it to Sexta!' uttered Octavia, appalled.

'Oh, Dess, how could you be so *stupid*?' Nona ejaculated.

'Will someone tell me what the devil this is about?' roared Quarto.

'I will tell you,' Septimus said quietly, and they all turned to look at him. 'Sexta suggested to Quint that if he married Louisa, then Dess might marry Millie.' Seeing his young brother's face of consternation, he patted him consolingly on the back. 'Yes, babe, it *was* your idea. But as I first suggested Quint in jest, I am as much to blame.'

'Good idea, though,' Quarto put in, 'if Lady Louisa would have him. But I dare swear she won't.'

'She will *not*, and it is a *terrible* idea,' Septimus snapped, causing his sisters to exchange one of their conspiratorial looks. 'If Dess cannot marry on his own merits, then he had better not marry at all!'

His young brother's face fell. 'That's dished me, then.'

'Oh, *no*, Dess,' Octavia said quickly. 'Louisa may come round in the end.'

'Yes, you must not give up *hope*, Dess,' instructed Nona.

'Listen, all of you!' begged Septimus. 'It is not Dess's chances that are exercising my mind at the moment, but Quint's possible actions.'

'What do you mean, Setty?' Octavia enquired, frowning. 'If Louisa will not marry him, there's an end.'

'I wish I could think so,' her brother returned, 'but —'

Quarto butted in. 'Hey, hey! Know you don't like the fellow overmuch, my boy, but he *is* our brother. Why shouldn't he be satisifed with a plain "no" like I was?'

'Because Quint, I regret to say, does not take kindly to losing. And as I understand that the discussion became somewhat acrimonious — and from what Louisa hinted at, I am not at all surprised — I am not too happy about what Quint might do.'

Nona was staring at him with popping eyes. '*What* might he do, Setty?'

But Octavia moved towards him and grasped his arm.

'Setty, we must do something! You are perfectly right. Quint is capable of anything. And after all Lady Louisa has done for us —'

'Precisely, Tavey. It would be too bad if her kindness was repaid with Quint's malicious mischief.'

'I think you're going too far, Setty,' Quarto protested.

'But even if Quint *did* try anything — and I don't see what he could do,' Decimus put in, 'I would think

Lady Louisa perfectly capable of sending him to the rightabout.'

'Oh, *yes*,' agreed Nona at once. 'Don't worry, Setty! Louisa is *so* capable. She will *never* be taken in.'

'That is all very well, Nonie,' Octavia said, turning to her sister, 'but you are forgetting Sexta.'

'Oh!' uttered Nona, her eyes wide. 'Sexta is mad enough for anything!'

'But damn it all,' Quarto exploded, 'you don't imagine Sexta and Quint will get into a plot against the woman, or anything so melodramatic?'

'There is no saying *what* Sexta will do,' Octavia said sternly. 'And as for Quint, have you forgotten how he was ready to cut up poor Lord Wherwell, all for nothing at all?'

'Gammon! Do you say he's going to draw his sword on Lady Louisa?'

'Oh, that would be *dreadful*!' exclaimed Nona fearfully.

'Don't be ridiculous!' Septimus snapped. 'Even Quint is not as idiotic as that.'

'Are you serious, Setty?' asked Decimus in a hushed voice. 'Because if you are, I think you ought to warn Lady Louisa.'

'What a good idea, Dess!' approved Octavia. 'Yes, Setty, tell her — make her understand — what Quint is like and tell her to be on her guard.'

'I doubt whether my word will carry much weight with her just at this present,' Septimus said with a wry smile.

'Nonsense, Setty! Louisa likes you.'

'That is comforting, Tavey, but I fear ——'

'Well, it can't be *us*,' Nona pointed out, with unusual perspicacity, 'because she thinks we are very silly and she wouldn't believe us.'

'And Dess is hardly in a position to speak to her on the matter,' Octavia put in.

'Don't look at me!' Quarto said hastily. 'I don't subscribe to any of this.'

Decimus grinned suddenly at his elder brother. 'That settles it, Setty. You are elected.'

The rotunda was packed when Louisa and Millie, closely following on Mrs Wavertree and her husband, with sundry other guests, finally managed to make their way through the vestibules and card-rooms into one of the boxes around the periphery overlooking the huge Assembly Room.

Eyes dancing through the slits of her mask, Louisa gazed with enjoyment upon the throng below. Harlequins, eastern potentates and all manner of historical figures mingled with shepherdesses, witches, goddesses and queens from the past, a surging mass of colourful imagery, heaving under the huge domed ceiling, weaving in and out of the pillared porticos under the balconies, and making a gay complement to the background of classical paintings that graced the ceilings and walls, in a style reminiscent of Raphael.

The Pantheon, as Lady Pyrland had informed her niece, was becoming quite outmoded, and—although it was whispered there was in planning an event scheduled to celebrate the coming of age of the heir to the throne in August—the proprietors had been forced to resort to getting up these masquerades in order to attract the skittish world of fashionables back to its rooms. The starchiest members of the upper crust condemned such frivolous entertainments for their encouragement of the licentious behaviour possible under the shadow of disguise. But since they were perennially popular the world and his wife attended them in droves, eager for the unmasking at midnight, when questionable conduct might be brought home to its perpetrators.

Louisa, trusting that the excitement might drive the clouds from Millie's eyes—for since catching her guardian in the arms of Septimus Berowne she had been wrapped in a pall of gloom—overbore Lady Pyrland's dictum and accepted Mrs Wavertree's invitation to make one of her party. Following that lady's advice, Louisa and Millie visited one of the Covent Garden warehouses that specialised in fancy dress, coming away with a Columbine consisting of a tight-fitting pierrot jacket and a brightly coloured petticoat for Millie, and a full-lenth pink taffeta domino for Louisa, ruched with ribbons and bows.

'This is delightful, Mrs Wavertree!' she exclaimed, turning to her hostess.

'Yes, I *love* masquerades,' agreed Mrs Wavertree, unmistakable under the mask and voluminous black domino by the red powder and the feathers in her coiffure. 'Such fun guessing who is who, you know.' She leaned forward, pointing. 'Gracious me, Louisa, isn't that Lady Pyrland?'

'Where?' It was Millie asking, her eyes scanning the crowd below, her fan fluttering anxiously.

Now why should Millie be concerned about Aunt Hebe's presence? Louisa wondered, glancing at her.

Quick suspicion kindled. Had she by some means arranged to meet Decimus here? Or one of the girls?

'Thought you told me she disapproved,' pursued Mrs Wavertree. 'That *is* her, ain't it? The thin stick got up like Queen Elizabeth.'

Louisa caught sight of her then. In fact the costume was little more than modern dress augmented by a ruff about the head and a profusion of paste jewels sewn on the bodice, and pearls decorating her red-powdered head. The mask only covered her eyes, so that she was recognisable by that jutting Roman nose.

'Yes, it is my aunt,' Louisa said evenly, 'and I imagine she is here to keep an eye on us. Yes, she must be, for she is not in a party. Oh, tush! She has my cousin Sedbergh with her.'

'And what does he think *he's* got up as?' demanded Mrs Wavertree contemptuously. 'Raleigh or Drake, I suppose.'

'Indeed, it could be either,' Louisa agreed, for Philip wore only a ruff and an odd-looking hat to signify his persona, and he had not even deigned to wear a mask.

The musicians on a dais at the far end struck up, and, almost by instinct, people began to move aside so that a space for dancing was cleared under the dome. Millie was solicited at once by one of the gentlemen in their party, but Louisa, casting about among the revellers below, was searching out anyone who might resemble Decimus Berowne.

The discussion she'd had with Millie had been both acrimonious and futile. Unable to speak of the matters that had led to that fatal embrace, for her involvement with the Berownes must be withheld from Millie for her own sake, Louisa had tried to make light of it, to no avail.

'I did nothing so compromising with Dess,' Millie protested with heat. 'And if I had, you would have *annihilated* me.'

'It is a very different matter in your case, Millie,' Louisa said placatingly.

'It would be!'

'Well, it is. I make no excuses for myself, for such conduct is disgraceful. I know it. But I *am* a widow, and as such may be expected to know how to curtail it before it leads on to dangerous ground.'

'I suppose *Mr Shittlehope* would agree with you!' Millie threw at her.

Louisa flinched. 'That was uncalled for.'

Millie flushed, biting her lip, but she offered no apology. Gruffly she said, 'You are determined to make me miserable.'

'On the contrary, I am trying to see to it that you will be happy.'

Tears stood in the green kitten eyes. 'I shall never be happy without Dess!'

'Millie, that is poppycock!' Louisa said tersely. 'You fancy yourself in love with him *now*, but ——'

Millie had looked at her then, a world of despair in her eyes, but a quiet confidence in her voice. 'I think you don't *know* about love, Louisa. If you did, you would not talk of "fancy".'

She had turned on the words and walked out of the room, leaving Louisa a prey to confusion and doubt. She did not know about love; how should she? She had become fond of Mr Shittlehope over the years, but in the way one might be fond of an uncle, perhaps. And she had been far too busy — and, in all honesty, far too practical — to indulge in any romantical nonsense elsewhere.

But she did love Millie. Enough to be cast into this slough of despondency and pain at the breach between them. Was *that* how Millie felt about her precious Dess? She and Millie were almost distantly polite to each other over these last few days. But only now did it occur to Louisa that Millie might possibly be using that coldness — even fostering it! — in order to engineer further clandestine meetings. And this was the ideal place.

Her eyes, roving the shifting figures below, began to spot now individuals instead of the characters they were portraying. Deliberately she joined Mrs Wavertree in her game of guessing, for that matron was far better acquainted with these people than she.

'There's Charlotte Childrey, just intercepting your ward, my dear. She would choose to be a nun! And there is her mother, all spangles and beads. Some sort of princess, I suppose.'

'Do you see any of the Berownes, ma'am?' Louisa asked, hardly conscious of the anxious note in her voice.

'Ah, afraid for Millie, are you?' guessed Mrs Wavertree shrewdly. 'Rather think they're all here. Saw Septimus holding court in one of the card-rooms as we passed. And over by the pillar there, look. That's Quarto in the Punchinello.'

'Of course, yes,' Louisa said, noting the large bulk and the red hat. Beside him she saw a figure in a dark

domino, whose sneering mouth marked him.
'Quintus!'

'Yes, and here comes Sexta in the blue domino.
She will never dress up.'

As Louisa watched, Quarto seemed to glance from
one to the other of his brother and sister. Then she
saw him shrug and stroll away as the blue domino
grasped the arm of the dark one.

'Ah, there is Nona,' Mrs Wavertree said, and
Louisa followed her glance to another part of the
room to see a shepherdess in a sprigged gown strung
up into puffs at either side, over a lacy petticoat that
indecorously exposed her ankles, with a flat chipstraw
hat over her brown hair and a pouting, melancholy
mouth showing under the mask.

'Why, whatever is amiss with her?' exclaimed
Louisa in surprise, becoming aware of the way the
girl leaned forlornly against a pillar, her gaze following the perambulations of a harlequin a few feet
away.

Mrs Wavertree looked and clicked her tongue.
'Fullands!' she said succinctly.

'Her husband? Who is he — the harlequin?'

'Flirting as usual.' Mrs Wavertree nodded. 'If he is
not careful she will end up just like her mother, for all
she's still head over heels in love with the wretch! No
woman will long bear such heartless neglect.'

'Oh, poor child!' Louisa uttered instantly, her
heart wrung. 'No wonder she is forever to be found in
her sister's company! And I thought *her* uncaring
from the things she let fall.'

'Pish! She worships the fellow,' Mrs Wavertree

assured her. 'But Fullands was ever a Lothario, and she hadn't the wit to see it.'

'How should she?' Louisa demanded, firing up. 'She was but a baby!'

Mrs Wavertree gaped at her. 'Why, Louisa, what a heat!'

Louisa's eyes were still on the miserable figure by the pillar. 'Well, it is all of a piece! Had she been watched and guarded as she should have been. . . And she is *so* naïve. They both are.' Her eyes began to flick back and forth. 'Do you see Octavia?'

Mrs Wavertree did. To some purpose. 'She's the Indian queen there, with that ogling Neptune.'

Louisa followed the direction of her pointing finger to where a country dance was being performed, in groups of four. In one of them was a pretty creature in a yellow gown lavishly decorated with gold spangles and lace, hair daringly powdered in bright saffron, spangled and feathered and topped by a richly jewelled crown. She was circling about a rather grotesque gentleman in Roman armour with a huge bush of hair at his chin and carrying—to the imminent danger of his partner's elaborate head-dress—a trident.

Louisa burst out laughing, but her amusement was short-lived. It was evident from the simpering and tossing of the crowned head that Octavia was encouraging Neptune's leers.

'Is the Neptune her husband?' demanded Louisa sharply of Mrs Wavertree.

'Lord, no! Kilgetty is still away.' Then she blinked as Louisa rose purposefully from her seat. 'My dear, where are you going?'

'To put a stop to this nonsense!' Louisa said flatly, and left her hostess gasping helplessly after her.

It took Louisa some time to make her way down into the Assembly Room, and even longer to weave through the groups of persons to the other side. But she found Nona still by her pillar, although she had moved around it, and was surreptitiously dabbing with a handkerchief at suspiciously wet cheeks — out of sight of her errant husband! Louisa noted with annoyance.

'Come along, Nona! It is no use moping here. That will not mend matters.'

'*Louisa*,' squeaked the girl, jumping. 'Is that you?'

'Yes, it is,' Louisa said, taking her hand and pulling her irresistibly towards the dancing.

'Pray don't say anything!' begged Nona. 'Jamie *hates* me to weep.'

'Jamie,' Louisa said in a voice of censure, 'is going to be given a good deal more than your tears to think about presently.'

As she went, she did not see Punchinello behind them, staring after her, his jaw dropping under the mask.

'Where are you taking me?' Nona asked fearfully.

'First to rescue your sister from her own folly!'

'Oh,' Nona said blankly, her eyes on what she could see of Louisa's profile.

Neptune, clanking a little as he twirled in the dance, was halted in the middle of it by a tap on his shoulder, and almost knocked himself on the head with his own trident.

'Eh?' he gasped, staring at the pink domino confronting him.

'Nonie, what in the world —— ?' began his partner, staring at the shepherdess.

'Octavia!' Louisa said sharply, bringing that lady's head round with a jerk. 'This dance is over, do you see? Now say goodbye and come with me.'

Octavia's mouth fell open, but Neptune flourished his trident.

'Now see here, ma'am — er — whoever you are!'

Louisa turned on him. 'Take your giant fork, sir, and go and swim in some other sea! Preferably with a mermaid who belongs to no other fish.'

Neptune's jaw gaped wide. 'Eh?'

'If you prefer it in plain English,' Louisa said clearly, 'take yourself off, sir, or I shall forcibly remove your beard!'

His trident came about as if for protection and he stepped back hastily, glancing briefly at his late partner, who had, regrettably, dissolved into uncontrollable giggles. Affronted, he turned about and clanked away.

'Oh, Louisa, how superb you are!' uttered Octavia in delight. 'And I had thought him so gallant. What a clumsy fool he is, to be sure!'

'Octavia, you are a very naughty girl!' Louisa told her crossly. 'Do you forget you are a married lady?'

'Oh, well, I was only cutting up a lark,' Octavia said airily.

'It will be well for Captain Kilgetty if he comes home soon! You must not do such things. It is a very dangerous pastime. Now I want you to look after Nona for a while.'

Octavia gazed at her. 'But Jamie is here.'

'Jamie has neglected her shamefully, and so I mean to tell him.'

Two masked faces looked at each other and back to Louisa, and then back to each other, shrugging.

'But if we cannot dance ——' began Octavia.

'You may do so presently, but *don't flirt*,' Louisa said sternly. 'For the present I wish you will do me the kindness to help me find Millie. I am very concerned about her.'

'But we thought ——'

'You *don't* want us to be with Millie,' Nona finished.

'I had rather you were with her than to see you moping, Nona, and you flirting, Octavia. By the by, is Decimus here?'

Nona and Octavia looked at each other in mute question. Then they both spoke together.

'I don't know!'

'I haven't seen him!'

Louisa eyed them. 'Well, if he is, and he comes over to speak with Millie, you two must *stay* with them, do you understand?'

The crown wobbled as Octavia nodded her head, and Nona at once reached up to try to secure it.

'Keep still, Tavey!'

'Leave that for now, Nona,' Louisa ordered. 'Come along. Millie was dancing, but I don't see. . .'

She had glanced about as she spoke, and now broke off as she perceived her ward, standing with her partner in a recess below one of the balcony boxes. Propelling her two charges before her, she made her way to the place and, ignoring Millie's astonishment, brought the three together. In an instant they were chattering away as of old, and Louisa was satisfied.

Leaving them together, she asked the gentleman of the Wavertree party who had danced with Millie to convey a message to her hostess that she would be with her presently, and then went back in search of Nona's husband.

Just as she reached the spot where she had last seen him she was accosted by a gentleman in a costume of silver and grey, loosely resembling a Vandyke painting, with an unusual white mask in the Venetian style.

'A masterly performance, Loulou,' said a familiar voice, 'but I fear your quarry has departed.'

CHAPTER NINE

'SEPTIMUS!' Louisa exclaimed, and an involuntary smile curved her mouth, which was just visible under the mask that concealed quite half of her face.

He bowed, but quickly grasped her elbow. 'Louisa, if you can bring yourself to speak to me for a moment only, I have something very urgent to impart.'

'Tush, how can you talk so?' Louisa cried. 'I am so glad to see you, for I wanted to apologise — again! — for the terrible things I said.'

His hand tightened a little on her elbow. 'Good God, *I* am the one who must beg forgiveness! But come. We cannot talk here. If you will trust yourself to me, there are some private corners to be found.'

'In this den of iniquity? I make no doubt of it!'

He laughed, but led her in silence out of the press of persons, through a vestibule, up a flight of stairs, and between a pair of velvet curtains, into a convenient alcove behind them that led to an outside balcony.

'The very place for a secret assignation,' Louisa commented drily.

'Is it not?' Septimus agreed, taking a taper from beside a single candle that lit the place, and lighting the other four in the candelabrum on the wall. 'That's better. Now it is far less improper.'

'I'm glad you think so. For myself, I am thanking God for my mask.'

Septimus laughed. 'And I was about to suggest that you remove it. I *hate* talking to a faceless vacuum.'

He was untying the strings of his own mask as he spoke, and as it fell away, exposing his comely face, Louisa experienced a jolt at her heart. How very odd! she thought, aware of her pulse quickening. Was she nervous of Septimus? Surely not.

'What is it, Loulou?' he asked gently, looking closely at her in the flickering light.

Louisa shook her head, suddenly aware that she had been staring at him through the slits of her mask. She reached behind her head and tried to untie her own strings with hopelessly unsteady fingers, uttering a soft, 'Drat!'

'Here, let me,' Septimus said, coming behind her.

Acutely conscious of his nearness at her back, Louisa fought for control over her suddenly unruly heart. The strings came loose, and his hands reached around to catch the mask as it fell. At the same instant Louisa's own hands came up and their fingers entangled.

Something like a ripple of physical shock zipped through Louisa's body, and she fumbled, dropping the mask. Septimus bent and picked it up for her, but his head was turned up, and his eyes sought hers, a question in them.

'Thank you,' Louisa uttered shakily, unable to meet his eyes, and reaching out to seize the mask as he rose. Breathlessly she uttered quickly, 'What was it you wanted to say to me?'

'Apart from begging your pardon?' he asked with a rueful twinkle.

'Oh, don't speak of that,' Louisa begged. 'I feel

quite dreadfully already, and if you begin to blame
yourself I shall feel worse!'

'Louisa, don't be ridiculous! You know very well it
was six of one and half a dozen of the other. Shall we
agree to forget the whole episode?'

'Yes, if you please,' Louisa said, feeling a little
calmer now that they were conversing with ease
again. It must just have been embarrassment that had
thrown her into such unaccustomed confusion.

'But will that mean,' he said, and the old teasing
gleam was back in his eye, 'that I dare not tell you
how becoming on you is that particular shade of
pink?'

'The one you have just put in my cheeks, you
mean?' Louisa enquired shakily, once more suffering
with an irregular beat in her heart. The poet's
response was to recite:

> '"O, blushing rose that crept unknown
> From Loulou's toe to Loulou's crown. . ."'

'Don't start that again!' Louisa told him, but her
lips quivered at the corners and her eyes danced.

He reached out and his finger brushed the edge of
her lip as he went on softly,

> '"For all she tries to mask the laughter,
> A crack appears, and widens after ——"'

'Septimus!' Louisa uttered warningly, choking on a
giggle. She moved to the curtain and lifted a hand as
if she would leave him.

'No, you don't!' The poet intercepted her and
captured the hand. 'Stay, Loulou! I have done.'

Louisa drew her hand away. 'Will you stop behaving in this fashion?'

He placed his hand on his heart and looked up to heaven. 'I swear it!' He added, as Louisa cast up her eyes, 'Don't you believe me?'

'The day I believe *anything* you say, Septimus Berowne, poet, I shall take myself to Bedlam!'

He laughed. 'As long as you have me incarcerated there with you.'

'Thank you, I should be mad enough without that! Now what was it you brought me here for?'

'Yes, I was rather forgetting that,' Septimus said, and the smile faded from his lips. 'It is this, Louisa. What *are* you trying to do? Ruin yourself?'

'Whatever do you mean?' she demanded, staring at him.

'You must know that the apparent incognito of such affairs as these is a farce,' he said forcefully. 'Everyone is perfectly aware of the identity of everyone else, and if you *will* so blatantly interfere — in your managing way — with my sisters' affairs you are bound to come under notice.'

'Well, but I *couldn't* stand by and leave them to make mincement of their respective careers,' Louisa protested. 'Which reminds me, I must find Mr Fullands.'

Septimus grinned unexpectedly. 'I tried to tell you earlier, Loulou. He has hidden himself. Quarto heard you and warned him off.'

'Oh, did he?' Louisa said wrathfully.

'He rather thought,' Septimus explained, 'that *you* would make mincemeat of poor Jamie.'

Louisa was obliged to laugh. 'Yes, I should. And I will, as soon as ever I catch up with him.'

'May the lord have mercy on his soul!' Septimus said devoutly, and she giggled. Then the mischief vanished from his eyes and he reached out to take her hand. 'But more importantly, Loulou, and *not* in jest, I promise you, I do have a word of warning for you.'

'About Jamie Fullands?' Louisa asked, frowning.

'Good God, no! About Quint.'

'Your brother? Why, what is he about?'

'That is just it,' Septimus said, holding her hand between both his own and drawing it close. 'I don't know. But I am *afraid* for you.'

He lifted her hand to his lips and kissed it, and Louisa's breath caught, control deserting her again.

'Afraid?' she repeated rather huskily.

'Of what Quint may try to do.'

'To *me*?'

Septimus gripped her imprisoned hand rather tightly. 'What did he say to you? Tell me!'

Louisa winced, looking away. 'I cannot repeat it.'

'I thought as much,' came the grated response.

She looked back at him, and her fingers moved within his hold so that they entwined with his. 'You need not be afraid. I told him what I thought of him. I know he was very angry, and he *did* swear some sort of oath about my not having heard the last of it. But I can't honestly see what he imagines he could do.'

'Well, my imagination positively races, Loulou,' Septimus said harshly.

'But Septimus, what do you expect me to do? Lock myself at home?'

'No, of course not.'

'Well, then.'

He sighed, and, kissing her hand again, released it at last. 'I entreat you to be on your guard, at least. Don't trust him!'

'I would not, in any event,' Louisa said, adding smilingly, 'even though he is your brother.'

Septimus smiled back at her. 'If that means that you trust me, I am glad of it.'

'We are friends, are we not?' she returned. 'Of course I trust you.'

'Then we had better go back to the public eye,' he said, 'for if I am alone with you for much longer I may well cease to deserve it!'

Louisa retied her mask, consciousness returning, together with the memory of his kiss the other day. For there was no doubt that that was what he referred to. It would be too much to say that she wished they might stay in this hiding-place so that he would repeat it, but she undoubtedly felt a thrill run through her at the thought of him doing so.

As they slowly re-entered the Assembly Room, once more obliged to push their way through the throng, Septimus leaned to murmur in her ear. 'You are about to be hoist with your own petard, Loulou! Here is your aunt, ready to manage you out of my company.'

Looking where he indicated, Louisa saw the gaunt Queen Elizabeth descending upon her. She turned her head to Septimus again, only to find that the poet had melted away. She was conscious of a feeling of disappointment, and determinedly ignored it, facing the onslaught of her aunt.

But before Lady Pyrland could reach Louisa a

figure in a blue domino darted at her, and Sexta's nervous titter came out from under the mask.

'Lady Louisa, stay a moment.'

'Yes, Sexta?' Louisa said, aware of her aunt halting in outrage a few feet off. 'What is it?'

'Oh, pray, Lady Louisa, I have to beg your pardon for my part in what occurred the other day.'

'It is of no consequence,' Louisa said shortly, having no wish to converse with this particular Berowne.

'But it is! Dolly is most anxious to make it up with you.'

'I can't believe *that*,' Louisa said curtly. 'And you certainly cannot have spoken to her.'

'No, no, it was her maid who told me,' Sexta insisted. 'She wants you to come and see her tomorrow. At ten, if you please.'

'Ten! She is not *up* at ten.'

'Oh, yes. Indeed, she wants you to come *early*, though she will receive you in her boudoir.'

Louisa eyed the woman, but Sexta's mask hid any clue to her thoughts.

'It sounds very unlike the Dolly I met,' Louisa said. 'You are not going to pretend she has had a change of heart, I hope.'

'Oh, no,' Sexta said readily. 'At least, I do not know. Only that the maid gave me the instruction. *Will* you come?'

In spite of herself, Louisa began to be intrigued. What could Dolly want? 'Very well, you may tell Dolly I will be there.'

'Oh, thank you,' uttered Sexta. 'You are very good.'

Next instant she had darted away again into the crowd, and Lady Pyrland was before her niece.

'*Dolly*?' she said in an accusing voice.

'Good evening, Aunt Hebe,' Louisa said hastily.

'So far it has been no such thing!' announced Lady Pyrland, her gimlet eyes boring into Louisa through the slits of her mask.

'I am sorry to hear that, Aunt,' Louisa said lightly.

'Sorry? *Sorry*? Louisa, you are *impossible*, and from this night I wash my hands of you!'

'Do you?' said Louisa evenly, but there was a heat of anger in her breast. 'Then you are as heartless as Dolly Berowne, and I can only say I am thankful that I had Mr Shittlehope's example to guide me, rather than yours!'

'Lou-isa!' gasped Lady Pyrland, outraged.

'Ask yourself, ma'am,' Louisa went on, 'whether your abandonment may serve only to hasten both my downfall and that of my ward. Were you, on the other hand, to lend us your support, in the face of our *questionable* friendships, then perhaps others might choose to follow where you led.' She shrugged. 'However, if *you* choose instead to be a sheep, it is all one to me.'

Turning, she left Lady Pyrland flat and went in search of Millie. Her aunt, her gaze sweeping a path around her, found several smirking mouths under masks, fans hastily lifting to hide them. She could not doubt that the interchange had been heard, and annoyance at her own lack of discretion made her glare about her until the masks became discomfited and looked another way.

'If that is how she speaks to you, Hebe,' said Lord

Sedbergh at her elbow, 'you will do well to leave her to her own devices.'

'Oh, be quiet, Philip!' snapped her ladyship. 'She was right. What is more, I was wrong. You are not at all suited, and I am sorry I ever tried to pair you off!'

Then she turned her back on him, and peered through the groups of people to try and find her niece. But Louisa had located Millie, together with the two Berowne girls, and was being subjected to the same request from three separate directions.

'I *know* you don't like us to meet, but ——'

'*Pray* let Millie come with us, Louisa.'

'It will be *such* fun, won't it, Tavey?'

'Oh, yes, and we *swear* we will not allow Dess anywhere *near* her,' Octavia promised.

'Oh, if you *please*, Louisa!' begged Millie, the green kitten eyes eager, just as if she had not been at outs with her guardian and sulking for days.

Louisa was too happy to see this change of mood to raise any objections to the proposed scheme. She could not see what harm there could be in an acrobatic display at Sadler's Wells.

'It is so *droll* to see the tumblers,' Nona was saying.

'The rope-dancing is so *very* clever,' Octavia told her excitedly.

'And they have promised an equestrian performance,' Millie added, her eyes shining, 'and a *real* mermaid in a tank!'

'Indeed?' Louisa said, her own eyes dancing. 'I do trust you will not, then, encounter your friend Neptune there as well, Octavia.'

That sent both Octavia and Nona into fits of giggles, while Millie cast them puzzled glances.

'Oh, *no*,' Octavia managed at last. 'There will be no *men*. Only Quarto, and he doesn't count.'

'I doubt he would agree with you,' Louisa said drily.

'We *are* pleased with him, though, for he said he would escort us,' Nona said in a tone of consolation.

'In that case I suppose I may safely give my consent,' Louisa said, smiling.

A chorus of high-pitched appreciation greeted this decision, and Louisa was obliged to put her hands over her ears. Having agreed to send Millie to Grosvenor Square at ten o'clock the next day, she firmly detached her and started back to rejoin Mrs Wavertree. In a corridor Lady Pyrland caught up with them.

'Louisa, wait!' she called breathlessly.

'Yes, Aunt Hebe?' Louisa said stiffly, turning.

'Louisa, don't be distant with me, I implore you!' begged her aunt with unaccustomed meekness. 'I have allowed myself to be too much alarmed by what has happened tonight. If I said. . .if I was overscrupulous, I am sorry for it.'

Louisa was never one to bear a grudge. She put out her hands at once. 'Don't say so, Aunt! I quite understand your scruples, even if I cannot myself adhere to the principles they embrace.'

'But you can go some way towards it, Louisa. Let us compromise. I do not *know*, in truth, if my credit can help you withstand your connection with the Berownes, but I am forced to admit that your influence over the younger girls at least can only be to the good.'

'Thank you, Aunt Hebe,' Louisa said, exchanging

a brief glance with Millie. She saw the burgeoning hope on the girl's face, and her heart sank. Did she imagine this olive-branch to be a prelude to approval of her choice of husband? 'I must point out to you, however,' she continued to her aunt, 'that I cannot befriend them and yet hold aloof from the rest. It is not in my nature. Besides being grossly impractical.'

Lady Pyrland sighed. 'I see the difficulty, Louisa. I would suggest that you may to some extent keep your involvement *private*, though. For instance, if you were to depart tonight *before* the unmasking, no one could say for certain that they saw you both in such company.'

A surge of violent resentment flooded Louisa's bosom, quite startling her. What, was she to indulge in a *clandestine* friendship with Septimus Berowne — not that he was particularly in her mind when she thought of the Berownes — and a secret connection with the rest of them, only to keep face with the *haut ton*? Despicable! But she bit back the hot words that rose to her tongue. If she had any hope of keeping Millie out of Decimus Berowne's clutches, it was the *only* way.

'Very well, Aunt Hebe. For this present occasion we will do so.' She held up a warning finger as Lady Pyrland heaved a relieved sigh. 'But I cannot promise that such discretion will always be possible.'

With this Lady Pyrland was obliged to be content, but before they parted she persuaded Louisa to agree to meet next afternoon for the purpose of discussing the matter further.

Louisa resolved to say nothing to Millie of her own planned visit to Grosvenor Square tomorrow morn-

ing. She would send Millie in a hackney—for the
Berowne family coach was to be put at the girls'
disposal—and follow herself in her own carriage at a
time when Millie would already have departed on her
expedition of pleasure. It would make her late for
Dolly, but that could not be helped.

Millie was punctual to her rendezvous, stepping
out of the hackney carriage almost precisely at ten
o'clock on the following morning. She tripped up the
shallow steps of the Grosvenor Square mansion, and
was just about to ring the bell when she was startled
by a plaintive cry behind her.

'Help me! Oh, pray, someone help me!'

Turning, Millie saw a female—well-dressed, in an
expensive furred velvet pelisse and a modish hat all
over flowers—holding on to the railings above the
area steps. She was evidently in some trouble, for she
looked as if she could barely stand, her head bowed,
and one hand pressed to her side.

'Oh, what is it?' Millie cried, running back down
the steps and coming quickly towards the woman.
'Are you ill?'

'A spasm!' gasped the girl, raising her head a little.
It was quite a young face, very pretty, but dreadfully
pale. 'A sudden pain. . .here.'

She indicated with a dip of her chin the place where
her hand still rested. Millie glanced down and saw
that the woman was with child.

'Oh, *dear*,' she uttered in a distracted way, wishing
that her guardian was here. Louisa would know just
what to do!

'Lean on me,' she offered, slipping an arm about
the girl's back and taking her weight.

The thought flitted through Millie's mind that the woman was not very heavy, for she was the shorter of the two and would have expected to find her weight a burden.

'Oh, thank you!' gasped the woman. Her voice was strikingly genteel, but with an oddly harsh timbre. 'You are very kind. I should—should not have. . . tried to—to walk so far.'

'You look as if you should not be walking at all!' Millie agreed.

'But the park looked so inviting,' the other said in a protesting way, 'and the doctor *did* tell me to. . . exercise.'

Her voice faded on the final word, and Millie said anxiously, 'Would you care to rest inside for a little? I am sure my friends will not object.'

'Oh, no, pray. . .don't trouble them,' the girl uttered, sounding a little frightened.

'But I think you should see a physician,' Millie said rather desperately, conscious of her own ignorance and afraid of what might happen in the woman's delicate condition.

'My—my house is just around the corner,' the girl ventured. 'Perhaps if you will be kind enough to—to lend me your arm, I can. . .can reach there safely.'

'Yes, but I don't know if you ought to *move*,' Millie said, frantic now.

The woman's head came up and a pair of beseeching gentle eyes met Millie's. She gave a wan smile. 'Please. I am a *little* better now. I should far, far rather get back to my own home.'

'I can understand that,' Millie said kindly, preparing to move. 'Let us try, then. But you must tell me if you feel yourself weakening.'

The girl agreed to this, and together they made their slow and painful way to the end of the Square. Millie was kept in a state of constant anxiety by her companion's gasps, the biting of her lip and the occasional little stagger as she almost lost her footing.

As they rounded the corner the woman paused. 'Oh, there is my husband's carriage!' she exclaimed. 'Oh, I had not dared to hope he would come in time.'

She began to hurry a little as she spoke, urging Millie forward, making not for the house outside which the coach was standing, but for the vehicle itself. Millie, worried by the quickened pace that the girl might injure herself, hardly noticed.

'Oh, take care!' she warned.

But the next instant the woman suddenly wrenched away, and the carriage door opened. Millie was pushed violently from behind so that she stumbled towards the coach, uttering a startled cry. A pair of strong arms came out of the vehicle's interior and seized her. At the same moment as she was lifted from in front, someone thrust at her back.

Shock suspended every faculty, and Millie, without the faintest murmur of protest, was hoisted into the coach like a sack of potatoes.

The door slammed. A whip cracked over the horses' heads. And the vehicle moved off.

As Louisa knocked imperatively on the door of the Berowne mansion in Grosvenor Square she was surprised to find in herself an uncommon degree of pleasurable expectation at meeting Dolly Berowne again. Was that what Mrs Wavertree had meant by saying that everyone always forgave her? She was selfish and heartless, but Louisa had been amused by her, and there *was* something about her that charmed. That something she had undoubtedly passed on to some of her children.

The picture of the poet's smiling face formed in Louisa's mind. But as the door opened just then she made no sort of connection of it with her thoughts.

'Oh, it's you again, is it?' said the surly general factotum.

'Are you not expecting me?' Louisa asked, stepping into the hall.

'Ain't my place to expect no one,' Andrew grumbled. 'Lot of use expecting, anyways. Comes and goes all times of the day and night, they does — all the more work for me! Who did you want?'

'I am here at Mrs Berowne's request,' Louisa said, repressing a strong desire to get into a gossip with this person. If anyone could tell her about the Berownes, Andrew could!

'This way,' said the servant laconically, and started to ascend the stairs.

As they approached the back parlour on the first floor Louisa heard girlish voices in the upper hall above them, obviously headed down. The girls! She had thought them long gone. Millie must not see her here! She darted forward and whispered to the butler.

'Quick, I must hide! I don't want them to see me.'

Andrew stared at her blankly. 'What, miss?'

'Oh, never mind!' Louisa said impatiently, looking quickly about for herself.

The girls were already on the stairs above. She saw

a door to one side and dashed over to open it. A dark empty saloon was revealed, all the furniture covered in dust sheets, the curtains drawn. Louisa went in and signalled to the astonished servant with a finger to her lips. Then she pulled the door and held it to, peering through the veriest crack.

'But where *can* she have got to?' Octavia was saying as they descended the stairs. 'I know she would never be late.'

'Perhaps she is *ill*,' Nona suggested anxiously.

'No. Louisa would have sent a message.'

Grasping swiftly that her ward had not arrived, Louisa was just about to burst out of her hiding-place and join in the prevailing discussion, when Nona spoke again, causing her to hesitate.

'Tavey, do you think it could be a ruse?'

'What do you mean, Nonie?'

'Perhaps she never *meant* to come with us. Perhaps she met Dess last night after all, and——'

'And arranged to fly with him this morning!' Octavia finished in an awed voice.

Louisa's heart plummeted. Could it be true? The two girls had paused at the bottom of the stairs, and from her hiding-place she could just glimpse their full pastel petticoats and flashes of their pretty worried faces under the lavishly decorated hats. Louisa strained to listen, hoping for some further clue.

'Nonie, she could not have done such a thing!' Octavia was protesting.

'Why not?' demanded her sister, suddenly excited. 'It would be so romantic.'

'Romantic? It would be shockingly vulgar!'

'Well, but I remember Dess saying to me once that it might come to that in the end.'

'He *didn't*!' exclaimed Octavia.

'But he *did*,' insisted Nona.

'He couldn't have *meant* it. Why, that would mean an *elopement*.'

'Well, have you *seen* Dess this morning? I have not.'

'No, but ——'

'He is not *here*, is he?'

Behind the door, Louisa was frozen with fear. Snatches of conversation, of argument, were tumbling through her brain. Images of Millie's face, with its changing expressions. She had been so altered towards her guardian suddenly last night when the girls had invited her to Sadler's Wells. Could it be that even then she had been planning this flight? She must have found an opportunity to meet Decimus, after all, and ——

A new voice interrupted her hurrying thoughts.

'My dears,' said the languid tones of Dolly Berowne, 'have you seen this *wretched* female who is coming to visit me?'

'You don't mean *Millie*, do you, Dolly?' demanded Octavia.

'Who?' asked Dolly vaguely.

'No, Tavey. Millie was coming to *us*.'

'Oh, I can't recall her name,' Dolly uttered irritably, 'but Sexta told me she wanted to beg my pardon for some reason.'

Nothing of the kind! Louisa thought wrathfully. What *was* Sexta thinking about?

'We don't know anything about that, Dolly,' said

Octavia dismissively. 'What *we* want to know is, have you seen Dess?'

'One of you, you mean?' their mother asked.

'Oh, Dolly!' Nona groaned. 'Decimus, the *baby*.'

'Oh, *him*. You can't call a grown man a baby; don't be silly.'

'Not if he has gone to Gretna Green,' Nona agreed.

'Who has gone to Gretna Green?' demanded Dolly.

'We think Millie might have done,' Octavia explained.

'Who is Millie?' asked Dolly.

'Oh, it does not matter, Dolly!' Octavia said impatiently. 'Come on, Nonie. Let's us go and consult with Setty.'

'Ah, the poet!' exclaimed Dolly in sudden animation. 'It is quite useless for you to try to speak to *him*.'

'Don't say he has locked himself in his garret again?' bodingly enquired Nona.

'I don't know, but I sent Andrew to fetch him to me not ten minutes ago, and the dratted fellow sent back a message that he is wrestling with his muse and cannot be disturbed.'

Is he indeed? thought Louisa. Well, he would not do so long. She had need of his services. After all, Decimus was his brother.

'But this is *important*,' Octavia was saying agitatedly.

A roar from somewhere downstairs signalled yet another arrival. 'Hey! Are you girls coming to Sadler's Wells or not?'

'Quarto!' exclaimed Octavia. 'Come on, Nonie. We will go down and tell him.'

'Oh, yes. Then we can *all* go in search of Dess.'

Their voices receded with the pitter-patter of their running feet as they descended. But Dolly Berowne was heard to seize on the butler.

'Andrew! Go and find Sexta. I cannot wait forever for this female, whoever she is. Bring Sexta to my boudoir at once!'

Then a door slammed, and Louisa cautiously entered the hall. The butler was on his way up the next flight of stairs.

'Psst!' Louisa hissed.

He halted on the stairs and turned. 'Yes, miss?'

'Never mind Sexta,' Louisa said. 'This is far more urgent. Show me up to Mr Septimus Berowne *immediately*.'

So commanding was her aspect that the servant did not hesitate. He beckoned and went on up the stairs, muttering, 'Gretna Green indeed! Whatever next? All the same, this here lot. Never a minute's peace.'

Louisa followed him to the second floor, thinking how fortunate it was that she had worn a pelisse — for the morning had begun with a light drizzle — over the chemise gown of her favourite pink. Andrew indicated a door on the right. Then he went back down the stairs, still muttering to himself. Louisa tapped on the door.

'Go away!' came in an irate tone from the other side.

'Septimus!' Louisa called, knocking again. 'I must see you. It is I, Louisa.'

There was a brief pause, then the sound of a chair scraping and a hasty footstep. A lock clicked and the door was flung wide.

'Good God!' ejaculated the poet, staring. 'What in the world are you doing here, Loulou?'

Louisa was momentarily distracted by his appearance. He was in his shirt-sleeves, and his hair, though loosely tied, had been disarranged by frustrated fingers. He became aware of her scrutiny and a gleam entered his eye.

'The poet at work, Loulou,' he explained.

'So I see,' she agreed, twinkling. 'I am sorry to disturb your *muse*, poet, but I need your help. At once!'

'What is it?' he asked in instant concern, reaching out to take her hand and drawing her into the room. He closed the door, and stepped across to his desk to pick up his long clay pipe. Turning with it in his hand, he said, 'Forgive me! I know it is mannerless to use this in your presence, but my—er—my *work* is excessively trying this morning.'

'That is fortunate, for you are about to abandon it.'

He frowned. 'Am I?'

'Yes, for I am very much afraid that my ward has eloped with your brother!' Louisa announced.

'*What*? You cannot be serious!'

'I don't know if I am or not,' Louisa said frankly, and proceeded to give him an account of what she had heard on the landing. 'I did not discover myself to your sisters, because I thought, if it *was* true, the fewer of us to become involved, the better.'

'Yes, of course,' Septimus agreed, laying down his pipe. 'But are we to assume it without looking for Dess? I know he is mad for Millie, but I can't believe that he would go to such scandalous lengths.'

'Can't you?' Louisa said sceptically. 'Well, you

know your brother best. I cannot say I feel as sanguine about Millie. She has been so rebellious over this whole affair that I don't believe I know her at all! And if *she* were to put forward the notion, do you suppose your brother's principles to be strong enough to resist it?'

'I'd like to think so, but I doubt it,' sighed Septimus, crossing to his desk and shoving a stack of untidy papers into a drawer. 'We had better try to find him.'

'Your sisters and Quarto are already doing so,' Louisa said. '*My* intention is to go after them at once. *Before* they get much further on their way. I have no wish to be obliged to chase all the way to Gretna Green.'

'I don't think that is likely,' the poet said, locking the desk drawer. 'It is five days' journey at least.'

'Five days?' exclaimed Louisa. 'Are you mad, Septimus? I *must* catch up with them before nightfall, or all will be lost. I would prefer it if you were to escort me, of course, but if you are prepared to waste time in a fruitless search beforehand, so be it.'

She marched towards the door, but Septimus caught up with her in two strides and, grasping her arm, swung her about.

'Louisa, if you think I will allow you to go off alone on such a mad errand, you much mistake the matter. Wait here!'

He left her where she was and went through into the adjoining chamber. In a few moments he was back, fully dressed in his blue frock-coat, with that grey cockaded hat on his head over tidied locks, his dramatic grey cloak over his arm, and a sword at his side.

Louisa, chafing even at this small delay, nevertheless caught sight of the sword and at once entered a protest. 'What do you want that thing for? Are you planning to fight your own brother?'

'Of course not. But we are going out of town, and it is as well to be prepared,' Septimus said shortly.

'I suppose you have a pistol about you as well?' queried Louisa sarcastically.

'Naturally,' he said, and grinned. 'Come, Loulou. Haven't you longed to go adventuring with a heroic figure at your side?'

'As it happens, I have not,' Louisa said flatly, but her eyes danced, in spite of the gnawing anxiety in her breast.

'You have no romance in your soul,' complained the poet.

'None at all,' agreed Louisa, walking through the door as he held it open. 'It is as well *one* of us is practical on such a jaunt as this. For pity's sake, don't go blowing off anyone's head!'

'Don't concern yourself. The only head that is likely to tempt me is yours, Loulou!'

She laughed, but made no answer, too urgent to be off to waste time in further banter. Septimus paused on the next landing.

'One moment. We had better let Dolly know what is happening.'

'If you think it will serve any useful purpose,' Louisa observed doubtfully.

'Probably not, but one can always hope.' He

popped his head through the door into his mother's room. 'Dolly!'

'Oh, it's you,' she uttered plaintively. 'Where is Sexta?'

'I haven't a notion, Dolly. I am off to Gretna Green.'

'Gretna Green? But I thought this Millie, whoever she is, went to Gretna Green.'

'Precisely. That is why I am going, too. If Dess should show his face — he's the *baby*, Dolly, remember? — tell him I am chasing Millie with Louisa.'

'Oh, *that* is the one!' exclaimed Dolly, pleased at recognising the name. 'The wretched female is supposed to be with me. Where is she?'

'She is with *me*, Dolly,' said Septimus, preparing to vanish again. 'She's going to Gretna Green.'

CHAPTER TEN

DOLLY was left staring blankly at the closed door. She could hear Septimus calling for Andrew to fetch the lady's carriage to the door.

'If she is going to Gretna Green,' Dolly said despairingly to herself, 'what does she want to come and see *me* for?' Groaning, she sank back on to her day-bed, groping for her bottle of smelling-salts.

A few minutes later the little parlour door banged open.

'Where is Lady Louisa?' demanded an anxious voice. 'Has she gone already?'

Dolly's eyes flew open. 'Sexta! Where is that wretched female you sent me?'

'That is what I am asking you, Dolly.'

'How in the world should I know?' Dolly demanded distractedly, clutching at her salts. 'Have I seen her? Has she come *near* me?'

'You mean she did not arrive?' Sexta asked, her nervous eyes flicking about the room as if she was seeking some shadow of Louisa's presence.

'I don't know. All I know is she has not been in *here*,' Dolly said firmly. 'And I am *waiting*, Sexta, to go to my maid. I *have* to dress.'

'But why didn't she come?' Sexta demanded, an unsteady hand creeping to her cheek.

'I tell you I don't *know*,' uttered her mother almost tearfully.

'I must find Quintus!' Sexta uttered, beginning to tremble.

'Is he the fat one?' Dolly asked. 'Because if he is, he *was* here. I know that because he took your sisters to Gretna Green.'

'Quarto took Nona and Octavia to Gretna Green?' shrieked Sexta, staring at her mother with wide eyes.

'Or was that the poet?' mused Dolly. Then she threw a hand to her brow. 'Stay! I remember now. It is *Louisa* who is gone to Gretna.'

'Oh, lord in heaven!' uttered Sexta wretchedly. 'It was a trick, then! He told me to get her here and then. . . Oh, he *can't* have been so vile!'

'Who?' Dolly enquired, her lashes fluttering at the woman. 'Setty?'

'No, Quint of course! I must *find* him.' She ran to the door, turning a haggard face back to her mother. 'If he is not at his lodging, then I fear the worst, God help us all!'

Dolly blinked as her daughter flew from the room. Then she became aware of a draught creeping into her parlour.

'Drat the girl!' she muttered plaintively. 'She has left the door open. People are so inconsiderate!'

Bestirring herself, Dolly rose to her feet, shaking out the voluminous négligé of muslin and lace that draped her person. Deciding that she might as well go up to her chamber and dress, she moved to the bell-pull with the intention of ringing for her maid. But the mirror above the mantel, reflecting her features, caught her attention, and she forgot about the bell as she peered closely within it, searching in the candlelight—for, as always, only candles were permitted to light her boudoir—for new wrinkles.

She had forgotten about the open door, too, and a hasty pounding of footsteps coming up to the hall outside startled her.

'Who is that?' she called out, moving towards the doorway.

The footsteps halted, and Decimus looked into the room. 'It is only I, Mama.'

Alone of her children, Decimus almost always called her by that title, a circumstance that ensured she always remembered at once which one he was.

'Oh, dear, I wish you would not,' she uttered, pouting. 'I was saying only this morning that you are no longer a baby, or you could not be going to. . .' Her eyes widened and she suddenly threw out an accusing finger. 'Why are you not at Gretna Green?'

Decimus blinked. 'I beg your pardon, Mama?'

'*Don't* call me that!' Dolly ordered, shaking a fist. 'I declare, the world is topsy-turvy today! I knew how it would be the moment I allowed myself to be drawn into the affairs of my children.'

'I am sorry, Ma—— I mean, *Dolly*, but I don't know what you are talking about.'

'*That* does not surprise me,' Dolly said acidly. 'I don't understand anything about it myself.'

'But what has occurred?' Decimus demanded. 'Why should I be at Gretna Green? I was just going up to see Setty.'

'Spare yourself the trouble,' recommended his mother. 'He is not there. *None* of them are.'

'Oh? Where, then, is he?'

'How should I know?' Dolly demanded, exasperated. 'Probably at Gretna Green with this Millie!'

'*What*?'

'Don't shout like that,' begged Dolly, covering her ears. 'My poor *nerves*.'

'I beg your pardon, but what was that about Millie?' demanded Decimus, quite pale about the mouth.

'It is no use asking *me*. All I know is that she has gone.'

'Didn't she arrive here, then?'

Dolly stared at him. 'Have you been consorting with your sister Sexta?'

'Mama!' exploded Decimus, anxiety making him impatient. 'Make a little sense, do! What has Sexta to do with it?'

'Ask her!' advised his mother crossly. 'Or chase after that dratted poet and ask him. He is the one who has taken Millie. . . I think.'

Decimus drew a painful breath. 'I'll kill him!' he said distinctly, and, turning, flew down the stairs.

Dolly tottered on her feet, grasping at the door-jamb for support. 'My salts! Andrew! *Andrew*. Oh, mercy me! Now they will all do away with each other, and I shall be blamed. Everything is always *my* fault. I never wanted children!'

The front door slammed, and Dolly shuddered, staggering back into the room and collapsing on to her day-bed. In a moment the butler arrived, walking straight in through the still open door.

'What do you want?' he demanded truculently.

'Andrew, they've all gone *mad*,' Dolly told him,

flinging her hands out. 'Fetch my maid! Get me a cordial!'

'Brandy, you mean?' Andrew snorted. 'You'll be lucky. The master has had all there is in the house.'

Dolly sat up with a jerk. 'Andrew! You know perfectly well you must never *mention* Mr Berowne to me.'

'Nor you to him neither,' retorted the servant. 'Husband and wife they calls it? I can think of another name.'

Before Dolly could annihilate him another set of footsteps sounded. Heavier ones. In a moment Quarto came puffing and steaming into the room.

'Seen Dess, Dolly?'

'Of course I have seen him!' his mother said crossly. 'He went off to kill his brother only a moment ago!'

'What? *Which* brother?' demanded Quarto, eyes popping.

'How in the world should I know?' Dolly uttered in a tone of total helplessness, falling back on her cushions. 'I wish everyone would not keep *asking* me things.'

Andrew the general factotum, casting up his eyes, manoeuvred his way about Quarto's bulk and left them to it.

'Sent the girls off to check if Millie's at Brook Street, after all,' Quarto announced.

'Millie again,' murmured his mother resignedly. 'Who *is* this Millie?'

'But if Dess is *here*,' Quarto went on, paying no attention to the question, 'they *can't* have eloped to Gretna Green.'

'*Someone* has gone to Gretna,' Dolly said positively, opening her eyes. 'That much I do know. Now was it perhaps Louisa?'

'Louisa?' exclaimed Quarto. 'Dash it all, she *can't* have done. It's Millie who is missing.'

'Don't keep talking about this Millie!' ordered Dolly, flinging her hands to her temples. 'I don't know *who* she is, and what is more I don't care. I am getting the headache.'

'Quarto! Quarto!' came shrieking from the stairs.

'That's Sexta,' said Quarto. '*Now* what's to do?'

'Oh, *no*,' groaned Dolly. 'Not her again, I *beg* of you.'

'*Quarto*,' uttered Sexta frantically, bursting through the doorway. 'Andrew said you were here! Oh, Quarto, what are we going to do?'

'Steady, girl, steady!' warned her brother, grabbing the hands that had seized his lapels. 'Expensive coat, this! What is the matter?'

'It's Quint,' disclosed his sister, her eyes wildly veering all over his face.

'Don't you get into one of your fits, Sexta,' Quarto said bodingly. 'Tell me what's amiss with Quint. And be quick about it, for I've enough on my hands as it is!'

'I can't find him, Quarto. And oh, I'm much afraid he may have abducted Louisa.'

'What? He can't have done!'

'*Yes*, I tell you.'

'Perhaps he has taken her to Gretna,' suggested Dolly brightly.

'Indeed I think so,' Sexta said, her eyes still on her brother. 'He — he made me ask her to come here to see Dolly this morning, but—but she never arrived. And I have just been to his lodging, Quarto, and he is not *there*.'

She ended on a note that promised hysteria, but Quarto hardly noticed. He was staring at her, horror in his face. Then an angry red flush suffused his cheeks.

'The *blackguard*!' he roared. 'By God, if this is true I'll kill him!'

'Not *another* one!' Dolly shrieked. 'For heaven's sake, I look *shockingly* in black!'

'I'm going after them!' Quarto said, ignoring this interjection. He grabbed his sister's arm. 'And you'll come with me! If he tries to deny it I shall have you there with the *truth*.'

'No, Quarto, *no*,' screamed Sexta. 'Quint will kill *me*.'

'No, no, *no*,' Dolly uttered. 'Oh, *pray* don't all slay each other in this tiresome fashion! My nerves will *never* stand it.'

Unheeding, Quarto was already dragging a protesting Sexta to the door. '*Andrew*!' he bellowed as he made for the stairs. 'My phaeton! Get the horses put to. This instant!'

Dolly had risen again in her anxiety, and now stood gazing after their retreating forms, listening to the shouting and shrieking echoing through the hall, until the front door once again slammed and quiet descended on the house.

'Besides,' she said in a plaintive tone, sinking down on to her day-bed, 'I *loathe* black. It is such a *depressing* colour.'

Nevertheless, she began to picture to herself an

appropriate mourning dress, wondering whether her dressmaker could create precisely the effect she wanted with the new modish muslin. Or would it have to be silk? She was just imagining the reaction of her current favoured cavalier to the agreeable image she had conjured up when her two youngest daughters tripped into the room.

'Dolly, where is everyone?' demanded Octavia, making her mother jump.

'Andrew tells us they have been rushing in and out like mad things,' Nona added.

'He may well say so!' Dolly uttered with an eloquent shudder. 'I declare, I would have supposed that if I were obliged to have children at all they would at least have had the courtesy to remain in possession of their senses!'

'Oh, Dolly, please keep to the point,' Octavia pleaded.

'And *we* are not mad,' Nona said indignantly. 'In fact it is only Sexta who is ripe for Bedlam.'

'Yes, she is *dreadful*,' Octavia agreed.

'You are *all* dreadful,' Dolly declared, sitting up. 'And never more so than today.'

'But what has happened?' Octavia insisted.

'Yes, where are they?'

'It is no use asking me,' Dolly said. 'They have all gone to Gretna Green to kill each other!'

Her two young daughters gaped at her.

'But you don't go to Gretna to kill people!' Octavia protested.

'No,' agreed Nona. 'You go there to get *married*.'

'Not in this family!' Dolly threw at them. Then she opened the smelling bottle that was never far from her reach and sniffed delicately at its contents, complaining in between. 'I wish to heaven I had not borne any of you! Now I shall have to wear black, and black is so *ageing*.' She looked at the girls, who were staring at each other in perplexity. 'Well, I do not know why you two are standing there! You had better go off to Gretna yourselves and be done with it.'

'Yes, Nonie!' Octavia exclaimed, seizing her sister's hands. 'We shall go after them! I could not *bear* to stay here, in any event, not knowing what may have happened.'

'No, indeed. We would end in *hysterics*, like Sexta. But how will we go?' Nona asked, round-eyed.

'In the family coach, of course. Quarto let us go alone to Louisa's house, so he cannot object to it if we follow.'

'Object?' echoed her sister. 'Why *should* he object? After all, if *they* can go to Gretna, so can we!'

Their mother was gazing at them, dumbfounded. 'But I did not mean it, you stupid creatures! For all I know, they may not be anywhere near Gretna. I could not make head or tail of what any of them said!'

'But we must go, Dolly,' Octavia said in distress. 'We know Millie is missing, and Louisa is not at home either. And if even Quarto thought he must go in pursuit, then there is every reason to be concerned.'

'Besides,' her sister put in, 'we are *not* going to be left out! Come on, Tavey.'

Next instant they were gone from the room, their excited voices rapidly receding down the stairs. Dolly heard them calling for Andrew, and with shaking fingers once more unscrewed the top of her smelling bottle.

'And that *lunatic* female thought I might exercise parental control!' she said bitterly.

Setting the bottle under her nose, Dolly inhaled far too deeply of the acrid aroma, and collapsed against her cushions in a dead faint.

Louisa and Septimus, meanwhile, were still on their way north, each as firmly convinced as the other of entirely separate conclusions. For enquiry at the Adam and Eve Tavern at St Pancras had elicited the information that a coach bearing a couple — the lady corresponding to Millie's description — had stopped there briefly. But at the Mother Red Cap Inn, which served as a halfway house on the route from London to Hampstead, where the coach had changed horses and also direction for Kentish Town on the Great North Road, it was reported that the lady was in tears, and the gentleman's description did not appear to tally with that of Decimus Berowne.

'One would not describe Dess as "big",' Septimus argued as they resumed their journey. 'Besides, it is ridiculous to suppose that a lady on the way to be married to the gentleman she loves would be weeping all over the carriage.'

'If I know Millie,' Louisa said tartly, 'the very consciousness of the atrocity of her conduct would be enough to set her off.'

For the sake of comfort, Septimus had elected to sit forward, his back to the horses, spreading himself in the opposite seat. They thus faced each other, and the spring sunshine, which had succeeded the early drizzling rain, was so obliging as to cast its rays through the glazed windows, so that they danced through the trees that lined the route and played over Louisa. Septimus was therefore able to enjoy an uninterrupted view of her expressive face, and a glimpse of the swell of her white bosom under the skimpy muslin neckerchief that but just covered it — for she had thrust her pelisse back to her shoulders as the day warmed up. This was a considerable compensation. And a far pleasanter occupation than the one the poet had left behind at home! But his conviction that they had come on a fool's errand never wavered.

'For my part,' he told her, 'the prospect of conveying all the way to Gretna Green a female suffering from the vapours would fast induce me to change my mind about the desirability of wedding her.'

'Yes, but you are not Decimus,' Louisa pointed out.

'And you, I thank God, are not Millie,' he returned.

Louisa raised her brows. 'How am I to take that?'

Septimus grinned. 'Any way you care to, Loulou.'

There was a silence as their eyes locked. Louisa felt her pulses quicken. Unconsciously she passed her tongue over suddenly dry lips, and was puzzled when the poet looked quickly away. The flurry of her heartbeat subsided again.

'You said Decimus was mad for Millie,' she ventured after a moment or two.

His eyes came back to her. 'And so?'

'Well, if that is so, and if she has persuaded him to this course, is it not possible that once she began to regret it — as these tears might indicate, after all — he would bring her home again?'

There was almost a plea in her voice, but Septimus answered without hesitation, 'No, Loulou.'

'But——'

'My dear ninnyhammer, *if* he has been so mad-brained as to begin the journey, he is sufficiently the gentleman—I sincerely trust!—to recognise that in honour he *must* pursue it, having compromised *her* honour.'

'Oh, "honour" again!' ejaculated Louisa impatiently.

'You may scoff, Loulou, but rules are rules,' said the poet firmly.

'But it is perfectly absurd! Besides making nonsense of this vaunted "Great Love" of theirs. Really, Millie has been behaving like a perfect Juliet!'

'Yes, I was rather reminded of Shakespeare's tragedy myself,' Septimus agreed. '"Wherefore art thou *Berowne*?"'

Louisa twinkled. 'And I the adamant Capulet, I collect. At least I have not attempted to thrust her into marriage with anyone else.'

'Good God, I should imagine you would be the last person to do that!'

The large eyes became serious at once. 'Because of Mr Shittlehope, you mean? He was very good to me, you know.'

'So I should hope!' said the poet austerely.

Her lips quivered on a smile. 'I wish he could hear you. He would say, "I owe the chit nothing! Choused out of my pennies only to be pecked at and nagged from morning to night!"'

Her rough mimicry of a deep northern accent made Septimus laugh, but he was conscious of a surge of resentment which made him say almost angrily, 'He did not value you as he should.'

'Oh, but he *did*,' Louisa contradicted, quite distressed. 'He did not mean a word of it, and said it only to tease me. *You* should understand that.'

A short laugh escaped him. 'So I should.' He lowered his voice a little, quite unconsciously. 'Did you love him, Louisa? He must have loved you.'

'We were not *in love* with one another, if that is what you mean. At least, I don't think so.' Louisa smiled wryly. 'I would not know how to recognise it, you see.'

'You mean you have never been in love?' Septimus asked incredulously.

'Not to my knowledge. Have you?' Then she laughed. 'What a silly question! You are a poet. Of course you have been in love.'

He grinned. 'Naturally. If you should care to be instructed in the art, I am your man!'

'Thank you, but just at this present the vagaries of that particular art are anathema to me.'

'God, yes, our mission!' He cast exasperated eyes to heaven. 'I had almost succeeded in forgetting it. What will you do with the runaways when — if! — we do catch them?'

Louisa threw up her hands. 'Oh, I don't know. Borrow your pistol and shoot them both!'

But by the time the coach lumbered into Highgate, anxiety had so far superseded anger that she prayed only to find Millie, and could not think beyond that. The carriage first pulled up at the Old Crown, but, on seeing that it boasted tea gardens, Louisa at once suggested they should rather enquire first at the Black Dog opposite.

'For they will scarcely show themselves in an inn of this size,' she explained as the coach moved across.

'Not if it is an elopement,' Septimus agreed. 'Not that I believe in such a fairy-tale for a moment!'

'We shall see which of us is proved right in due time,' Louisa said, eyeing rather doubtfully the seedy establishment at which they now halted. 'I don't care much for the look of this place, I must say.'

'Decidedly unsavoury,' her companion conceded, assisting her down from the coach. 'I should not be surprised to find that it had been the headquarters of Dick Turpin.'

'Did he roam these parts, then?'

'Good God, this whole area is infested with highwaymen! Why do you think I came armed?'

'Oh, I see,' Louisa said, and gave him a mischievous look. 'In that case I am glad that I dragooned you into accompanying me.'

'You are abominable, Loulou!' Septimus told her, a gleam in his eye. 'However, it is undoubtedly rich fodder for some more "doggerel" concerning your managing ways.'

'More?' she echoed, laughing, and preceded him into the rather dingy hall of the Black Dog. 'In that case I need have no scruple in managing you into procuring for me a private parlour, some refreshment and a landlord to interrogate.'

'All of which I would naturally have left to you, being the mannerless clod you evidently think me!' Septimus said sarcastically.

Hardly knowing that she did so, Louisa reached

out her fingers and lightly caressed his cheek. 'Proceed, clod!'

He turned to her, searching out her face in the dimness that had engulfed them as they stepped out of the sunlight. But before he could speak, a skinny individual with bandy legs, and wearing an apron over an ill-fitting tarnished waistcoat and breeches, came with a rocking gait into the hall from an almost empty tap-room.

'Ah!' he said, looking his visitors over out of gloomy eyes in a cadaverous face under a black scratch wig. 'Thought as that carriage must have brought quality.' He leaned forward, resting his hands on his thin hips, adding direfully, 'Only I don't want no more riot and rumpus! This is a respectable house, this is.'

'I am glad to hear it,' Septimus said smoothly, only the faintest tremor informing Louisa of his amusement. 'Kindly show us to a private parlour — if you have one.'

But Louisa stepped forward and grasped the man's arm. 'What sort of riot and rumpus? Who has been here?'

'Louisa!' hissed the poet warningly. 'Not here.'

'Septimus, this is no time for discretion,' Louisa told him impatiently.

'Do you know the meaning of the word?'

Ignoring him, Louisa turned back to the man, but she was forestalled.

'Knew it, I did!' he said lugubriously. 'All one, the quality. Here we go again. You might as well come in. I can see as how it's no use fighting the inevitable.'

He turned as he spoke and led them past the tap-

room to a door further down on the opposite side of
the hall. He threw it open, gesturing them inside.

'You can use this. Ain't what you'd call a parlour,
but it's private as you please.'

'Thank you,' Louisa said, moving into a large
apartment.

It was furnished with two long deal tables and
several straight-backed chairs. The windows had
been opened, and the remains of a fire glowed in the
grate, but a stale odour hung about the place, and it
could have done with the services of a broom and
duster.

Septimus looked the room over with disfavour
from the doorway, and then brought his eyes to the
man's face. 'You are the landlord?'

The man nodded. 'Tuffley's the name.'

'And this, Tuffley, is the best you can do, I take it.'

The man bristled. 'T'other party were content
enough!'

'What other party?' Louisa demanded at once.
'The cause of the "riot and rumpus"?'

'*He* weren't,' the man explained. 'Not at first, that
is. Sat in here until the coach come. I'm not saying he
weren't a surlyboots, but he kept hisself quiet
enough.'

'I don't understand,' Louisa said, glancing at
Septimus and back. 'A man was here *waiting* for a
coach?'

Septimus came forward into the room, laying his
hat and cloak on one of the chairs. 'Can you describe
him?'

Tuffley looked at him in a little perplexity.
'Weren't unlike your honour, now I think on it.'

'Oh, my God!' Septimus said softly.

'A younger man, though?' Louisa asked.

Tuffley shook his head, his eyes on the poet's face. 'Older, I reckon. Nor he weren't so pleasant-spoken, neither. Calling on the devil every other word, he was.'

Septimus and Louisa looked at each other.

'It can't be them. That does not sound at all like Decimus,' she said.

'It sounds like Quint!' Septimus said harshly.

'*Quint*? But for pity's sake, what could *he* want with Millie?'

Septimus did not answer. He turned to the landlord. 'Was there a lady with him?'

Tuffley shook his head. 'Not as I seen. But the fellow what came in the coach—rough big 'un he was—he says as how he brought *her*. Now I ain't saying,' added the landlord, warming to his tale, 'as there were or there weren't no lady *in* the coach. But the gent goes out and pokes his nose in it. Next I know, the two of 'em are back in here, argufying and shouting fit to bring the ceiling down!'

'But this is fantastic!' Louisa cried. 'Either your brother has taken leave of his senses, or we have got the wrong people altogether.'

'It begins to seem like it,' Septimus agreed, but there was a troubled look at the back of his eyes. He nodded to Tuffley. 'Perhaps you would be good enough to bring coffee for the lady.'

'Coffee?' The landlord scratched his chin. 'Ain't much call for coffee, but I'll see if we've any in the house.'

The poet's lips twitched. 'Your efforts will be very

much appreciated. You may fetch ale to me. That should not be beyond your powers, I think.'

'Oh, we've ale aplenty, your honour,' Tuffley told him reassuringly, and rocked himself out of the room.

Louisa sank into a chair, throwing back her pelisse again. 'Have we lost the scent, do you think?'

'We never had it, Loulou,' Septimus said drily. 'What do you want to do now? Go on or go back?'

Louisa sighed, shaking her head. 'I don't know.' She looked up at him, the large eyes cloudy. 'All I know is that Millie left my house in a hackney at ten minutes to ten to go to yours. She did not arrive. If she is not with Decimus, *where is she*?'

Septimus came over to her and, cupping her face with his fingers, smiled at her. 'We'll go on.'

She winked wetness away, and smiled back rather tremulously. 'Thank you, dear poet,' she said huskily.

Footsteps signalled the return of the landlord, and, releasing her, Septimus moved away. The door opened.

'Setty, you villain!' thundered Decimus from the doorway, his eyes blazing fiercely. 'What have you done with Millie?'

Louisa jumped up, starting forward, but Septimus reached out and detained her with a hand on her arm. His eyes were on his brother, whose mud-spattered boots bore witness to a furious ride.

'We might ask you the same question, Dess,' he said quietly.

But Decimus had already taken in his companion. 'Lady Louisa!' he gasped, his wrath ludicrously arrested. His stunned gaze went from one to the other. 'B-but. . . I thought. . . Dolly said——'

'My babe,' Septimus drawled, 'you surely have not come haring after us on Dolly's recommendation?'

'Well, no, but she said you had taken Millie to Gretna Green, and I thought——'

'Decimus!' Louisa burst out. 'Where is Millie? Pray, pray tell me! I will not be angry, only that I know she is *safe*.'

'But I don't *know*,' Decimus said. 'Dolly told me she had gone, and. . .' He broke off, paling. 'Is she missing, then? Oh, God, *no*!'

'She never arrived at the house this morning,' Septimus told him, his eyes flicking back in concern as Louisa seemed to wilt where she stood. 'Sit down, Louisa! This is no time for swooning.'

'Oh, no, I-I will be all right in a moment,' Louisa said, sinking back on to her chair. But she felt sick to her stomach. Until now she had been held up by the thought that Millie was with Decimus. An elopement she could deal with. But Millie had *disappeared*. Shock for the time being suspended every other thought.

'Setty, what has *happened* to her?' Decimus demanded, coming up to grasp his brother by the coat.

'Softly, my babe,' Septimus warned, removing the frantic clutch on his costume. 'We will get nowhere with panic.'

Decimus drew a steadying breath. 'No. Of course. I'm sorry.' He bit his lip, but anguish throbbed in his voice. 'Only it's *Millie*, don't you see?'

'I do see, babe,' Septimus said gently, putting a

hand on the young man's shoulder and squeezing it. Then he looked at Louisa. 'I think our first course must be to return to town.'

'What good will that do?' Louisa asked shakily, her eyes coming up.

'I have an idea,' he said, 'and I can find the truth of it in London.'

'But we *know* Millie was on this route,' Louisa protested, her brain beginning to function again. 'That man at the Mother Red Cap described her *exactly*.'

'You have news of her?' Decimus asked eagerly.

At this moment the landlord appeared in the doorway, bearing a tray with a coffee-pot and its various accoutrements, and a jug of ale.

'Ah, you found 'em, then,' he said, nodding at Decimus. Then he jerked his head to the rear as he moved inside. 'These two are yourn as well, are they?'

Sexta appeared in the doorway, her eyes casting wildly about the room. They fixed on Lady Louisa, who, like the Berowne brothers, was staring at her blankly. Sexta flung out a pointing finger.

'She is here, Quarto. Look!'

Quarto's bulk pushed in from behind her, shoving her out of the way. 'Where's that blackguard?' he roared, his gaze sweeping the room. Catching sight of his brothers, he stopped dead, eyes popping. 'Setty, you here? Dess, too! Hello there, infant. Thought you'd gone to Gretna.'

'Of course I have not gone to Gretna!' Decimus snapped irritably, hunching out of his greatcoat.

'How do you two come here, I should like to know?' Septimus demanded.

Tuffley, who had placed the tray on the table near Louisa, was gazing from one to the other of the gentlemen. 'Dang me!' he muttered. 'Three on 'em, and all as like as peas!'

'Came in my phaeton, Setty,' Quarto explained. 'Dash it, you must know I'd never leave town any other way.'

'Oh, Quarto!' Decimus said impatiently. 'He means *why* have you come?'

'Oh, I see,' said his brother. He threw an apologetic glance at Louisa. 'We came after you, Lady Louisa. Sexta would have it that *you* were missing instead of Millie. Got it into her silly noddle that Quint had abducted you. Ha, ha!'

But Septimus was not amused. He had gone deathly pale. His eyes found his sister and he went up to grasp her urgently by the shoulders.

'Sexta, what reason had you for thinking so? Tell me at once!'

'Let me go, Setty!' she uttered, her eyes swivelling as she squirmed in his hold.

'Well, you *know* why she thought so,' Quarto burst out impatiently. 'Mad as a hatter! Doesn't need a reason.'

'Oh, she had a reason,' Septimus said harshly, his eyes boring compellingly into the frightened ones of his sister. 'Now are you going to tell me, you little fiend, or do I have to shake it out of you?'

'Here, Setty!' protested his elder brother.

'Septimus, don't!' Louisa cried.

But the poet only grasped the struggling woman the more strongly. '*Tell* me!'

Sexta began to scream. And pandemonium broke out.

Tuffley, who had stood gaping at the turn of events with the coffee-pot in his hand, jumped violently. The coffee-pot flew from his nerveless grasp and dashed its contents over the table, splashing Decimus and Quarto, and crashed into pieces on the floor below.

'Damn it to hell!' bellowed Quarto, leaping away.

'Look out!' shouted his youngest brother angrily, brushing at the stains on his coat.

'Be quiet, Sexta!' yelled Septimus, at once brought to a sense of his own inept handling of the woman.

But Sexta's shrieks continued unabated, and she began to rock and pull wildly at her coiffure.

Louisa, jerked out of a shocked stupor — for the implications of Quarto's words had set up the most horrifying possibility in her brain — had risen sharply to her feet, the pelisse dropping from her shoulders, and her eyes flying to the landlord, who was backed against one wall, his dumbfounded gaze on the wrecked coffee-pot and the brown liquid streaming along the surface of the table and swilling about the floor.

'Fetch a cloth!' she ordered, waving at the man to attract his attention.

But Tuffley's head was turning back to the cause of the fracas, who was still shrieking, pressed into a corner, while all three brothers advanced upon her, trying to top her with their vociferous demands for her to stop.

Louisa came around the table to the landlord, and, seizing one arm, she shook him. His head jerked round.

'Fetch a cloth!' Louisa said clearly over the cacophony. 'Hurry, man!'

Like an automaton under a hypnotic command, Tuffley made for the door. Just as he reached it, two flying bodies entered and sent him reeling back.

'I knew it was Sexta!' cried Octavia, stopping as she took in the mêlée within the room.

'Oh, Tavey, she is in hysterics again!' Nona said despairingly beside her. Then she, too, noted her brothers surrounding Sexta. 'Oh! They are all here, Tavey.'

But Octavia had already seen Louisa. 'Have you got Millie?' she shrieked over her sister's screams.

Louisa was staring blankly at them both. What, was everyone come on this crazy adventure? Her practical side reasserted itself as she recognised the useless nature of the gentlemen's efforts to quiet their sister. Turning, she pushed through them unceremoniously, and, reaching the woman, who was by now threshing about against the wall, she lifted a hand and dealt her one sharp slap on the cheek.

The screams ceased abruptly, and with them the other voices. Into the silence that followed, as Sexta gazed stupefied into her assailant's face, Louisa's clear voice fell like balm on the troubled waters.

'That will do, Sexta! This situation is far too serious for self-indulgence.' She saw the eyes begin to roll again and held up a finger. '*Stop*. I said that will do.'

She paused a moment, but Sexta stared at her wide-eyed, apparently cowed by the implicit threat.

'That's better,' Louisa said more gently. 'Now listen to me. You asked me to visit Dolly today at Quint's request, didn't you? Then, when you thought I had not arrived, you became suspicious of his motives. He *meant* to abduct me, didn't he?'

'I didn't know,' Sexta uttered in a distracted way. 'He didn't tell me. I tell you I didn't know.'

'But you might have guessed,' Louisa said flatly. 'Only, you see——' turning to look at the rest '—she didn't know about Millie's engagement with Nona and Octavia.'

The three gentlemen followed her gaze and, turning, beheld their young sisters standing behind them, and Tuffley the landlord, his hand pressed to his head as if he was in pain, just making for the door. He caught their glances and eyed them with loathing.

'These more of yourn, are they? You'd best take over the whole house then and be done with it,' he said bitterly, and tottered out of the door.

'Oh, the devil!' ejaculated Quarto, eyeing his sisters. 'Not you two as well!'

'Bravo, Louisa!' Octavia said admiringly, ignoring her brother's comment. 'None of us can *ever* manage her.'

'Don't you *dare* object, Quarto,' Nona uttered, squaring up to her brother. 'Dolly told us that you had all gone to Gretna to kill each other, so what *could* we do but follow?'

'You peabrains!' Quarto said disgustedly. 'You should know better than to listen to anything Dolly says.'

Septimus turned back to Louisa, his jaw set. 'My guess is that you are right in every particular. I had a feeling Quint was behind this.' He cast an unloving glance at his sister Sexta on the last words, and she shrunk away into her corner, flinching.

'Eh?' Quarto uttered, his attention caught. 'You are not suggesting that Quint —— '

'My God!' interrupted Decimus, horror in his face. 'He took Millie by mistake!'

'I fear so,' Louisa said, glancing at him. 'My appointment was for ten, but I put it back. I did not want Millie to know that I was coming to see Dolly.'

'For fear that she would think you were softening towards me,' Decimus guessed in a hard voice.

'Oh, Dess!' uttered Nona in a disappointed tone, removing her short cloak. 'How unromantic of you! I thought you had *eloped* with her.'

'Oh, be quiet, Nonie!' Octavia snapped. 'This is *serious*. Don't you understand? Poor Millie is in Quint's hands.'

'Hell and the devil confound him!' roared Quarto suddenly. 'He'll ruin us all! I've a damned good mind to kill the fellow, brother or no brother!'

'No need of that, Quarto,' Decimus snapped. 'For *I* intend to kill him!'

Quarto shook his head. 'Won't do, infant. He'd carve you to ribbons! Better leave it to me.'

'Neither of you will do anything!' Septimus said firmly. 'At least not yet. The first priority is to get Millie back safe.' He glanced at Louisa, who had gone pale, sinking into the nearest chair, and quickly turned back to his elder brother. 'Quarto, fetch Tuffley back in here!'

'Who?' demanded his brother, blinking.

'The landlord. He may have information that can help us.'

Louisa raised her head at that, hardly noticing as Nona and Octavia converged on their young brother, twittering with sympathetic comments and reassurance. She watched Quarto walk out of the room, bellowing for the landlord, and her eyes came back to Septimus. He made his way over to her and she rose as he came up, automatically putting out her hands.

'Don't look so haggard, Loulou,' he said softly, taking the hands in a strong clasp. 'He won't hurt her. And at least we know where she is.'

'With whom, you mean,' Louisa corrected, a distinct tremor in her voice. 'Not *where*.'

'We'll *find* her.'

Her large eyes searched his face. 'Septimus, why did he not let her go at once when he discovered his mistake?'

'That is precisely what I think Tuffley may be able to tell us,' he answered, squeezing the hands he held. 'If it *was* Quint who was here today, then he only found his mistake when the coach arrived.' His voice hardened. 'I should have guessed he would hire someone to do his dirty work for him.'

But Louisa's eyes were still fearful. 'What if he thought he might as well have Millie?'

'Not Quint,' Septimus said positively. 'She's not a rich enough plum to tempt him.'

'Ransom, then?'

'What, and risk gaol? Your wits have gone begging, Louisa!'

The large eyes misted over. 'I know. I'm b-being a n-ninnyhammer, am I n-not?'

'You *are* a ninnyhammer,' he said caressingly, and his eye gleamed. 'But an *adorable* ninnyhammer, none the less.'

A rather watery chuckle greeted this sally, as he put an arm about her and drew her close. He became aware then of silence about them, and his eye caught his young sisters studying them both with interest.

Decimus was also looking at him, but there was no vestige of speculation in the anguished brown eyes. Septimus gave him a reassuring smile, and released Louisa. But his cheeks nevertheless coloured faintly.

'Don't look so desperate, my babe,' he said gently, coming forward to grasp his young brother's shoulder. 'We *will* find her, and that right speedily.'

'Are you sure, Setty?' Octavia asked, her own eyes anxious.

'Poor Millie!' uttered Nona distressfully. 'You *must* find her, Setty.'

Just then Quarto returned with the landlord. 'Hey! This fellow has a dashed interesting story to relate!'

'Yes, we've already heard it,' Septimus said. 'Tuffley, did your visitor leave *with* the coach?'

The landlord opened his mouth, but Quarto butted in. 'That's just what he's been telling me. Left here not an hour ago, and the coach went *on*. But Quint — if it was him — was riding behind.'

'Keeping himself incognito,' Septimus grated.

'It won't do him any good,' Decimus said through his teeth. 'We *know* he did it.'

'Very well, then,' Septimus said in a decisive tone. 'Quarto, you and Dess go forward in your phaeton. If you're not back within the hour, we'll assume you've had to go further and follow. Meanwhile, I'll institute enquiries in this village. For all we know she may have escaped and hidden herself hereabouts.'

'Come on, man!' urged Decimus, snatching up his greatcoat from a chairback, and propelling his elder brother into the doorway.

'Very well, very well!' grumbled Quarto. 'No need to jostle me, infant.'

'Well, if you don't hurry I'll take the phaeton myself!' Decimus promised, squeezing past him and marching out of the room.

'Hoy!' bellowed his brother, puffing after him. 'Just you wait for me, you young hound!'

'Tuffley!' Septimus called, turning to the landlord, who was watching all this and shaking his head as if he did not believe he was seeing it. 'Clean up that mess, will you? And bring the ladies more coffee.'

'*She* ain't getting any,' growled Tuffley, pointing at Sexta. 'Oughter make *her* clean it up.'

'Get on!' Septimus ordered, thrusting him from the room.

'Can't we help?' Octavia asked, taking off her mantle and moving to put a pleading hand on her remaining brother's arm.

'Yes. Stay here and watch Sexta!' Septimus told her.

'Oh, no!' uttered Nona, pouting, and glancing across at her elder sister.

Septimus leaned towards them both, lowering his voice. 'And keep Louisa from driving herself into a frenzy with worry!'

This was much more to Nona's taste. She brightened. 'Oh, yes! You may rely on us, Setty.' She sped towards Louisa's chair and pulled another up in which to sit by her.

Octavia watched Louisa glance up and blink at Nona's bright smile, and her hand tightened on Septimus's arm as he began to move.

'Wait, Setty! Poor Louisa looks quite wretched. Are you sure you should leave her?'

Septimus eyed her suspiciously. 'I must. But not for long, I hope.' He added a trifle acidly, as his sister gave him a sidelong glance, 'Don't jump to ridiculous conclusions, Tavey! I am still a *Berowne*.'

Quarto and Decimus, bowling along in the elder brother's phaeton, with two fresh horses harnessed, made excellent time. Several miles flashed by without a sign of a coach. But Decimus, labouring under a weight of dread, could not prevent himself from anxiously scrutinising every vehicle and every chance wayfarer that they passed.

His eyes roved a lumbering covered wagon taking goods to market. He leaned to inspect two women with ducks under their arms. There were three lone horsemen, interspersed with a ragged urchin at the heels of a vagabond, and a yokel in homespuns with a straw in his mouth. The drayman hauling a cart of barrels did not escape his eager glance, nor a solitary country parson in a gig. Then it swept over the farmer and his family forking hay in a field, and a bedraggled female with a muddy dress and hair falling down her back, a squashed hat in her hand.

'Quarto, stop!' he cried out. 'For the lord's sake, stop! *That was Millie.*'

CHAPTER ELEVEN

MILLIE sat within the circle of her guardian's protective arm, relating her story to all the Berownes around them. Her adventure had concluded when her captor had suddenly halted the horses, opened the door, and pushed her out of the carriage, so that she had stumbled and fallen on to the muddy verge.

'At first I was frightened,' she told her attentive auditors, making Decimus, hovering a foot or so away, clench his hands and scowl blackly, 'for besides not knowing where I was, the place seemed quite a wilderness. But then, when it came to me that I was *free*, I was so thankful that I did not *care* any more.'

Decimus was heard to mutter under his breath, but Nona, in a chair opposite, piped up, 'How *brave* you were, Millie!'

Beside her Octavia asked, 'But what in the world could you *do* in such a sorry situation?'

Millie smiled. 'Walk, what else? I knew in which direction we had been travelling, so I turned around and began the other way.'

'Very sensible,' approved Louisa, giving her a hug.

Millie groped for her hand, looking into her face with all the old admiration. For this dreadful occurrence had wiped out all misunderstanding between them.

'I asked myself what *you* would do, Louisa, that is all.'

'You would not have done had you seen me an hour since, Millie, darling,' Louisa said ruefully. 'I was quite *useless* with dread. You may thank Septimus for your deliverance——' with a grateful glance cast at the poet, who was standing by the fireplace, leaning one arm along the mantel '—for all my fine common-sense had deserted me, and he was the only one of us who could think what to do.'

'Don't be ridiculous, Louisa,' Septimus said, but his eyes twinkled. 'If *you* had not dragged me out to rush off to Gretna Green——'

'And if *Dolly* had not got it all wrong,' Octavia put in.

'Dolly?' ejaculated Quarto. 'She is more bird-witted than the two of you put together.'

'How *dare* you?' gasped Nona.

'Yes, that is *most* unfair,' Octavia averred. '*You* are worse than we are!'

'For my part, I am thanking God for Dolly's vagueness,' Decimus broke in. 'Without it, I should not have thought of coming here. *None* of us would have, and I dread to think of what might have happened to Millie if we had not found her when we did.'

'Ah, there you are, Millie,' the poet said triumphantly. 'You owe it all to Dolly!'

Everyone burst out laughing, with the exception of Sexta, who was still sitting in an isolated corner, an empty cup in her hand, darting fearful glances from one brother to another. For the feeling against Quintus was unanimous among the rest of the assembled Berownes, and certain threatening remarks had filled her with apprehension. Of them all, she most feared the poet's vengeance, but she was a little comforted to see that his demeanour was as calm and pleasant as usual.

She could not have guessed — as indeed none of his siblings could — that a white heat of rage was smouldering below the placid surface. This, however, was not the moment to release it. He called the meeting to order.

'Come, my babes. It is time we all returned to town. I am sure Millie would be glad of a period of quiet, so you may take Sexta in the family coach, Tavey and Nonie.' The girls rose, donning cloak and mantle, and the poet looked at his young brother. 'And you, Dess, had better accompany them, for your horse must rest here overnight. I will go with Quarto, and Louisa and Millie can be ——'

'No, poet.' Louisa released her hold about Millie's shoulders and rose, smiling at Decimus. 'I think Millie had far rather enjoy *your* company, Dess. Nona and Octavia may come with me. I dare say Sexta will prove an adequate chaperon.'

Millie's mouth fell open and she stared at her guardian. But Decimus glanced first at his inamorata, and then back to Louisa, colouring vividly.

'Th-thank you!' he stammered. In an instant he had seized Millie's hand, leading her from the room in haste, as if he feared this heaven-sent opportunity might be snatched away from him.

'Tavey!' Septimus urged quickly. 'Go with Nonie and get Sexta into that coach!'

His two sisters, too stunned for speech by Louisa's extraordinary change of face, grabbed their elder sister and, ignoring her instant whine of complaint, dragged her out of the room.

Quarto was draining a flagon of ale. He finished it and looked about. 'Are we off? Come on, then, if you're in my phaeton.'

Louisa had started for the door, her pelisse in her hands, but found her way blocked by the poet, who looked at his brother. 'Go on, Quarto. I will be out in a moment.'

Quarto glanced from him to Louisa's face, which was rather grave as she, in turn, watched Septimus. He shrugged and went through the door Septimus was holding open. The poet shut it behind him, and turned a heavy frown on the lady.

'What in God's name are you doing, Louisa?'

'Don't scold!' she begged. 'I am not going to renege on what I have started.'

'I am not afraid of that. But have you considered how rash this is? Apart from the obvious disadvantages, do you know what you are letting yourself in for?'

Louisa's eyes danced. 'I rather suspect I am about to take on the role of surrogate mother. Not to *you*, of course.'

'Heaven forbid!' He eyed her. 'You know Dess has no money?'

'I shall have to make them an allowance,' Louisa said, shrugging. 'Though Millie's portion is not contemptible.'

'Don't try to pull the wool over *my* eyes,' Septimus warned. 'Her portion is as considerable as you choose to make it.'

'Well, yes. But I am not a fool in business, Septimus. I have learned my lessons well.'

His eye gleamed, and he took her pelisse out of her hands and shook it out. 'You are a fool in love, though, I think.'

Louisa opened her eyes at him. 'How do you know? I told you I have never been in love.'

'There is more than one kind of love, ninnyhammer! I am speaking of Millie,' he said, slipping the pelisse about her shoulders. He cocked an eyebrow. 'And just possibly Nonie and Tavey. Am I right?'

Louisa laughed a trifle self-consciously as she grasped the edges of the cloak. 'I *have* grown fond of them both, poor things. They stand in crying need of guidance, you know — which they will not get from their husbands.'

'Nor from Dolly,' he agreed drily. 'So you will manage them into respectability. And Dess, of course, together with his bride. What of the rest of us?'

Louisa sighed. 'Well, there is not much I can do about Quintus.'

'Him you may leave to me!' Septimus said in a hard voice.

'What do you intend, poet? More "honourable" feats?'

'Never mind. That is my business,' he said harshly. Then he grinned at the suspicion in her eyes. 'You will not manage *me*, Loulou, so don't even try! And I don't hold out much expectation for Quarto, either. He will undoubtedly batten on you, but you can deal with that.'

'Yes, I can. But I have to tell you, I *cannot* promise

anything for Sexta,' Louisa said seriously. 'She really
is a hopeless case, I am afraid.'

'Good God, Loulou, don't bay for the moon! Fifty
per cent is a pretty good average.'

Louisa laughed. 'Three out of six, you mean? I
suppose it is.'

That gleam entered his eye. Softly he asked, 'And
the seventh?'

Louisa's large eyes glowed all at once and she put
out her hands to him. 'The seventh, poet, is my
dearest *friend*.'

Septimus took her hands and, folding them within
his own, held them high against his chest. His eyes
seemed to search hers for a moment or two. Then he
smiled, lifted the hands to his lips and kissed each in
turn, and then released them.

'I'm glad of that, at all events,' he said lightly. 'You
are likely to need one when your Aunt Pyrland gets
wind of this!'

'Louisa you *cannot* allow it!' exclaimed the matron in
great distress.

'Well, I am allowing it, Aunt Hebe,' Louisa said
flatly.

'But to give your ward in marriage to the worst
possible *parti*!'

'I am giving her to the man she loves, and who, in
turn, loves her.'

Lady Pyrland gazed at her in a desperate way for a
moment. Then, as if the sight of that determined
countenance was unbearable, she brought up her fan
and flicked it once or twice, turning away to pace
about the little parlour.

Louisa watched her in silence from her position by the desk. Since her aunt's arrival had followed hard on the heels of her own, there had been no time to speak to Millie. Instead she had left it to Nona and Octavia — for Decimus, fearful of outstaying his welcome and alienating this new and accommodating Lady Louisa, had departed after depositing his love on her doorstep — to see that she changed her dress, and had herself brought her aunt in here with the intention of enlisting her support, before actually informing her ward that she might marry the man of her choice.

As if she read her thought, Lady Pyrland halted behind the sofa and looked at her. 'You have given your permission, then?'

'No, but I intend to,' Louisa said calmly.

With a rustle of petticoats her aunt came quickly around the sofa and urgently grasped her wrist. 'Then let me beg of you to consider well before you do so!'

'I have made up my mind, Aunt Hebe,' Louisa said apologetically. 'I know it will not be easy, but with your help ——'

'*My* help?' repeated the matron, releasing her wrist and drawing herself up. 'I will have no hand in assisting Millicent to an alliance with a pauper, who is not only a younger son several times over, but whose family connection renders him totally ineligible!'

'And I,' returned Louisa with a flash of anger in her eyes, 'will have no hand in making Millie miserable for the rest of her life.'

'As she will be if she marries Decimus Berowne!' riposted Lady Pyrland swiftly.

There was a silence as they eyed each other in mutual defiance. Then Louisa broke into a chuckle.

'This is quite absurd, Aunt! Come, may we not discuss this sensibly?'

'I would do so, if you were prepared to be sensible.'

'But to be fighting in this way over *Millie*. Had I left her at home, she would probably not have married at all. Are we not being rather too ambitious for her?'

Lady Pyrland looked struck. She shifted her shoulders, and moved away to the fireplace. 'Yes, that is all very well. She may not mind it, but what of us?'

Louisa sat down by the desk. 'Ah, yes. The Berowne connection.' She glanced in a speculative way at her aunt. 'You know, Aunt Hebe, it strikes me that between us, did we put our minds to it, you and I might do something about the Berownes.'

The gimlet eyes were turned on her. 'I? Do something for the *Berownes*? Have you taken leave of your senses?'

Louisa felt her temper rising, but she knew that would not help. With forced calm she said pleasantly, 'I was thinking more of the younger ones. Were we, dear Aunt Hebe, to suggest — quite quietly and confidentially, you know, so as to spread the word more rapidly — that they need not all be tarred with the same brush, that some of them might just be reclaimable, don't you think that perhaps —— ?'

'Don't try me too far, Louisa!' interrupted Lady Pyrland. 'You are attempting to inveigle me into spreading my patronage over those wretched girls,

and their idiotic brothers, just so that your precious
Millie may marry into the dratted family.'

'Well, yes, I am,' confessed Louisa with a twinkle.
'You could do it, Aunt Hebe, if you chose to.'

'There's the rub,' said the matron. 'I may *not*
choose.'

Thankful for the 'may', Louisa added persuasively,
'Think of it as a challenge. What a triumph to bring
into respectability the hopeless offspring of Dolly
Berowne!' She read a retort in her aunt's eye, and
went on quickly, 'And I promise you I will see to it
that they deserve it. If they fail, you may blame me.'

'A lot of good that would do when I had already
taken them up,' said Lady Pyrland acidly.

Louisa got up out of her chair and came to stand
before the lady, her large eyes pleading. 'Pray, *pray*
help me, Aunt Hebe. I could never do it without your
support, and we are family.'

Lady Pyrland was quite aware that she was being
manipulated, for her niece had touched on precisely
those matters that moved her. Family was important
to her. And she did pique herself on the extent of her
influence in Society. She felt herself weakening.

'I declare, I am almost sorry for that wretched
Shittlehope!' she said crossly. 'I dare say he could not
call his life his own.'

Louisa giggled. 'Poor Mr Shittlehope. He did try to
withstand me.'

'Fighting a losing battle. Like me,' said her aunt
bitterly. 'Very well, do as you wish. Only don't count
on me to find a husband for that hysterical Sexta!'

Millie—respectably decent in a clean dimity
gown—when informed of Lady Pyrland's conversion

was moved to fling her arms about that lady's neck in an ecstatic embrace. Called to order, she turned shining eyes on her guardian instead.

'May I marry him indeed, Louisa?'

'Indeed you may,' smiled her preceptress.

Octavia and Nona let out excited whoops as Millie hugged her, but subsided on catching Lady Pyrland's eagle stare. They looked at each other and then at Louisa.

'May we go and fetch Dess?' Octavia asked.

'Oh, *do* let us,' begged Nona. 'I can't *wait* to see his face when we tell him.'

Permission was granted, and the girls set off on foot, for the April afternoon was still fine, with the result that Lady Pyrland had barely left the house when Decimus Berowne came flying back to claim his betrothed.

'Oh, Millie!' he uttered, devouring her face with his eyes as he held her clasped in his arms. For Millie's guardian had, most reprehensibly, given in to sentiment and left them alone together. 'I never thought this day would come. I love you so much!'

'And I love you, dearest Dess,' Millie told him, mistily smiling. 'I am so happy!'

'But what made Lady Louisa change her mind?' he asked some time later, when the first flush of joy had abated a little and several vows and kisses had been exchanged.

'I can't *think*,' Millie said blankly, holding tightly to his hand as they sat close together on a sofa. 'Unless it was the dreadful happening today.'

Decimus drew her closer as she shuddered. 'Don't think about it, sweetheart.'

'But I must, Dess,' she protested. 'For how are we ever to know if it *was* your brother? I never saw him, you see.'

'But you saw the man who brought you to Highgate, where Quint was waiting at the Black Dog,' Decimus said firmly. 'And I am quite certain you will recognise the female who tricked you.'

'Oh, yes, certainly,' Millie agreed. 'Only how are we to find her?'

'We *have* found her.'

'What? But ——'

'We have found her, and we know it was Quint,' he said, and his voice went hard. 'He has not yet returned, but we are all of us going tomorrow to his lodging to bring him to book.'

Quintus Berowne was just finishing breakfast when his brothers burst in upon him. He glanced up as the door to his parlour jerked open, a cup of coffee halfway to his lips.

'Good morning, Brother,' Septimus said calmly, walking into the room.

'What the devil do you want at this hour?' demanded Quintus sourly.

He sat still, watching the entrance of Decimus, who was literally trembling with anger, and behind him Quarto, who eyed him bodingly as he shut the door after them.

'Well, well, a family deputation,' Quintus drawled as he put the cup to his lips. But wary eyes looked over it as he sipped, travelling to the swords buckled about each of the three waists.

'Where were you yesterday, Quint?' Decimus burst out, coming up to the table.

'Steady, infant!' warned Quarto, lounging against the door. 'We agreed to let Setty handle this.'

Quintus glanced across at the poet, who pulled up a chair to the table, turned it about, and slung a leg across to sit so that he could lean his arms along the back of it.

'Well, Quint?' he said softly. 'Where were you?'

Quintus put down his cup. 'Out of town, if it is any business of yours.'

'*Where* out of town, dash it?' snapped Quarto impatiently, forgetful of his own advice.

'Devil take you, mind your business!' growled his brother.

'Oh, but we are, Quint,' Septimus said, his eyes narrowing. They never left his brother's face. 'We are all minding our business. We are all here, in fact, on behalf of our separate businesses.' He glanced briefly at his eldest brother. 'Except perhaps Quarto. He is merely here in support.'

'Hey!' called Quarto. 'It's my business too, I'll have you know. Wasted a whole day on the dashed affair!'

'So you did, Quarto.' Septimus looked back at Quintus. 'So you see, Quint, your business *is* our business.'

Exasperated, Decimus butted in. 'Stop talking in riddles, Setty, for God's sake! This isn't a *game*.' He placed his hands on the table and leaned in to his brother. 'Quint, you black-hearted villain, you abducted my betrothed!'

'Oh?' Quintus raised his brows. 'Your betrothal comes as news to me. Who is the lady?'

'Oh, damn you!' uttered Decimus, hitting the table with his fist. 'Stop hedging!'

Septimus reached out and grasped his wrist. 'Enough, babe! Leave this to me.'

'Well, get it over, then!' snapped his young brother, flinging away to glower from across the room. 'I'm not enjoying this, if you are.'

'Patience, babe,' Septimus said reassuringly. Turning back to Quintus, he explained, 'Louisa has consented to the marriage, Quint. Of Millie to Decimus, to make it quite clear to you. But that is not the issue here.'

Quintus watched him, the sneer marked, but he leaned back at his ease. 'What is the issue, milksop?'

Septimus met his eyes. His voice was cold steel. 'That nickname, Brother, I shall presently force down your throat.'

'You may try,' sneered Quintus.

'But first,' Septimus went on, ignoring the interjection, 'you will tell us where you were yesterday.'

'Make me!' Quintus said softly.

'Dash it, Quint, don't be so stubborn!' Quarto roared. 'We *know* where you were. You were on the Great North Road, travelling to Gretna Green.'

Quintus looked from one to the other of them as they waited expectantly for his response. Then a thin smile curved his lips. 'Prove it.'

'Hell and the devil!' Quarto swore, and Decimus started forward, growling, but Septimus held up a hand.

'You choose your tools very ill, Quint,' he said

calmly. His glance went across to the bedchamber door. 'A cold night, Brother? No warming-pan to bed?'

For the first time, Quintus frowned. 'What the devil are you talking of?'

'He's talking about your mistress, you dunderhead!' Quarto snapped.

'She told us she would not stay to suffer retribution,' Decimus put in.

'But you must not blame Lily, Quint,' Septimus said. 'She tried very hard to be loyal to you.'

'Only I remembered she had been an actress,' Quarto said grimly. 'Lily Levant she was when she was on the stage.'

'And when we put it to her that Millie's pregnant lady was not pregnant at all. . .' Decimus added.

'Threatened her with being an accessory and she broke down at once,' Quarto finished. 'Told us everything.'

'Yes,' Decimus agreed. 'She was more concerned with saving the neck of your bully-boy than your own, Quint.'

'Probably found him for you, did she?' Quarto added. 'Been tipping you the double with the fellow, I dare say. At any rate, we can find her and we can find him — if we have to. We know you're our man.'

There was a long pause. Quintus had recovered his poise, but a glitter in his eye told how livid he was at this betrayal by Lily Levant. He said nothing, however, merely eyeing his brothers.

'So you see,' Septimus said at last, rising from his chair, 'you *treacherous* demon, we, your loving brothers, are here to ensure that such conduct does not go unpunished.'

'Are you indeed?' Quintus said silkily, rising also. 'And which of you is going to make the attempt? Or are you all three intent on vengeance?'

'I wanted to kill you, Quint!' Decimus uttered in an overwrought way. 'But Setty has a better idea.'

'Damned sight better!' corroborated Quarto. 'Fond of you, Quint, and I'll miss you. But I'm not willing to be ruined for your sake, my boy. You're a dashed nuisance, and the sooner you go the better.'

'Go?' uttered Quintus, his composure deserting him. 'Go where?'

'To join Tertius in the West Indies,' Septimus told him.

'The devil I will!' snapped Quintus. 'Who the devil are you three to tell me to leave the country? Damn you to hell, the lot of you!'

'I thought you'd say that,' Septimus told him calmly. 'Then there is nothing for it but to persuade you.'

With a scrape of steel he drew his sword and, lunging, pointed it towards his brother's heart. All trace of his easy manner was gone. His brown eyes were like chips of granite, his jaw set, his voice chilling.

'Arm yourself, Brother!'

Quarto leapt forward. 'Hoy! Not here, Setty.'

'Why not here?' Septimus grated. 'It's as good a place as any.'

'Setty, you said you wouldn't fight him!' expostulated Decimus, concerned all at once.

'I said I wouldn't *kill* him,' Septimus corrected 'Though I shall be hard put to it to refrain.'

Quintus had not moved, his eyes riveted to the sword's point. He watched as Septimus pulled back laid the sword on the table, and began to unbuckle the belt.

'What the devil is it to you, this matter?' demanded the culprit suddenly. 'I might fight Dess, if he chooses to name his bread-and-butter Millie as a cause.'

'I'll fight you, Quint. I'm not afraid!' Decimus said at once.

His brother ignored him, his puzzled eyes still on the poet. 'But what in Hades has this matter to do with you?'

Septimus was in the act of removing his dark blue frock-coat. He paused with it in his hands, and a flash of sudden fire lit his eyes as they flicked across at Quintus. His voice was like a whiplash.

'Louisa! Your plot was made against Louisa. That is what it has to do with me.'

'Louisa!' echoed his brother, and both Quarto and Decimus turned to stare at the poet. 'What the devil is Louisa to you?'

'*Everything*,' answered the poet.

A hush fell. Quarto and Decimus looked at each other in astonishment, their eyes almost popping out of their heads. Then Quintus began to laugh jeeringly.

'You cannot be serious. You and the Shittlehope woman?'

The point of the poet's sword was suddenly at his throat. 'Take up your weapon, Brother!' ordered Septimus softly. 'You enquired of me my business here, did you not? My business is to see Louisa safe from you. If that means that you must go into exile, then into exile you will go!'

Quintus glared at him in defiance over the steel point that still just touched his neck. He began to remove his coat. 'Try if you can force me.'

Septimus lowered the sword, and set it down so that he could take off his boots.

'You can't fight in here!' Quarto said again.

'We can,' Septimus contradicted. 'There are two of you to see fair play.' He glanced at his young brother. 'Clear a space for us, Dess. You had better act for me. Quarto may serve Quint.'

'I think you're mad!' Quarto told him, but he went to Quintus's side and received his clothing, while Decimus pushed aside the table and chairs, leaving the centre of the room clear.

In a few moments the two brothers faced each other, in shirt-sleeves and stockinged feet, two yards of cold steel between them. After the briefest of salutes, their swords clashed together.

Louisa and her ward, who was going about in a haze of happiness, were just completing their morning meal when Millie's prospective sisters-in-law arrived.

'We told Dolly that you and Dess were to be married,' Octavia informed her, after exchanging a warm embrace.

'It was the *drollest* thing,' Nona exclaimed, sitting down next to Millie.

'Why, what did she say?' asked the latter, absently picking up her discarded bread and butter and putting it down again.

'She would keep asking who you *were*,' Octavia put in as she moved to a chair nearer Louisa on the other side of the table.

'Yes, every other sentence she said, "Who *is* this Millie?"' Nona disclosed.

'And, "I thought you said Dess was a baby",' quoted Octavia, mimicking Dolly's distracted manner to perfection. '"How can he be getting married?" So of course we had to explain everything ten times over.'

'We did not even *begin* to try and tell her what really happened yesterday.'

'No, for the first thing she asked was how many of us were dead!'

Louisa joined in their laughter, but added, 'I trust you reassured her?'

'Oh, yes,' Octavia said blithely, 'but she only wanted to know so that she might order the necessary black gowns from her dressmaker.'

'But how callous!' exclaimed Millie. 'And Dess is her youngest son!'

'Never mind, Millie,' Louisa said, smiling across the table. 'From now on Dess has you to worry over him.'

Millie's face clouded. 'Well, I do *hope* there is no need to worry. He told me not to.'

'Whatever do you mean, Millie?' demanded Octavia, frowning.

'There is no danger *now*,' Nona put in.

'Yes, but I am not at all sure about that,' Millie uttered, concern in her eyes. 'After all, your brother Quintus did not balk at kidnapping.'

'Millie, what is the matter?' demanded Louisa, a

frisson of apprehension running through her as she recalled Septimus saying harshly that she might leave Quint to him.

Her ward turned to her. 'Dess told me they were all three going this morning to bring Quintus to book.'

'*What*?' screeched Octavia.

'Oh, *no*,' Nona groaned. 'Oh, Tavey, they will get in a fight, I *know* they will.'

'Undoubtedly,' agreed her sister, jumping up from the table.

'Oh, for pity's sake!' cried Louisa disgustedly.

But Millie rose too, her eyes wide with fear. 'Not Dess. Oh, pray, not *Dess*.'

Nona was up now, seizing her hands. 'Oh, dear, Millie, he was so *furious* with Quint. And he is *no* match for him.'

'Be quiet, Nonie!' snapped Octavia, pushing in as Millie paled. 'You need not fear, Millie. Neither Quarto nor Setty will allow Dess to fight Quint.'

'I should think not!' Louisa put in furiously. 'I should hope none of them will be so foolish as to get in a fight.'

Octavia turned to her. 'But they *will*, Louisa. You know what gentlemen are. And our brothers are *particularly* foolish.'

'Indeed, I begin to agree with you,' Louisa said, throwing down her napkin as she got up out of her chair.

'But Tavey, you don't think *Quarto* will fight Quint?' Nona argued. 'Why, they are the best of friends.'

Octavia did not look at her, for her eyes were on

Louisa as she answered. 'No. I think it is Setty who will fight Quint. And you know what *that* means.'

Nona nodded portentously, but Louisa did not notice. She was staring at Octavia, the colour draining from her face. There was a buzzing in her ears and a heave of nausea in her stomach. Instinctively she gripped the edge of the table to stop herself from falling.

'Setty will fight Quint?' she repeated faintly, as if the words were meaningless.

'I am *sure* of it, Louisa,' Octavia told her, a world of understanding and sympathy in her pansy eyes. 'There was that in his face yesterday, and — and Quint intended harm to *you*, remember?' Mentally she willed Louisa to understand, for she dared not say it outright, not after Setty's warning.

Louisa was past understanding. A horrifying mental image imprinted itself on her dizzying brain. Of the poet, deathly pale, eyes closed, one slender hand at the hole in his breast, welling blood.

She cried out then, and, lifting shaking fingers to her lips, she pressed back the threatening sickness, shutting her eyes tight as if she might eradicate the vision.

All three young ladies were gazing at her, Nona and Millie amazed and shocked. Only Octavia, in an instant recognising the signs, came quickly forward to grasp Louisa by the shoulders.

'Don't, Louisa! He is a very fine swordsman, I promise you.' She shook Louisa gently, saying again, 'I *promise* you. It is rather Quint who will be in danger.'

Louisa opened her eyes. Shuddering, she dragged

herself together a little. But her voice was rough with pain, the large eyes haggard. 'Ring the bell, Tavey. . . My carriage.'

Octavia looked about, but it was Millie who ran for the bell-pull.

'Are you ill, Louisa?' asked Nona anxiously, entirely missing the inference which was right before her eyes.

'Yes, we will *all* go!' Octavia decided, not even hearing her sister's question. 'Nonie, go with Millie and fetch cloaks. Louisa's, too, Millie.'

The two younger ladies hurried from the room, and Octavia turned back anxious eyes to Louisa, who had sunk down on to her chair again.

'I am all right now, Octavia,' Louisa said, managing a smile.

'Are you sure? I have some sal volatile in my pocket,' offered Octavia, reaching beneath her overgown.

'Burnt feathers and smelling-salts?' Louisa asked with a shaky little laugh. 'No, I thank you. I am not like Dolly.'

Octavia giggled. 'Very unlike.'

But Louisa's lip was trembling and she felt cold and shivery inside in spite of the warmth of the day. A weight of dread seemed to hang in the air above her, as if in preparation to descend into the hollow space that appeared to have opened in her chest. Her breath came with difficulty and her heart shrivelled within her as she tried to banish the thought of Septimus Berowne. . .dead.

But the poet was very much alive, lunging and thrusting and parrying with ease as he fought his brother in the confines of this small upstairs parlour of a lodging house in Clarges Street. The light of battle in his brown eyes, he seemed to thrill to the hiss of steel on steel, to take pleasure in the dextrous twists of his arm, the fleet and springy footwork that seemed to make his lithe body take wing as he advanced to the attack and sprang back again out of range.

Quintus, by contrast, heavier on his feet, and aware of his brother's superiority, took his time, weighing carefully each of the poet's moves that he might parry successfully and deflect the point as it threatened him time and again.

Watching from the sidelines, Quarto lost sight of the real point of this bout, as he saw with admiration Septimus open a line with a feint of the direct thrust. Quintus met it in quarte, then, almost quicker than the eye could see, the poet's point flashed in a circular movement, as if to aim high again. But as Quintus brought his blade up to meet the threat in tierce, Septimus deceived, lunging in the low line to aim for the stomach.

A gasp of fright left the lips of Decimus, looking on with his heart in his mouth, and Quarto made a quick movement of the hand as if he might intervene.

With lightning presence of mind, Quintus leapt back, swinging his arm up so that the poet's sword met his foible and glanced along the blade to the forte, hitting the guard about his hand.

There was a double sigh of relief from the onlookers as Septimus pulled back, still on guard, his eyes on his brother, who had stumbled as he saved himself. Sweat dotted his brow and his breath came short and fast.

In a grating voice Septimus asked, 'Are you ready to leave us, Quint?'

The familiar sneer contorted his brother's features, and in a panting snarl he responded, 'Damn — you — to hell, *no*!'

Decimus almost cried a warning as Quintus flew at the poet with a direct thrust in sixte. But Septimus caught it counter-quarte, riposted, deceived the parry again, and once more slipped under, lunging from below.

In the nick of time Quintus caught the blade, but only just. He was fighting for breath and knew himself beaten, but sheer stubborn fury drove him on. Steel clashed again, and again Quintus was driven back.

'He is near spent,' Quarto murmured to his youngest brother.

'Setty won't stop,' Decimus whispered back. 'Not until he yields.'

'Yes, but the damned fool won't yield!'

They watched the thrust and parry with increasing misgiving. Decimus followed the wicked hiss of the blades, the driving back and forth, with fast-beating heart. But Quarto, impressed by the younger brother's prowess, began to lose himself in the beauty of the fight.

Quint was a good swordsman, but Setty far surpassed him. Dash it, the damned poet was welded to the foil, like an extension of his arm! The weapon seemed peculiarly his own. Setty would no doubt say it appealed to his artistic soul. Who was to say he wasn't right, eh? Rarely did a man see such dash and brilliance. And there was no deadly purpose in his swordplay, nothing to acknowledge this was simply a solution to a dispute. The man was enjoying the art of it; anyone could see that!

But all of a sudden, as the blades met and disengaged again, a sudden scream shattered the heavy, concentrated atmosphere. Quarto and Decimus turned instantly to the doorway. Sexta stood there, her eyes wild.

By the greatest misfortune, Septimus had his back to the door, so that the piercing sound distracted his attention. In the instant that he glanced behind, his guard wavered.

Quintus seized the opening, feinting in tierce. Recovering, the poet just managed to take his blade for the envelopment.

Sexta moved forward as the point of Quintus's sword slid over the poet's in a lunging thrust. Septimus brought up his wrist, deflecting the blade.

A shout of warning came too late, for at the same instant Sexta ran in on the fight, and received the point of her favourite brother's sword in her bosom.

CHAPTER TWELVE

TIME froze. As one in a dream, Sexta saw the sword wrenched back, took in the horror on her brother's face, looked down at herself, and lifted a wavering hand to the red stain appearing on her grey gown, a little above her heart. Her glance came up again.

'It w-was not your f-fault, Quint,' she said unsteadily. Then she swayed, her eyes closing.

Decimus, like his brother Quarto a helpless spectator of this appalling tragedy, shot forward and seized his sister as she fell.

'You villain!' roared Quarto, turning an ugly glare on his brother Quintus.

Septimus, who had scarcely had time in which to take in the extraordinary turn of events, instantly threw aside his own weapon and began to hunt for cloth.

'Fetch the nearest surgeon, Quarto!' he ordered and, going to the table that had been pushed to one side, he swept the remains of his brother's breakfast on to the floor in a crashing welter of broken crockery, and seized the cloth that covered it.

Quarto hurried out, bellowing for the porter downstairs, as the poet began to rip the cloth from end to end, tearing it into strips.

Decimus, meanwhile, making a pad of his handkerchief, was pressing it to the wound. Urgently, he

265

called, 'Help me, Quint!' as he struggled to keep his
sister's slack body from sliding to the floor.

Quintus, whose dawning horror had by now trans-
muted into the deepest remorse, dropped his sword
and dashed to his junior's aid. It was he who lifted the
woman into his arms and carried her through to the
adjoining bedchamber.

'Keep that pad tight!' he instructed his young
brother, who was hurrying beside him, still trying to
staunch the blood.

Laying his burden gently on the bed, Quintus
kneeled beside her, pushing Decimus out of the way.
He ripped open the front of his sister's gown and laid
bare the wound. It was more a gash than a deep,
thrusting hole, and he heaved a sigh of relief.

'It is in the shoulder, thank God!' he uttered.

'Then it has touched no vital part?' Decimus asked
anxiously. 'Heaven be praised!'

'Amen!' Quintus uttered grimly. 'It is not deep
enough to be really serious.' He glanced up at his
brother, and took the blood-soaked handerchief out
of his hand, snapping, 'Get those bandages from
Setty!'

Already the bleeding had lessened, but he pressed
the pad to the injury nevertheless, uttering heavily,
'Sexta, I did not mean it.'

'She knows that,' said Septimus from behind him.
'Only Sexta would be so idiotic as to run in on a fight!
Here, take this.'

Quintus received the fresh wedge of cloth and
threw away the bloody handkerchief, and, while he
held it to the wound, Septimus, with the help of his

youngest brother, bound it tightly about Sexta's shoulder and chest with his improvised bandages.

'Thank God you deflected his sword, Setty!' Decimus said as they worked. 'If it had been with the full force of his arm —— '

'Then it would have gone into *him*, and not Sexta.' Quintus broke in angrily.

'Well, don't sound as if you wish it had!' Decimus growled. 'This is all your fault, Quint!'

'I do wish it had,' returned his brother, glaring at the poet. 'And I don't need you to tell me it is my fault.'

Septimus glanced up from tying his bandage. 'This makes no difference, you know. If necessary, we will fight again. And again, and again.'

'Until I consent to go?' Quintus asked, the old jeer back in his voice.

'Until you *do* go,' Septimus corrected.

'What, do you mean to drive me up the gangplank at the sword's point?' demanded his brother with a flash of humour.

'Hoy!' said Quarto from behind them. As they all three looked round, he grinned. 'Just had a brainwave. He can take Sexta with him, and that will get her off our hands as well!'

Quintus glanced up at him. 'Where's the damned sawbones, you idiot? What the devil do you imagine Sexta would do in the West Indies?'

'Keep house?' Quarto suggested, making the others laugh. 'Surgeon's on his way, by the by.'

'Good,' Septimus said, sitting back and surveying his handiwork. 'That should suffice.'

'She's coming round!' Decimus warned, his eyes on Sexta's pale features.

Quintus reached for her hands and held them, gazing into her face. 'Sexta! Sexta, can you hear me?'

Her lashes fluttered and she opened her eyes, looking full into his face. 'Quint?'

'Don't try to move,' he instructed. Without glancing at his brothers, he added, 'Fetch brandy, one of you! In the cupboard back there.'

Decimus dashed to do his bidding, and Quintus leaned to kiss his sister's brow. 'God help me, my sweet, I *hate* myself for this.'

'Oh, no, Quint,' uttered Sexta, a flutter in her faint voice. 'You must not say that! I was—I was so *afraid* for you, and when I saw it was Setty. . .' She broke off, tears starting to her eyes.

'Don't weep!' begged her brother, kissing her fingers. 'No harm came to me, though it *should* have done.'

Her fingers clung to his. 'Quint, *pray*. I would not care if you had killed me, only that it had saved *you*.'

'Oh, God!' groaned the man, writhing under his conscience the more. But Sexta's fingers came wavering up to touch his cheek, and he was moved to bid her lie still again.

Thereafter their conversation was conducted in too low a tone to be overheard either by Septimus or Quarto, standing back and watching their brother and sister crooning at one another.

'You know, Quarto,' Septimus murmured, 'that isn't a bad idea.'

'It's a capital idea! Always thought we ought to get

rid of the wench. We won't marry her off. Who'd have her? Better send her with Quint.'

'If she will go,' his brother said drily.

'She'll go,' Quarto said confidently. 'Go anywhere with *him*. God knows why! Mad as hatters, both of them.'

'But will Quint have her?'

'He will if we get the pair of them off at once,' Quarto said, lowering his voice confidentially. 'Look at him. Full of remorse, don't you see? If we give them no time to get in a quarrel, they'll go together all right and tight.'

'We can but try.' He looked at Quarto. 'Do you think he *will* go now, or will I be obliged to fight him again?'

'Don't think so,' Quarto said with some regret. 'Dashed good fight, Brother! No, Quint knows he's beaten. He'll not resist any longer. Not now he's speared his own sister!'

The surgeon arrived in good order, and the brothers, with the exception of Quintus, who would not leave Sexta, retired to the parlour.

Thus it was that when the Brook Street party arrived a short time later they found only Decimus and Quarto quaffing ale. Also Septimus Berowne, poet, still half dressed, who was sitting on the table, one booted leg swinging, the other clad only in a stocking as it rested on a chair on which reposed the other boot. On his raised knee was his pocketbook, in which he was scribbling away with his pencil.

'What has happened? Is it all over?' demanded Octavia, dashing into the parlour through the still open door and coming to a jarring halt.

'Where is Quintus?' demanded Nona, close behind her.

'Dess! Oh, Dess!' cried Millie, rushing straight to her betrothed to be gathered into his willing embrace.

In the doorway Louisa halted, her glance sweeping the scene. Finding the poet, it became riveted, while wave after wave of quite dizzying relief swept through her so that she was obliged to grasp the door-jambs for support.

Septimus did not look up, or appear to notice the new arrivals. But Quarto hailed the girls at once.

'You're too late. Missed all the excitement. Mind you, I could have done with missing it myself!'

'Why, what has *happened*?' squeaked Nona.

'Don't screech like that!' complained her brother. 'As bad as Sexta.'

'Is *she* here?' Octavia asked.

'I should say she is! To some purpose.' He jerked a thumb in the direction of the bedchamber. 'She's in there with Quint.'

'In his *bedchamber*,' gasped Nona.

'Don't be silly, Nonie!' uttered Octavia crossly. 'You don't suppose she is in his bed, do you?'

'Well, she is,' Decimus said in rueful tones, suddenly entering the lists. With his arm still about Millie, he explained, 'She ran in on the fight. The doctor is with her. Quint, too.'

'Oh, *no*!' Nona exclaimed. 'Oh, poor Sexta!'

'Is she much hurt?' demanded Octavia anxiously.

'Shoulder,' Quarto said succinctly. 'Won't die of it.'

Nona and Octavia, closely followed by Millie, rushed towards the bedchamber, twittering with anxiety, and disappeared through the door. Decimus followed, but remained just outside, watching the two girls begin to fuss over their elder, with Millie hovering about them.

From the main parlour doorway a clear voice spoke. 'Septimus Berowne!'

'Hush!' uttered the poet, without looking up. He threw up a hand with finger warningly lifted. 'My muse, Loulou!'

Louisa marched into the room and came to stand before him, the large eyes blazing. 'To *hell* with your muse, poet!'

Septimus dropped his pencil, and his startled eyes came up. '*Louisa*!'

'Septimus Berowne,' she said bodingly, her breast rising and falling with emotion under the tippet she wore over her gown, 'what have you been doing in this room?'

His eyes gleamed. Blandly he answered, 'Fighting, Louisa.' He added in a kind voice, 'With swords.'

'Septimus, I am in no mood for your quizzing!' raged Louisa. 'If you have been dabbling with "honour" —— '

'But it was all on your behalf,' protested the poet. He flung a hand to his brow. 'Ah, me! All that energy wasted!'

'You are wasting energy *now*,' Louisa pointed out. Fury had been an inevitable reaction, but, confronted with the poet's usual manner, it was deserting her fast. Her voice was unsteady. 'I w-wish you would not tease me, Septimus. If you knew how my imagination has been playing upon me!'

'Aha, at last! I *knew* there was romance in your soul. It needed only my influence to bring it out.'

'Oh, stop!' begged Louisa, but a choke of laughter escaped her. Still her fine eyes menaced him. 'I have come here half expecting to be presented with your lifeless body!'

The poet twinkled at her. 'But my body is not lifeless, Louisa.' He reached out his hand and rested the back of it against her cheek. 'See? Warm blood runs yet in my veins.'

She seized the hand and grasped it tightly. Her voice husky all of a sudden, she said, 'Do you realise the *anguish* I have suffered, fearing you dead?'

The poet stilled, his glance catching and holding her own. A slow smile spread across his face, and a warm glow lit the brown eyes. His hand curled about hers.

'Loulou,' he uttered softly, 'you have just made me the happiest man on this earth!'

She stared at him blankly. 'How so?'

Septimus squeezed her hand and grinned. 'That you shall see. Come! These lines can wait.'

Louisa shook a puzzled head. 'What lines?'

'Louisa, for shame!' he said in mock-reproof. 'I have been composing a verse, you must know, on the devotion of brother and sister.' He waved a hand towards the bedchamber. 'Sexta and Quint.'

'Devotion?' echoed Louisa, for the first time casting a glance in that direction.

It was Quarto who answered. He had been standing to one side, a silent and appreciative spectator of the little comedy being enacted before him. But it was scarcely a puzzle now that he had heard the poet's views on Lady Louisa Shittlehope. And seen, what was more, his violent revenge!

'Sickening, it is,' he said jovially. 'Sighing and ogling each other as if they were lovers! Won't last, of course. Once she's back on her feet, they'll be at it again, hammer and tongs.'

Louisa had scarcely taken in the story of the end to the duel, for her whole mind had been concentrated on the magic of finding Septimus alive. Now she demanded to hear it, and Decimus, coming away from the door, assisted his brother Quarto in the telling.

'And they will really go to the West Indies?' she asked at the end.

'Setty says so,' Decimus told her.

'And I'm sure of it,' Quarto agreed. 'That is, if we act fast. Eh, Setty?'

Septimus had been pulling on his other boot, but he glanced up at this. 'Oh, certainly. Not that I care much one way or the other.'

'*What*?' uttered Quarto, staggered.

'Setty, have you gone completely mad?' demanded Decimus.

He grinned. 'In the last five minutes, yes!'

Louisa was making for the door to the bedchamber. Leaping off the table, Septimus went after her and seized her arm. 'No, you don't!'

'But I must go and see if——'

'You must do nothing of the kind,' argued the poet. 'Sexta does not need you.' He grinned. 'But I do, Loulou. Find my coat, will you? It is somewhere about.'

To the astonishment of his two brothers, Louisa

immediately looked about the room as Septimus tugged at his disarranged waistcoat and pulled down his shirt-sleeves. But it was Decimus who located the errant coat, for he had been the one to place it on the top of a cupboard near the door where it had rested ever since the beginning of the fight. Louisa took it from him and went across to hold it for Septimus to put on.

He turned his back and slid his arms into the sleeves, glancing at his brothers as he did so. Smiling to himself at the looks on their faces, he said, 'I am taking Louisa home now.'

'But what about ── ?' began his younger brother.

'There are quite enough of you here to succour our sister in her hour of need.' He held up a hand as Decimus made a move towards the bedchamber. 'No, no, don't call *any* of them. You can take care of your betrothed, Dess. And you may see to the girls, Quarto.'

'That's it!' Quarto said, suddenly grinning. He winked at Septimus. 'Know what you're about, and I wish you better fortune than I had. Yes, yes, get along and settle the matter! We'll manage here.'

Louisa threw him an odd look as she came around to straighten the dark blue frock-coat at the front. 'What in the world ── ?'

Hastily, Septimus interrupted, 'Concentrate, Louisa!'

'Well, but this is perfectly useless,' she said, brushing at his neckcloth. 'I cannot make you respectable. Your cravat is ruined.'

'Never mind my ruined cravat!' said the poet, taking her firmly by the hand. 'As for respectability, that is past praying for. In any event, we have more important matters to talk of.'

'What matters?' she demanded as he led her unresisting towards the door.

Just then Octavia came out of the bedchamber, stopping short as she saw the pair leaving. She opened her mouth to call out, but Quarto's hand touched her shoulder and she looked round, a question in her eyes.

'Keep mum!' he murmured, and laid a finger to the side of his nose, grinning.

Octavia shot a glance at the door, where Louisa had suddenly halted.

'We have forgotten Millie!'

'Have you not been listening, Louisa?' Septimus demanded. 'Millie is coming later with Dess.'

'And you dare to say *I* am managing!' Louisa exclaimed.

'You are,' the poet said.

Behind them, Octavia was beaming as she watched her brother drag Lady Louisa willy-nilly out of the parlour.

'You are quite the most managing female of my acquaintance,' Septimus was saying, hustling her down the stairs, 'and I can see that only the most domineering of fellows will do for you.'

'Don't be absurd! Mr Shittlehope was quite domineering enough, let me tell you, and I —— '

'Managed Mr Shittlehope,' he finished. 'Yes, I know. But Mr Shittlehope, my dear Loulou, has departed this life. You are going to have to learn another tune.'

'Septimus, what in the world are you talking about?' she asked, exasperated.

The poet, however, would not explain himself. The drive in her coach back to Brook Street did not occupy many minutes, and he infuriated Louisa by using them to describe his fight with Quintus in graphic detail. Icily informed that she did not understand one word about this so-called art of fencing, he instead gave her a more exact account of Sexta's wound.

But by the time he had forcibly bullied Louisa all the way up to her little parlour, and they stood face to face alone, his bravado collapsed on him.

'Louisa. . .' he began, and stopped, eyeing the questioning look in her face. 'I want — will you. . .?'

Louisa frowned. 'What is the matter with you?'

She stood, as was her wont, by the fireplace, dressed, as it chanced, in the same bright yellow gown that she had worn that far-off day — as it now seemed to him — when she had come to rescue Lord Wherwell from Quint. They had stood together in this very room and her warmth had knocked him off balance, just as he was now.

He turned away from her, afraid to give in to an overmastering desire to seize her in his arms. For that might jeopardise everything!

At the window by the desk, he stood looking out. 'Louisa, yesterday you spoke of — of friendship between us.'

Louisa did not answer. Some intuitive sense warned her, although its message was not clear. A shaft appeared to slice across her midriff, and her breath caught. Her limbs went weak. She could feel herself trembling, and one hand reached out to grasp the mantelshelf for support. A slow, heavy pumping began in her bosom and she waited, her mind blank.

'Louisa,' began the poet again, turning his head, 'you said — today, just now, at Quint's lodging — you said. . .' Once more he broke off. A self-conscious laugh escaped him. 'Good God, I am as tongue-tied as a schoolboy!'

'What. . .?' Louisa ran her tongue over dry lips and began again. 'What is it you are — you are trying to say?'

Septimus looked at her. 'Trying? You would never believe, would you, that words are my livelihood?'

'Your *livelihood*?' Louisa repeated, startled.

He uttered a short laugh. 'How do you imagine I live? I don't gamble as my brothers do. We none of us have an allowance — there is no money for that.'

'But you cannot possibly live on a poet's income!' gasped Louisa.

'Alas, no,' he agreed. 'One day, perhaps — I *hope*.' He drew a breath, and said with the air of one making a confession, 'Meanwhile, I am a hack writer, Loulou. I earn my crust in Grub Street.'

'I don't understand,' she said, leaving go of the mantel and moving closer as the distressing symptoms in her body faded a little.

Septimus grimaced. 'I wish I had not to explain. But clearly I must.' He looked away. 'I will pen anything, from political pamphlets to lurid tales for the delectation of the masses. Whatever the purveyors of such stuff request of me. I was actually engaged in writing a blood-curdling tale of the hangman's noose when you broke in on me yesterday.'

'The hangman's noose?' echoed Louisa, amazed.

He glanced at her. 'Just so. Extremely vulgar, is it not?'

'I did not say so.'

'Others would.' With a touch of bitterness he went on, 'Because I was born a gentleman — though that cachet brings more custom — I am obliged to ply my trade in the greatest secrecy. Had I been a novelist or a learned scholar, it would be different. And poetry is of course acceptable, and has even won me some little acclaim. But one whiff of the rest, and I may kiss goodbye to Society.'

'Oh, for pity's sake!' exclaimed Louisa. 'That is absurd. Why, I have been married to a tradesman and yet I am accepted.'

The poet smiled slightly. 'You, Louisa, had a marquis for a father. *My* family, as you well know, hovers daily on the brink of ostracism.'

He could not face her then. For it had come home to him how impossible was the thing that had, for a few brief moments of sheer insanity, seemed so easy. Good God, how could he have dared to suppose he might have the temerity to —— ?

His thought was arrested as Louisa began to giggle. Startled, he whipped about to stare at her. 'Louisa!'

The big eyes were dancing madly. 'Oh, Septimus, how can you be so *stupid*?'

The poet came quickly forward, grasping her hands. 'Loulou, my dearest, you don't understand! I would give *anything* to be worthy of you, to be able to —— '

'No, *you* don't understand,' Louisa said, interrupting him without ceremony. She retrieved one of her hands and touched her fingers to his lips. 'Hush a moment!'

Septimus seized the fingers and pressed them close to his mouth. 'As many as you please,' he said, twinkling involuntarily.

'Dear poet, I have said I managed Mr Shittlehope,' Louisa uttered, the large eyes merry, 'but the truth is I also managed Mr Shittlehope's business interests. I still do!'

'What?' Septimus cried, a sudden grin lighting his features.

'Yes. I almost blurted it out to you once. But my aunt made me swear I would mention it to no one, for, even for the daughter of a marquis, the merest *whisper* and. . .' She drew a hand across her throat, clicking her tongue to indicate an end.

'Oh, God, Loulou, that is priceless!' the poet said, bursting into laughter. 'And I thought my deep, dark secret must utterly *disgust* you!'

'You know me better than that, I hope,' Louisa said, smiling.

His eyes softened. 'I *should* have done. But oh, Louisa, you don't *know* how much I. . .' He paused, and the quizzical gleam was back. 'No! I shall do this correctly—in true romantic style.'

'Septimus, what are you doing?' cried Louisa as he suddenly slid his arm under her shoulders and lifted her bodily from the floor.

'Set me down!' she ordered, laughing, but nevertheless finding the sensation of helplessness surprisingly enjoyable.

Septimus did set her down—in some disorder, on the piano stool. Then he threw himself on to one knee before her as she righted herself, breathless and chuckling.

'You have gone quite mad!'

'I know,' he agreed, reaching into a recess inside his coat and bringing out a crumpled sheet of paper.

'Oh, no, not a poem!' she protested.

'Hush, Louisa!' he begged. 'You will listen in silence, if you please.'

'And if I don't please?'

'You will listen in any event.'

'*Very* domineering,' murmured the lady.

'Very *docile*,' returned the gentleman.

Louisa raised her brows and made to rise. 'Oh, indeed?'

Septimus put a hand to her knee, pleading seriously, 'No, *pray*, Loulou. Give me this opportunity!'

A certain quality in his voice not only halted her, but caused that uncomfortable series of strange physical reactions to start up again. She was glad to be sitting down, for she feared her unruly legs, which began to feel like jelly, would not carry her. With fast-beating heart, she waited as the poet unfolded his paper.

He glanced at it only fleetingly as he read, the velvet tones deep with emotion,

> '"All eyes she seemed that night we met, blue eyes alight and twinkling;
> Of hearts surrendered up, as yet we neither had an inkling —— "'

'But this is of quite different quality!' ejaculated Louisa, interrupting suddenly.

The poet grasped her hand and shook it to silence her, as he resumed,

> '"But lo! She crept, she snailed her way beneath
>   my soul's defences;
> She lit the spark, and sailed away with all my
>   tender senses."'

'Septimus, I had no idea,' Louisa uttered in awed tones. 'Why did you not tell me you could write like this?'

'Louisa, for God's sake!' cried the poet, jumping up.

'But I am amazed!' Louisa persisted, rising also. 'That is no doggerel. It was *beautiful*.'

'Louisa,' Septimus uttered frenziedly, 'is this a moment to be discussing my literary merits? I am trying to tell you that I love you!'

She fell silent, paling. In a hushed voice she asked, 'Is that what it means?'

The poet raised his fists to heaven. 'Lord, you have saddled me with a ninnyhammer! My *tender senses*, Loulou.' He grasped her shoulders and gave her a little shake. 'I *love* you. Not merely in friendship, dear fool. And I thought — after what you said you had suffered thinking me dead. . .'

'You mean *that* is love?' Louisa asked, blinking at him.

'That is love,' he answered, smiling with rueful tenderness.

'But it is so *painful*.'

'Don't I know it! My Loulou, I did not understand myself until yesterday. But when I realised what Quint had planned — when I thought what it would mean had he succeeded. . .!' He broke off suddenly, and dragged Louisa into his arms, kissing her fiercely.

Fire streaked through her, and she gave a muffled groan. Almost she fought him, but his hold tightened, and warmth flooded her being. Septimus slackened his grip slightly, and Louisa sank into him, answering the quest of his velvet tongue with a rush of heat to her veins.

Somewhere at the back of her consciousness floated a new-found wisdom, and she knew that this was not only where she belonged, but where she had longed to be.

The kiss came to a reluctant conclusion at length, but the poet kept his arms about her.

'How does love feel now?' he asked, with a gleam in his eye. 'Still painful?'

'Oh, no,' Louisa answered, nestling contentedly. 'It is simply heaven!'

Septimus kissed her again. 'By all the rules of honour I know I should not ask you, Loulou. But I love you too much to care for that.'

'You know *my* views on your precious honour. What do you wish to ask me?'

'Don't be obtuse, my darling ninnyhammer! Will you marry me?'

Louisa twinkled at him. 'Is not that the natural *romantic* progression?'

The poet's eye gleamed mischief. He loosened his hold and stood back a little. 'It may be, but it is not why I ask you. The truth is, my heart is quite wrung with compassion.'

'For me?' Louisa demanded with some misgiving. 'Dare I ask why?'

'I cannot reconcile it with my conscience to allow you to spend the rest of your life as Lady Louisa Shittlehope!'

She choked. 'I see. You feel perhaps that Lady Louisa Berowne has more of a poetic ring?'

'It could hardly have less!' he retorted.

Louisa sighed soulfully. 'What an altruistic person you are, Septimus! You realise, of course, that if I say yes it is only because I am similarly moved by compassion.'

His brows rose, and a quiver disturbed the corner of his mouth. 'For my family connection, no doubt.'

'Not at all,' answered Louisa without a tremor. 'A poet needs a patron, does he not? And it is high time you ceased to waste your very considerable talent on — on gruesome tales or whatever it is.'

'You are perfectly right!' declared the poet. 'You will manage the Berownes, and I will wander the grounds of our demesne, feeding my muse.' He frowned. 'Do we have a demesne?'

'We can always acquire one,' Louisa said.

'And do you suppose Mr Shittlehope would have approved of your sponsoring the arts?'

'Well, he liked me to play the pianoforte,' Louisa offered.

'Then that is settled. You may marry me with a clear conscience!' He stepped back all at once and added gravely, 'Except for one thing.'

'What is that?' Louisa enquired, her large eyes suddenly anxious.

'There are certain conditions I must impose,' said Septimus in a serious tone, but the teasing light was back in his eye and a tell-tale twitch of the lips gave him away.

'Septimus,' Louisa warned, noting these signs, 'you are treading dangerous ground. Conditions, indeed!'

'Yes, but this is *vital*, Loulou. Unless you can guarantee not to grow gouty and fat, I am afraid that——'

'Septimus Berowne, you may be thankful you left your sword at Quint's lodging!'

Laughing, he seized her firmly by the waist and pulled her close again. 'Enough of this frivolity. To more serious matters, madam!' His smile was tender. 'I love you. And if you don't say it back to me this minute——'

'I love you,' Louisa said obligingly, and lifted her face for his kiss.

'And now, Loulou,' said the poet in a moment, drawing her to the sofa, 'you are going to redeem your promise and listen to my poems about you.'

'*Now*?' Louisa asked in a plaintive tone, seating herself reluctantly. 'But I was just warming to that particular theme. Could we not——?'

'Louisa,' Septimus said firmly, 'you may manage the rest of my family, but you will not manage me!'

She fluttered her lashes at him. 'No, Septimus?'

'*No*. That particular theme can wait for a little.' He perched beside her so that he might half face her, and this time extracted a whole sheaf of papers from his inner pocket.

'All those?' groaned Louisa. 'Do you always carry them about with you?'

He grinned. 'This batch, yes. For it is so private

that I am fearful of leaving it anywhere but on my own person.'

'You alarm me!' uttered Louisa, opening her eyes at him.

'Hush, listen!' He selected a page and began to recite.

'"*O, daffodil* —— "' He broke off as Louisa shifted. 'What are you doing?'

'Only getting comfortable, dearest poet,' she said, lifting her legs and sliding them behind him. She disposed herself in a languishing pose against the back of the sofa, looking at him expectantly.

His eye ran over her face and down to the gauze that veiled her bosom — which had lifted enticingly as she lay back — above the exact yellow gown that had inspired this verse. With difficulty the poet dragged his eyes back to the paper in his hand, and began again.

'"O daffodil, whose yellow robe becometh. . ."

Louisa, will you stop fidgeting?'

Louisa had been straightening her petticoats. She desisted, and, widening her large orbs, she put a finger to her lips. His eyes lingered there, and she smiled invitingly.

'No, Loulou!' said the poet, and resumed.

'"O, daffodil, whose yellow robe becometh that unfolding globe. . ."'

He looked up again as if impelled, although Louisa had lain still and silent, and met those eyes — so large, so soulful, so serious! His gaze became riveted, and, only half realising that he did so, Septimus leaned the hand which held his sheaf of poems on the sofa's back and found himself slowly, slowly moving towards those mesmerising eyes.

'Loulou,' he murmured against her lips, 'what was that particular theme you spoke of?'

'This one,' she uttered softly, and began to kiss him.

Above his head, a stealthy hand twitched the sheaf of papers from between his fingers, and pitched it over the back of the sofa. They scattered like so many autumn leaves, floating to the carpet.

But the poet, his lips engaged in a far more pleasurable activity than the reciting of verse, did not even notice.